"Fun and flirty [...] ion to your summer vacatio[n ...]
- Sarah Monzo[n, author of ...] [...] of You

"Mikal Dawn's debut novel is such a fun combination of tenderness, romance, and tickle-your-funnybone humor. Combine an adventure-loving hero and his sordid past with an accident-prone, feet-on-the-ground heroine and her mountain of worries, and you have a delightful romance that shows how love gives us the courage to soar beyond our insecurities. Allegra is such a likeable and relatable heroine, second-guessing herself, but working hard to help others achieve their dreams. Ty is a kind-hearted hero who's learned the value of what matters most. Don't miss out on this delightful debut!"
- Pepper Basham, author of *Just the Way You Are* and the Penned in Time series.

Count Me In

MIKAL DAWN

121 PUBLISHING HOUSE
I lift my eyes to the mountains...

Copyright © 2017 Mikal Hermanns
All rights reserved.

All rights reserved. No part of this publication may be reproduced, stored in a retrieval system, or transmitted in any form or by any means — for example, electronic, photocopy, recording, for personal or commercial purposes — without written permission of the author(s). The only exception is for brief quotations in printed or electronic reviews.

This novel is a work of fiction. Names, characters, places, and incidents are either products of the author's imagination or used factiously. All characters are fictional, and any resemblance to real events or to actual persons, living or dead, is coincidental. Any reference to historical figures, places, or events, whether fictional or actual, is a fictional representation.

Scripture quotations are from the ESV® Bible (The Holy Bible, English Standard Version®), copyright © 2001 by Crossway, a publishing ministry of Good News Publishers. Used by permission. All rights reserved.

Cover photos:
Back cover design: Perry Elisabeth Design
                perryelisabethdesign.com
Seattle Panorama: Natalia Bratslavsky/shutterstock.com
Paraglide: Vitalii Bashkatov/shutterstock.com
Couple: Halfpoint/shutterstock.com
Author photo: Jeffrey Conger Photography, 2016
                jeffreycongerphotography.com

Edited by: Dori Harrell, Breakout Editing
         doriharrell.wixsite.com/breakoutediting

First edition, 121 Publishing House, 2017

ISBN-10: 0-692-88574-9
ISBN-13: 978-0-692-88574-1

For Jesus. Always first. This is all because of You.

For the best husband I never could have imagined. Mark, I love you. Thank you for your support, provision, encouragement...and the espresso machine.

For Ethan, Van, and Elliette. You guys bring so much laughter and joy to my life. I'm so thankful for you!
I love you.

Chapter One

The little hairs on the back of Allegra Spencer's neck stood at attention. He was behind her. She could feel his presence as sure as she could smell the beans being ground by the barista on the other side of the reclaimed-wood counter.

The barista who was staring at her. "You okay, Allegra?"

"Huh?" So eloquent.

"I was saying I heard what happened at your firm. And saw on the news how the Feds shut it down. I just about choked on my spaghetti."

Allegra knew how that felt. When she showed up at work last Monday to see federal agents carrying computers and cardboard banking boxes full of files out of the downtown Seattle office, she'd stopped in her tracks, choking on the Kit Kat latté she'd just taken a sip of.

"It was a...shock."

Jael, the barista, snorted. "Uh, yeah." She tamped the ground beans into the portafilter and inserted it into the espresso machine. "So what are you gonna do now?"

Allegra groaned. Behind her, the air stirred and warmed. Was he getting closer? She pulled her lips between her teeth. She'd noticed him weeks ago when he'd signed some napkins for a few people—he looked familiar, though she couldn't place him, which was no real shock since she rarely watched TV—but all they'd ever done was smile at one another. And oh, what a smile that man had. She shivered.

What had Jael asked? Oh! She lifted the tablet in her hand and showed a job-search website. "What else can I do? Job hunt." She rolled her eyes. "Have I mentioned how much I *loathe* job hunting?" And paying college tuition. She sighed. But it was worth it for her sister to get a good education.

As long as Allegra was still able to afford her coffee.

"At least there are tons of jobs for accountants here." Steam swirled around Jael's head as she held the paper cup under the frother. The noise put a damper on Allegra's reply, but the back of her tingled, pulling her attention to the man behind her. He'd moved closer and was in her personal space now. He wasn't a stalker or anything, was he?

"Here's your caramel macchiato, Allegra."

She watched as Jael slid the cup into a sleeve. Allegra wrapped her hand around it, proud of herself for taking a step outside her comfort zone from her regular Kit Kat latté. She turned...

Oomph.

"My coffee!" Did she really just yell for her coffee, more worried about it than the man she'd known was close behind her?

Something was wrong with her.

She snorted. No. She just loved her coffee. Though the man currently gripping her upper arms in his strong hands...

"I..." The words died on her lips as she peered up into lush green eyes gazing down at her. "Sorry," she squeaked.

The man looked down at her hand, still holding tight to her latté. "No harm done. Looks like the barista put the lid on tight."

Allegra glanced over her shoulder at Jael, who was standing behind the counter watching them with a grin on her face.

"You're welcome." Jael lifted a brow, tilting her head to the man.

Allegra rolled her eyes. Though if it meant the guy talking to her, she'd have to remember to slide Jael a big tip.

A very big tip.

Tyler Hawk wasn't the nosy type. But when he'd overheard the barista mention accountant jobs, his ears perked up and he leaned in.

Apparently a little *too* close.

Close enough that he caught the faint whiff of something sweet and floral. He inhaled through his nose. It must have been her shampoo. While her attention was on the barista—Jael, if he'd heard right—he'd studied her dark glossy hair, secured up high on her head in a loose bun, with wisps grazing her ears and neck.

And right in the middle of his study, she turned and laid the most beautiful sapphire-blue gaze on him.

Heat swirled in his belly, as if he'd just downed a full pot of boiling water.

"Hi." He stuck out his hand. "I'm Tyler."

The woman's pink lips formed an *O* before she shrugged, lifting both hers, showing the coffee in one hand and her tablet in the other.

Oh yeah. He lowered his hand. "Sorry."

He was not making a good first impression here.

"No problem. I'm Allegra."

"Allegra...that's an interesting name." He grinned. "Kind of like the allergy med—" Her cooling gaze stopped him before he fully inserted his foot in his mouth. "Sorry. You probably get that all the time."

She blinked. "Often enough."

That hole he was digging was getting deeper.

"Before I make a complete fool of myself"—*if it isn't already too late*—"I couldn't help but overhear that you're out of work." He pointed his chin toward Jael. "She mentioned you're looking for a job as an accountant?"

Allegra pulled her bottom lip between her teeth before she answered. "I am." She lifted her tablet.

She tilted her head to look past him. When he glanced over his shoulder, he saw a few people waiting to place their orders. His grimaced an apology to them before turning back to Allegra. "Were you planning to get a table? Would you mind if I joined you?"

She narrowed her eyes and took a moment to answer. She must have decided he was safe enough—or at least they were in a public enough place that she would be okay—because she nodded. "Sure. But, um...aren't you going to get a coffee?"

Huh? He looked back at Jael, whose hand was covering her mouth, her shoulders bouncing. Oh. Coffee. Right. They *were* in a coffeehouse. But the line behind them...

He grabbed a bottle of water from the ice-filled barrel in front of the counter. "I'll take this." He threw down a few dollars and followed Allegra to a table in the middle of Bean There.

As soon as Tyler sat down, a younger kid—probably about fourteen, with bright-red hair and braces—approached. "I can't believe it's you. Can I have your autograph, Mr. Hawk?" He thrust a napkin in front of Tyler's face.

From a table several feet away, a woman, probably the kid's mom, admonished him. "Bennett, give him some space."

The boy's rounded gaze stared at him. "Please."

Tyler laughed. "Sure, buddy." He took a pen from the boy and scrawled a message and his signature on the napkin before giving both the autograph and pen back to him. "Thanks so much."

"Thank *you*." The awe on the kid's face made it all worth it. Despite his retirement from the Seattle Seahawks a year earlier, the city still supported him and greeted him with enthusiasm. The love and friendliness of Seattle was one of the reasons he'd stayed.

He turned back to Allegra, who had watched the exchange with a question in her eyes. It seemed she didn't know who he was, and that was fine by him.

He needed to get down to business. "So, I run an outdoor-adventure company and am in desperate need of an in-house accountant. But I have one problem."

Allegra's eyes widened. "You need an accountant?" She drummed her fingers on her thigh. "What's the problem?"

"I hate interviewing."

She laughed, the sound floating around him. "What a coincidence. I hate being interviewed."

And that was what he'd been hoping to hear. "So I have a proposition for you."

Her countenance darkened. "Look. I don't do—"

"What? No! No, nothing...like *that*."

She closed her eyes for a quick moment before she spoke. "Okay then. What's your proposition?"

"I need an accountant, and you need a job. So tell me where you graduated, give me two references, I'll tell you you're hired, and we'll talk like old friends."

Allegra laughed again. "That sounds like an interview."

Tyler lifted a finger and wagged it in front of his face. "Nope, not an interview. A conversation. And the only part I really need is your two references. I'll call and interview them instead."

She quirked a brow. "This is a little unconventional."

"Because we don't like interviews."

"Valid point."

"So? What do you say?"

She took a deep breath, her shoulders rising. She held it in, then released it. Slowly. "Deal." This time, her hands were free. He stuck out his own, took hers, and shook.

Chapter Two

Allegra looked past the flicking windshield wipers, through the Seattle rain, and squinted at the sign attached to the two-story building.

Um, *what?*

Hawk's Flight Outdoor Adventures mocked her in giant red lettering. But no. That couldn't be right. Allegra thought back to the conversation she'd had with Tyler at Bean There. He hadn't mentioned the company's name. Did he tell her what his company did? She couldn't remember. Those blasted green eyes of his had captivated her.

Tyler Hawk. His name sounded familiar, but she couldn't quite place it.

Allegra glanced at the clock on her dash. She should have Googled Tyler's name to see what kind of business he ran. Now with only five minutes until she was supposed to show, she had just enough time for a few more sips of her Kit Kat latté and a breath mint. Breathing deep, she popped the mint into her mouth and eyed herself in the rearview mirror. *Calm, cool, and collected, Allegra.* Tyler had called an hour ago, telling her his partner thought he was crazy for hiring someone without interviewing the person.

His partner was right.

Thank goodness Tyler had assured her it was just a formality, but still. She needed this job. For her sister.

Already shivering at the thought of the cold spring rain, she ducked out of her car, opened her umbrella with a snap, stuck some quarters in the parking meter, and walked into Hawk's Flight. The vintage charm from the overhead jingle of doorbells was the only sound within the cozy space. To her right, a myriad of brochures lined half the wall in a colorful display. One sticking up slightly had a picture of a man on top of what looked to be a *very* tall mountain. Nope. Allegra shook her head. Not for her. She felt dizzy just looking at the photo. She'd keep her feet planted firmly on stained concrete floors at—well, not quite sea level, but whatever the elevation was in this Seattle neighborhood.

Past the brochures, a line of photographs hung on the wall—people on mountaintops, deep-sea diving, rock climbing, and even heli-skiing. Nope, nope, nope.

She rolled her eyes at her lack of adventurous spirit...only to see a canoe hanging from some wood beams on the ceiling. What? This place was an outdoorsman's paradise. Definitely *not* hers. Give her white sandy beaches and crystal-blue oceans. A girl could relax to the sound of waves lapping the shore...*not* the bedlam of hundred-mile-per-hour winds as she fell to the ground after jumping out of a perfectly good airplane.

She drew in a long breath, and the faint smell of spearmint teased her. On her exhale, she said, "Hello?" She huffed at her timid voice. Clearing her throat, she called out again. "Hello?"

"Be right out." The familiar deep voice echoed from a door at the back of the room. "Take a seat. Can I get you anything? Water, coffee?"

"No, thank you." Allegra walked over to a desk against the wall and sat in one of the two midcentury modern chairs, her fingers worrying the strap of her purse. Footsteps sounded behind her. She shot out of her chair and turned, arm extended. "Hi—"

Oomph!

Water soaked Tyler's T-shirt. Where was her rewind button? *Ugh.* She was so fired before she even started.

His eyes widened in shock. "Wow, that's...cold."

"I am *so* sorry." Mortification poked its fiery fingers at her cheeks.

Then...he laughed.

His belly laugh filled the room. And kept going. And going. Until she couldn't contain her own chuckles.

He lifted large hands to his face and wiped drops of water from his emerald-green eyes. "It's okay, really. Thankfully it was just water." Tyler sat in a chair behind the desk, causing it to squeak. "Are you ready to start?"

Allegra slid her hand down her black skirt. "If I'm not fired for that stunt, then absolutely."

He grinned, his even, white teeth pulling her gaze to his

lips. Movement drew her gaze down where his hand reached across the desk. "Then let's start over.

"Hi. I'm Tyler."

She couldn't help the laugh that escaped. "Hi. I'm Allegra." She took his hand and shook it.

Allegra's warm hand in his felt good. Soft. And it fit perfectly. A hum zipped through his core. Considering his drenched tee, he'd better be careful.

Not gonna go there.

Tyler cleared his throat and lowered his gaze to the paper lying on his desk. Not that he hadn't already studied her résumé before she'd arrived, thanks to his partner's insistence, but...

"Like I already told you on the phone, this is just a formality, and I'm so sorry to even have to do this." He rolled his eyes. "But let's start with the usual. Tell me about yourself."

Allegra clasped her hands in her lap before she answered.

"I'm a graduate of the University of North Carolina at Chapel Hill, magna cum laude. I moved to Seattle after accepting a job offer with an accounting firm where I interned back in North Carolina, and worked there for five years."

Allegra's gaze drifted down his chest, a hint of pink coloring her neck, before she flicked it back up to him. Ah, so he wasn't the only one affected.

"When I arrived at work last week, and the firm was closed. Permanently." She chewed her bottom lip again.

Oh yeah. Something to do with the Feds. He squirmed, the shirt uncomfortable. He remembered overhearing that part of the conversation between the barista and Allegra at the coffee shop. Since he was already uncomfortable, now was probably the best time to talk salary.

"So...you probably know I can't pay you what you're likely used to. Are you sure you want this job?"

The sound of midday traffic filtered through the window. Behind him, Tyler could hear the clock ticking. Allegra looked down, fingers playing with a ring on her right hand. Seconds ticked by before she took a deep breath.

"I despise interviews, and going through the motions to get into a larger firm takes time. And honestly? I needed a job quickly. My sister is in college, and I'm paying her tuition."

That brought a horde of questions. Where were her parents? Why weren't they footing the college bill? Or the sister herself? He couldn't ask, but there had to be more to it, and it didn't look like she was going to spill.

"Do you like spending time outdoors?"

A snort escaped before she slapped a hand over her mouth. "Um, it depends on what you mean."

Tyler lifted a brow. He'd said Hawk's was an outdoor-adventure company, right? "You know, do you have any experience rock climbing, scuba diving, whitewater rafting? That kind of thing."

Allegra dropped her gaze and smoothed her skirt. "I can't say that I do, no." She looked back up. "Is that a problem?"

He picked up a pen and started twisting it between his

fingers. No experience with anything his business offered. But she would just be the bookkeeper. Then again, his policy—

"Mr. Hawk—"

"Tyler."

She hesitated. "Tyler. I may not have the outdoor experience, but I can guarantee you'll be more than happy with my work. I'm an excellent accountant—"

"You're already hired. On one condition." Tyler watched as her eyes narrowed.

"What?"

Here goes nothing. "You need to try every adventure Hawk's Flight offers."

Allegra's brows shot up. Though he'd already given her the job, they hadn't signed any paperwork. He was free to change the terms. But still. Tyler Hawk was officially crazy. "Pardon me?"

His lips spread over bright-white teeth into a little-boy grin, and his green eyes sparkled. An adjective from one of her Regency romances popped into her thoughts: rake. The man was a rake.

Well, maybe not quite. She didn't know enough about him to say whether he was a womanizer. But he was definitely a charmer.

"The job is yours. *If* you agree to try every adventure we offer." He shrugged an apology. "Bo's condition. And since he's my partner, I have to roll with it." The chair creaked as he leaned back, lifting his muscular arms to rest behind his head, his still-wet T-shirt clinging to his chest.

She raised her palms up. "You can't be serious."

"Perfectly serious." He laughed. "Come on! It'll be fun. And really, what's the harm?"

Allegra's stomach rolled. The image of an officer at the front door flashed through her mind. *What's the harm? Seriously?* She pushed the image back and took a deep breath. "But...I'm an accountant. I'll be here"—her hands flitted around her, indicating the storefront—"working on the books. I won't be involved in selling, guiding, or whatever else you do. Just the books."

Tyler lowered his arms, a hand brushing over his blond crew cut on its way down. "I need someone in house, and Bo and I have made it our policy to never hire anyone who doesn't appreciate an adventure. We can make an exception to the policy, but not without you giving a little too. So what do you say?"

"Every adventure?" She hoped he didn't hear her voice quake.

"At least the ones here in Washington." He leaned forward and held out his hand. "Deal?"

Allegra pasted on a smile. If she accepted, she might be able to talk him out of the adventures. Or he might forget. At this point, though she despised risk, it was one she'd have to take. If her sister didn't appreciate this ultimate sacrifice of love, Allegra was going to kill her.

If she lived long enough to commit such a crime.

She stuck out her hand. "Deal." And look at that...she even did it without spilling anything.

Count Me In

Hashtag: winning.

Chapter Three

"I'll have my lawyer write the addendum to the employment contract over the weekend. You can sign it when you come in Monday morning, eight a.m."

"Thank you. I'll see you then."

"This will be good." Tyler shook her satiny hand... *Don't go there, man.*

Her smile didn't reach her eyes. Hesitancy marred her forehead before she turned.

Allegra opened her umbrella and stepped out the door, a curtain of rain sweeping into the shop as the door closed.

"That went well." Tyler grinned, his relief sliding down his back, releasing the tension of muscles that had been bunched.

He picked up her résumé, glanced over it, and set it back down. He hadn't been kidding when he told her his policy was to hire only those who loved adventure. He also wasn't kidding that he needed someone. Quick. A deep sigh expanded and deflated his chest.

His damp chest.

Oh yeah. He couldn't believe he interviewed her with a wet T-shirt.

Jumping off his chair, he moved to the back room, passing climbing gear, gloves, and hiking boots. Kenny Loggins's "Footloose" sounded through the floorboards of the dance studio upstairs. It was a good thing he liked '80s music—and "Footloose" was one of his favorites.

Opening the locker door in the back room, he grabbed an extra shirt. Bluish-gray…like Allegra's eyes.

Don't go there, Ty. Employee, remember?

He shook his head, dispelling the image of her finely shaped brows over those eyes, and her swept-back dark hair showing off high cheekbones and full…

Argh.

But those curves. His hands would fit perfectly around her, and if those curves were as soft as her hands—

Nope. Remember: blessed are the pure in heart, for they will see God. The verse from Matthew 5:8 cleared his mind and eased his soul.

He hadn't been tempted like that since his NFL days.

Tyler peeled off his shirt, bunched it up, and threw it in the laundry basket close by. After shrugging into his clean one, he closed the door and glanced at his watch. Whoa! Bo was likely already at the gym, annoyed that Tyler was late. Knowing Bo, however, he wouldn't stay mad for long when he heard Tyler had hired an accountant.

Allegra slid onto the front seat of her Pacifica and sat for a moment, the steady rain beating on the metal roof of her car, soothing her.

A contract. For adventure. What had she been thinking? If it weren't for Caprice and her almost $44,000-per-year tuition at Parsons School of Design... Memories of watching her baby sister bent over the kitchen table with colored pencils in hand as she drew fashion designs filled Allegra's mind. To see her sister happy after a hard few years made risking her own life totally acceptable.

Almost.

Definitely.

She hoped.

Allegra started her car and drove toward home. All she wanted right now were her yoga pants and espresso machine. A hot Kit Kat latté sounded heavenly.

Rosemary Clooney's "Sisters" blasted through the Bluetooth. Allegra pushed the phone button on her steering wheel. "Hey, sis."

"Hi!" Caprice's bubbly voice sounded through the speaker system. "Whatcha up to?"

She still hadn't told her sister about her job loss. "Coming from a job interview."

"A...what?"

"An interview. I got a new job."

"But why? I thought you loved the firm."

"Uh, yeah. About that. They went belly up a week ago."

"What?"

Allegra flinched at her sister's shriek.

"Don't worry, Capri. I just nailed the interview. I got the job."

"What firm? When do you start? Do you think you'll like it there? What happened to the old firm?"

Allegra pumped her brakes to stop for a red light. "I don't know what happened. I went to work one morning to have the building receptionist tell me—and everyone else—the firm was closed. A total shock."

"Why didn't you tell me?"

"Because I didn't want you to stress out. Your job is to get good grades and graduate, not worry about your tuition. That's my job."

"Alleg—"

"I mean it. Don't worry." She tried to inject some cheer in her voice. "This new job will be *great*." *A real adventure.* She tried to ignore the hard twist in her stomach.

"Well, tell me about it."

Allegra swallowed past the fear clawing her chest. "It's an outdoor-adventure company. I'll be the in-house accountant. I start Monday."

Caprice's laughter echoed throughout the car. "An outdoor-adventure company? Seriously? That would be so fun! Where?"

Fun. That was not how she'd describe it.

"This is a career move. Not something for fun. And it's at Hawk's Flight Outdoor Adventures."

"Oh, come on, Allie. You need to have some fun in your life! All you do is go to work, church, and the gym."

Allegra almost choked on her own saliva. *The gym?* Uh,

sure. The gym. "Yeah. Well. Who has time for anything else?"

Her sister snickered. "You wouldn't have to go to the gym if you went on those adventures. They're probably killer."

She was about to faint. Right there, driving her car down through rush hour traffic in the rain. *Killer.* Exactly. "Can you please use a different adjective?"

"Huh?"

"Never mind." She took a deep breath and slowly exhaled. "What are you up to?"

"Oh, yeah. I almost forgot! Guess what happened today?"

She couldn't help the grin. Caprice was always so positive and found excitement in every little thing. Allegra needed that kind of attitude, but she had too much to do. "What?"

"I was offered an internship at J. Wong!"

Thankfully, Allegra was already at a stop light, or she would have hit the brakes. "What? J. Wong? The fashion designer?"

"Yes!" Caprice started rattling off details. "It'll be totally crazy hours, no doubt until midnight—maybe later. And get this! I've even been asked to design one dress and give input on other designs for the spring show next year in—are you ready?—*Paris.* Paris, Allie! And that's not even all. I'll be working under J. Wong's head designer for a *week.*" The rapid-fire words gave just a slight hint to her excitement.

Allegra laughed. "That's amazing! Oh, sis, I'm so happy for you." Pride lightened her mood. Taking this job, putting her life at risk, was worth the hives she might end up breaking out in.

Maybe.

The light turned green, and she moved her foot to the accelerator.

Caprice took a breath on the other end of the line. "Whatcha think?"

"What do I think? I think it's fantastic! Such an incredible opportunity." A thought struck, and her hands went clammy. "Uh, is this going to cost money?"

A moment's pause answered her question. Her stomach dropped. "Capri?"

"I'll be earning a wage...a small one."

"Enough to cover living expenses?"

Another pause. "Um...no."

Fabulous.

"But I'm taking a second job, Allie."

"No. Your job is school and now this internship. Don't worry. This opportunity is way too great." Hopefully, Caprice believed that injected pep in Allegra's voice. She ground her teeth. Her parents should be worrying about these costs. If only they'd valued their kids—and their lives—more than their hobbies.

"No, I don't want you stressed out. And you haven't even started your new...wait. Did you have to take a pay cut for this job?"

Allegra crossed her fingers and sent up a silent prayer for forgiveness. "Nope."

A sigh, probably of relief, sounded. "Oh good. And...hey! Did you say *Hawk's Flight*?"

"Yes."

"There in Seattle?"

Where was her sister going with this? "Where else?"

"As in, the owner is Tyler Hawk?"

"How did you know?"

Capri's tinkling laugh flitted through the car. "I remember an interview with him when he retired, and he mentioned that name."

"An interview? He retired? What?"

Caprice groaned. "Sis, you really need to get out more. Tyler Hawk. *The* Tyler Hawk. Tight end for the Seattle Seahawks. Brought home the Super Bowl. Ringing any bells?"

Oh good gracious. *That's why his name seemed familiar.* "Oh yeah. That Tyler Hawk."

"Is he as good looking in person as he was on TV? Those eyes of his pop off the screen. And his lips." Her sigh came heavy over the line.

Flames licked the back of Allegra's neck. Thank goodness her sister wasn't there in person. She'd never hear the end of her blushes. "Sure. He's okay."

"Mm-hmm. I bet he is."

She needed to end this call. Quickly. "I need to run. I'll talk to you soon. Love you."

"Love you too. Drive safe."

Allegra pushed the phone button on her steering wheel to end the call.

She was so excited for her sister's internship at the high-end designer, but with Caprice not taking summer classes, Allegra had been hoping to save up money during the summer break to pay tuition for Caprice's final year. Apparently, she'd keep living paycheck to paycheck. Again. *Only one more year. Just one.* She could do this. The bit of weight gain from all the ramen only made her figure...curvier. Yeah. She glanced in her rearview mirror and moaned. Curvier was probably putting it nicely. What had once been a size six figure was now a twelve.

She looked down at her thighs. *Scratch that twelve and make it closing in on a fourteen.*

"But I'm healthy," she whispered. Her blood pressure check at the last doctor's appointment told her so. So did her bloodwork.

The number on the scale... *Bygones*, she thought.

Besides, if Tyler held her to this contract—and deep down she knew he would—she'd be exercising her hip size down in no time.

Speaking of hip size, she needed food. Good food. Food to give her the energy and endurance to forge ahead through all the upcoming *adventures*.

Good food equaled coffee. She grinned when she saw her condo building up ahead. That second Kit Kat latté she'd been dreaming of earlier would do nicely.

Clanking metal and a few loud grunts greeted Tyler when he walked through the door of Seattle Elite Fitness. Sweat fouled the air. The guys were working hard today.

He checked in, stored his things in a locker, and walked into the weight room, searching for Bo. Over in the corner doing some free-weight bicep curls, Bo looked madder than a sacked quarterback.

Tyler approached him silently, waiting until he'd dropped the dumbbells before talking. "Hey, man."

Bo turned, glaring. "You're late."

Ouch. He was *really* mad. But Tyler didn't think this was about being late. "Sorry. The interview you made me do ran a little long."

Bo's tense shoulders relaxed. A little. "How'd it go?"

"We have a new accountant."

"Good." Bo bent to pick up the free weights off the floor, wiped them, and placed them back on their stand. "Tell me about him."

"Her."

Bo grunted.

Okay then. "Allegra Spencer. Worked for Goldson and Murdoch until a few weeks ago. She's smart, beautiful, and seems like she'll be a great fit." Except the not loving the outdoors bit. But Bo didn't need to know everything.

Bo stilled, watching Tyler with a smirk on his face. "Beautiful?"

"What? Dude. I can't say that. It could be considered sexual harassment if she heard."

Bo laughed outright. "I didn't say it, man. You did. 'Smart, beautiful, and seems like she'll be a great fit.'"

Heat crawled up Tyler's neck. "No I didn't."

"Yeah." Bo slapped him on the chest and walked past him. "You did."

Tyler stood there, staring out the window of the weight room.

Yeah. He was in trouble.
Mind on the work, man. Not on the woman.
Now to make himself believe that before Monday.

Chapter Four

Monday morning arrived way too fast. Allegra woke to her alarm blaring some '80s hair band. She opened her eyes only to stare at the ceiling. What was she thinking, accepting a job at Hawk's Flight? Seriously. She was out of her mind. Maybe she should check herself in for an evaluation. She reached for her phone on the table beside her bed, tapped in her password, and opened the browser. Thumbing a search for doctors, she ticked off the reasons she shouldn't go in. *One, it's an* outdoor-adventure company. *Two, the boss is too good looking and a celebrity, for crying out loud. Three, it's an* outdoor-adventure company. Reasons one and three alone should get her checked in.

Her clock rang a second alarm.

She tapped on the phone icon and scrolled through her contacts. Maybe Dr. Smalley would meet her at the office early and check her out. She'd clearly lost her mind.

As she was about to call, a text chimed.

Caprice: **Good luck 2day. God's got this!!**
Allegra: *Thanks, sis. Love.*
Caprice: **Luv**

Very timely. Allegra turned her eyes heavenward. *Thanks for that reminder, God.* Not that she was thankful at the moment, not with risky trips in her future. But she should be thankful. *I'll work on it. Promise.*

After she showered and dressed, she made herself a latté—oh so grateful for that machine!—and grabbed an apple before she walked out the door. Nerves bunched her stomach into knots. The job she could do. The contract though...

You can do all things through Me, Who strengthens you.

"Okay, God. I get it. I can do this." She grinned as one of her neighbors opened her door a crack and peered through. "I'm okay! Just talking to...well, God."

The eye widened before the door rapidly shut.

Allegra reached her car outside the building, tossed her bag on the passenger seat, and climbed in. She looked down at her outfit. Tyler had been almost too casual when she'd interviewed—the memory of the wet T-shirt burned her cheeks. She shook her head clear. Anyway, she hoped her clothes were appropriate. Her navy ankle pants and white with blue polka-dot wrap shirt were less formal than she'd worn at her previous job, but wearing a suit to Hawk's Flight didn't seem right either.

Oh well. Here went nothing.

―――∞―――

He was a bundle of nerves and didn't know why. It wasn't like he'd never hired women before. Story worked by his side in the store almost every day. Tyler glanced over to where she stood talking with Bo.

There was a story there. Ha! No pun intended. He chuckled and watched as Story walked off, with Bo watching her every move. That guy had it bad.

Just then Bo turned to face Tyler and glared when he saw him watching. Yep. Real bad. Tyler brushed a hand over his head and down the back of his neck, rubbing it at the base. Those two should just go on a date already, but Bo kept insisting there was nothing there. Tyler knew that wasn't true on Bo's part, but Story was pretty good at keeping a straight face. Who knew?

The bells over the door clanged against one another as a breeze carried the scent of flowers. Allegra was here.

She cleared her throat behind him, and he turned. Her eyes were huge.

"You look as scared as a coach whose star quarterback was just injured."

She blinked. "Um..."

"I'm not making you go skydiving today, you know."

If it was even possible, her eyes grew larger. He tried not to laugh, but the panic on her face... Before he knew it, his laughter echoed throughout the shop. But there was something under his laughter...a light, melodic sound.

Allegra had joined in.

His heartbeat picked up speed. What he wouldn't do to hear that sound again. Tyler patted her shoulder. "Come on. I'll show you where you can put your things. Then we'll get started." He took a few steps toward the back room.

"Thanks. And…I am so relieved. No skydiving!"

Tyler stopped and glanced over his shoulder. Her sapphire-blue gaze traveled the products featured around the store before it stopped on a display of skydiving harnesses and a main canopy.

He grinned. "I said 'today.' You're not going skydiving *today*."

Her mouth fell open.

Working with her was going to be fun.

But first things first.

"We have storage lockers for the staff in the back." As he spoke, Story came out from the room he was pointing at. "Story, come meet Allegra, our new accountant."

"Oh hi! It'll be so good to have another woman in here. It's been overrun with testosterone for far too long."

The tinkling laugh floated around him once more.

Story's blond hair was caught up in a top knot, and her dark-brown eyes peered at Allegra from behind tortoise-rimmed glasses.

"How long have you worked here?" Allegra said, keeping her focus on Story as Bo approached the group, his own focus intense on Story, though she didn't seem to notice.

"About a year now." Her eyes flicked to Tyler, then back. "Too long." The corner of her mouth quirked up, belying her words.

"Hey! Not cool, Story. Remember who signs your paychecks." He winked at her before turning to Allegra. "Truth be told, this place wouldn't function without her." He pointed his thumb over his shoulder at Story. "She holds it together when Bo and I are out on excursions."

"Hm. I think you're sucking up, Ty. What is it you need me to do now?" The twinkle in Story's eyes gave her away.

"Set up a paraglide session." He darted a look at Allegra just in time to see her pale. "For tomorrow." He didn't think it was possible, but she paled even more. "For two." Was she about to pass out?

"Names?" Story looked between him and Allegra, a brow raised in question.

He smirked. "Me and"—he paused—"All—"

Allegra gasped before he could finish. He caught her elbow just as he thought she might go down. "Whoa! Fainting is *not* part of the employment contract, you know."

Her once-white face reddened. "I wasn't going to faint. I just…I didn't have enough water this morning."

"Ah, is that it?" He grinned. "Have no fear. We have water aplenty."

Leaving her in Story's care, he hustled to the back room and grabbed a bottle of water out of the mini-fridge. He turned, almost colliding with Bo. "Dude, sorry." He looked Bo up and down. His flattened lips and squinted eyes told Tyler he wasn't happy about something. "What's the story with you and…well, Story?" He laughed at his own joke.

Yeah. He was lame.

"Nothing." The frown lines on Bo's forehead deepened.

"Right."

Bo huffed. "That girl drives me mad."

He couldn't help but laugh. Again. Man, he was doing a lot of that the past couple of days. It felt good. "She's a woman. And really, you probably drive her mad too."

One side of Bo's mouth quirked up in a half smile. "Probably."

Tyler clapped him on his shoulder. "We'll hit up the gym later and work it off. Yeah?"

"Yeah."

"Good. Now I've got to get back to Allegra and show her around."

"Tyler." Bo's serious voice caught his attention. "She looks stressed. Don't mess with her too much."

Tyler considered Bo's words as he walked back into the shop. He was right. Allegra just about passed out when he mentioned the paraglide tomorrow. He should probably tell her he was talking about Allister Evans.

The mortification ran deep. *Allister Evans.* She'd almost passed out, and he'd been about to say *Allister.* Would she ever recover?

Probably not. But the sheepish grin on his face made her flushed cheeks worth it. Talk about *cute.*

Her mouth formed a silent *O.* "Allister Evans. Not…"

"No, not you, Allegra. I wouldn't do that to you." He quirked one blond brow and hiked his lips up into a grin. "You need a safety class first."

Before she knew it, Allegra whipped her arm out and smacked him in his bicep.

"Ouch!"

Could the floor actually open up and swallow her whole? That would be preferable to standing there, facing her new employer after *hitting* him. Talk about jeopardizing her job before she even started. Sheesh.

"I am *so* sorry."

"You know, you happen to say that to me a lot." A chuckle rumbled from his chest. "But I admit—I deserved that."

She drew in her bottom lip and chewed it. "No, you didn't. I really am sorry."

Tyler clapped her on her shoulder. "We could stand here all day debating this. Let's get to work instead."

Relief sagged the shoulders she didn't know she'd been clenching. "Perfect."

Tyler walked her around the shop, pointing to gear for rock climbing, rafting, camping... Finally, he walked her over to the activities display she'd seen when she came in for her interview. He grabbed one of each of the pamphlets, then turned to her, holding them out. Allegra took them and looked down at the top one: heli-skiing.

"Oh, wow. Heli-skiing?"

Tyler's eyes lit up. "It's one of my favorites. We take groups up to the North Cascades—the American Alps! They have the most glaciated peaks!—and are dropped anywhere between seven thousand and nine thousand feet. The best skiing conditions. The vertical drop? Oh man, fifteen hundred to four thousand feet. It's such a rush!"

Uh, it didn't sound like a rush. How many feet? Vertical drop? No. No way.

"I can't wait for you to try it."

"*What?*"

The man had the nerve to laugh. He really was a joyful sort, it seemed. "Your contract? Heli-skiing is one of the adventures we offer."

The need to faint almost overwhelmed her again. Yes, other companies, non-life-threatening companies, were hiring accountants right now. But really? She'd already committed to this job, and the thought of interviewing—long searches online, writing even more cover letters, and personalizing her résumé...putting herself out there? Just *no*.

"Right. The contract."

Tyler eyed her, a question in his eyes. "Are you okay?"

"Yeah." She forced what she hoped was a bright smile. "Peachy."

"Allegra, I'm kidding. Heli-skiing isn't something you can do unless you're really good at skiing. I mean, *really* good. No one in their right mind would send a newbie jumping out of a helicopter to go skiing down a mountain."

"Ah." Could a person die from relief?

He watched her for a moment before he shrugged his oh-so-muscular shoulders. "Your desk will be in the back, but if we ever get busy in here, would you mind stepping out to help?"

"No, of course not."

"Great. Okay, let me show you your space."

Allegra followed him through the storefront into the back room. To her left was a bank of lockers and a counter with an espresso machine—this was definitely Seattle—and a fridge. There was also a small table with a couple of chairs, and a door that likely led to a bathroom. On her right were two rooms with large windows—each office had one window facing into the back room and one overlooking the small park nestled on the other side of the street. She caught glimpses of green grass and some colorful flowers in between cars passing by. Each room held a desk and computer. Tyler walked into the farthest office and turned to face her.

"Welcome to your home away from home." He patted the back of the chair behind the desk. "Come sit. This used to be Bo's office, but his role is changing a bit, and he's rarely here anyway, what with the excursions he leads."

"He doesn't mind me taking his office?"

"Nah. He's good. He'd rather be outside." Tyler walked a few feet and rapped his knuckles on a file cabinet. "The files you'll need are in here. There's a key inside one of the drawers of your desk that'll open it. Oh, and the password for your computer. Hand me that pen and paper?"

Allegra handed him a pen and scrounged for a scrap of paper in the top drawer of the solid-wood desk. Tyler scribbled some letters and numbers down and passed the paper back to her. "I'll have Bo come in here in a few and show you the software and its setup. We need to get your paperwork filled out first though. Come over to my office." He motioned for her to precede him. They walked two feet to his office, and she sat in a chair across from him.

His space was surprisingly neat. She didn't know what she'd expected, but it wasn't that. Framed photographs hung on one wall—pictures of Tyler with other pretty large guys. His teammates? Other photographs showed him in different outdoor settings, from boats to mountains to...was that a cave?

She glanced over at Tyler and saw him watching her.

"Where was that last photo taken?"

His eyes narrowed slightly before he sat back, folding his arms across his broad chest. "Ah. That was the Naracoorte Caves in South Australia. Some amazing sights in those caves. If you ever get to Australia, you have to go."

Passion colored his voice. The man definitely *loved* the outdoors.

Better him than me. "Sure," she said. "So, the paperwork?"

"Right." He pulled out a small stack of papers and slid them across the desk. "You can sit here and fill them out. Just come get me when you're finished."

"You bet."

He grinned and clapped her shoulder as he passed her on his way out of the office. Her shoulder tingled where he'd touched it, pebbling the flesh on her arms.

She was in serious trouble.

Chapter Five

The first week flew by. Allegra spent more time with Story than anyone else, learning all the ins and outs of the business and meeting clients as they came in to shop or get information about upcoming trips. Tyler and Bo, it seemed, were out more often than not, which suited Allegra just fine.

Juggling the large insulated travel mug of her homemade latté in one hand and some files she'd taken home for the weekend in her other hand, she fingered her key ring, trying to find the right key to unlock the shop. She twisted her lips. Monday was not her favorite day of the week.

"Having trouble?"

She jumped and screeched, the files dropping to the ground along with her keys as she whipped around. Tyler's green eyes were as round as her biggest gold hoop earrings. A slow smile formed, creating a shallow dimple in his right cheek.

Oh, so delicious.

Stop that train wreck before it leaves the station. He was her boss. Off limits.

Forbidden fruit.

Allegra, no.

"Did I startle you? Sorry." His grin belied his apology.

"I can see how sorry you are."

He laughed outright, the sound setting off butterflies in her stomach, before bending to pick up the papers.

"Thanks."

"The least I can do." He stood and handed her the files with a wink.

Tyler unlocked the door and held it open for her. "After you."

"Charmed, I'm sure." She cast him what she hoped was a saucy grin and sauntered in. Her mind raced, however. What was she thinking, flirting—more like trying to flirt, with her limited experience—with her boss? *That's some dangerous ground, Allegra.* As if she hadn't already warned herself.

She picked up her pace and headed straight for her office, intent on avoiding him. After setting her things down on her desk, she glanced up to see Tyler leaning against the doorframe, watching her. She huffed. "Can I get you something?"

"Nah." He stepped into her office and plopped down in a chair in front of her desk. "I just wanted to see how things are going for you. Sorry I was out most of last week. With summer just around the corner, people are anxious to get started after being cooped up all winter and most of spring."

"No problem." Really. The last thing she'd needed was a distraction during her first week, and Tyler distracted her, no matter her inner pep talks. "Things are good so far. Story's been a huge help."

"Good, that's good." He looked down.

Allegra followed his gaze. He was picking at his fingernails.

When he didn't talk again, she reached to turn her computer on. The beep of the laptop was the only sound in the room. For a second.

The floorboards above their heads creaked with a footstep only a moment before the beginning beats of Simon & Garfunkel's "The Sound of Silence" filtered through.

Appropriate.

"Interesting choice of song for a workout."

Tyler laughed. "Yeah. Their music is pretty eclectic. They're probably in between classes right now."

She nodded. "Do you need anything else?"

He hesitated before answering. "We do need to talk."

Allegra's stomach dropped. Her mind raced over the prior week. Had she done anything wrong? She'd asked a lot of questions, but Story hadn't seemed annoyed by them. As a matter of fact, she'd told Allegra she'd rather be asked those things instead of going back and having to correct a mistake. Tyler had been out most of the week, as had Bo, so she didn't think she'd done anything to upset either of them.

"Oh?" She tried to keep her voice even. "Have I done something?"

Tyler shook his head before answering. "No, nothing like

that."

She swallowed, relief settling her stomach.

"We just need to plan our first adventure."

Her stomach dropped.

The music upstairs switched to "Fear" by One Republic, as if someone were listening to their conversation.

"First adventure?"

"Yep. We need to get started on some of these excursions before summer kicks into high gear and we get swamped. We can start with something easy, like surfing."

She sputtered. "Surfing? Easy?"

Tyler continued as if he hadn't heard her. "Mind you, surfing will take time to learn. I can teach you safety and techniques for rock climbing probably a little easier than surfing."

"Rock climbing?"

It was like the man didn't have ears.

"Kayaking is safe and easy. Kind of tame though, unless you're in some good rapids."

"Tame is good."

Tyler didn't acknowledge her part of the conversation. Why did she even try?

"Oh, or downhill biking Cypress Mountain up in Vancouver. That's a lot of fun."

She'd heard of downhilling. One blogger said you could hear the screams of mountain bikers riding downhill right before their thuds. Not a chance.

"There's our five-day bike trip down the coast."

That didn't sound scary.

"But you're just learning the job. I don't want to take you away for that long while you're still new."

Of course.

"Of course—"

Was there an echo in here?

"—there's always skydiving."

She felt the blood draining from her face. But did Tyler notice? Of course not

"Oh! I know. Paragliding. That's always a blast." He finally really looked at her, expectation full in his face.

He really did love this stuff. Huh.

"Um..."

"Paragliding it is."

Her stomach heaved. Maybe she could burn that contract.

Tyler couldn't help it. He lived for adventure. Loved it. And really, everyone should. God gave them this earth to enjoy, and He gave people spirit and personality, so He must want them to get out there and take life by its proverbial horns. People just got in the way of themselves.

He watched Allegra's face as she tried to work her mouth to form words. He'd never understood some people's lack of desire to scale new heights. Fears were made to be conquered. There was no joy in life without being on the move and succeeding in things you never thought you could do. His job was to make people see they could do it.

"Allegra?"

She chewed her bottom lip before taking a deep breath. "Paragliding?" Her voice ended on a squeak. An adorable squeak.

"Yeah, it'll be fun. Picture it: running off a cliff and soaring through the air, just you and the sky. It'll give you a small idea of what skydiving will be like. You'll love it."

He didn't think it was possible for her to pale even more, but she did. Even the blush staining her cheeks seemed to change from pink to white.

"Trust me. It'll be tons of fun. And safe."

She snorted. Actually snorted.

He rapped his knuckles on her desk and stood. "I'll leave you to it. I'll get the excursion organized and let you know. I'd rather do these one-day trips on Saturdays so I don't take you away from work, but you'll get paid for them. Consider it overtime. *Fun* overtime."

"Uh-huh. Sure. Fun."

He grinned as he left her office. He had no doubt she'd love it. He was pretty sure under that carefully applied makeup and subdued clothing was a woman itching for adventure. She just didn't know it yet.

"Hey, Ty."

Tyler stopped and glanced over his shoulder. Story stood at the counter, stirring a cup of coffee. Hmm. A cup of espresso sounded perfect. He turned and walked over. "Hey, Story. How's it going?"

"Good. How was your weekend?"

"Fun. I took that group skydiving on Saturday, then church yesterday. I don't remember the last time I went, but it was a great sermon." He watched Story carefully. She'd stopped going to church well over a year ago with no explanation. She didn't owe him one, but he'd hoped she would talk to him about it. She never did though.

She blinked. "That's nice."

He grabbed a coffee cup from the cupboard and waited while she emptied her coffee grounds and rinsed the portafilter before handing it to him. He filled the double-shot filter, placed his cup, and pressed the button before he turned and leaned back against the counter.

"What about you?"

Story avoided looking at him, instead glancing into Allegra's office, where his accountant focused on her laptop, clicking the keys. Probably returning an email at the speed she was typing.

"Not much. I spent Saturday out shopping with my mom, then yesterday cleaning my apartment and reading a book."

"Anything good?"

Story shrugged. "The book was okay. Some dystopian novel-turned-movie."

Behind him, the spurting of coffee finished. Faint music sounded overhead, along with creaking floors and lots of footsteps. The first class must have started. Coffee scented the air, offering comfort...and inspiring a keen need for caffeine.

"Story, you okay? You and Bo seemed to be having words last week. You both kind of looked upset."

She still didn't meet his gaze, but instead shrugged. "Yep, I'm okay. And Bo and I...we're fine. Just my boss." She flipped him a small smile and walked back into the storefront.

Tyler shook his head. That girl was a closed book if he ever met one.

"Tyler?"

At the sound of Allegra's hesitant voice, he turned to face her. "Hey, what's up?"

She didn't answer for a moment, instead looking toward the doorway Story just exited. When she turned back to him, she walked a little closer. Speaking softly, she said, "I overheard your conversation with Story. I..." She hesitated. "She seemed pretty distracted last week. I don't know her, but sometimes it's easy to tell when something is wrong with someone."

He nodded slowly and pursed his lips. "Yeah. She's been off since last fall. And she and Bo haven't been getting along as well as they used to."

She offered a small smile. "She looks like she needs a friend."

Tyler watched her a moment. Allegra's dark glossy hair was swept back off her face and in a loose bun low on her head. High cheekbones and arched eyebrows framed her blue eyes and delicate nose. The concern in her eyes highlighted her beauty. His heart thumped hard. She seemed to really like Story, even care about her, a woman she hadn't known more than a week.

"Maybe you can be that friend."

Allegra looked like she could use a friend herself. She held herself tightly. He wondered what kind of pain she'd endured to be—or at least seem—aloof. He was sure that aloofness wasn't snobbery.

A bigger smile lifted her full cherry-red lips. "Yeah. Maybe." She turned and walked back into her office.

Tyler stayed at the counter, grabbing its edge. For the first time in a long while, he had a deep impulse to follow a woman, grasp her arms, and kiss her soundly.

Forget his need for caffeine. He had to get out of the store before he did something he'd regret. He hoofed it to his locker, grabbed his running shoes, and readied himself for a long jog, leaving his espresso behind.

Chapter Six

She watched Tyler stretch against the brick exterior from the comfort of her office window before he jogged off. He'd looked pensive before he'd walked out of the back room.

But he was right. Maybe she could be that friend for Story. Goodness knew Allegra could use one herself.

She let out a gentle sigh, sat at her desk, and stared at the computer screen. Jumbles of numbers stared back. It was hard to concentrate when her good-looking employer had shown a soft side.

Allegra rolled her eyes. *Get a grip, woman. Time to get to work.*

But first she needed fortification.

She stepped out into the common area and made herself a latté. The tinkling of the bell at the front of the store caught her attention, but she ignored it knowing Story would respond. She added a bit of salted caramel flavor to her drink and stirred.

"Allegra?"

She dropped the spoon with a clatter, her heart jumping into her throat.

"Oh, sorry! I didn't mean to scare you."

"No." Allegra turned to face Story. "It's okay. What's up?"

"Someone's here asking for you."

Me?

She stepped out of the back room and was immediately swallowed up in a ferocious hug. Honeysuckle floated in a cloud around her. She gasped and stepped back out of the hug.

"Capri? What are you doing here? How did you get here?"

"Can't a girl surprise her big sissy?" She laughed, the low chuckle the complete opposite of her feminine high-pitched voice. "A friend's mom works at the airline and gave her some buddy passes. She gave me one of those. Who wouldn't want a free trip? Especially to see their sister."

"Well, yeah, but...what about school?"

"Spring break, sis. I don't have to show until Thursday—and only then because I have a paper due next week that I want some quiet to write, so I thought I'd come up here and hang out with you." Caprice tilted her head back and looked straight up. Kayaks and oars hung from the ceiling. "This is quite the place. I can't believe you work here."

"Yeah. Tell me about it. Not the job I expected, but I'm actually liking it." At least until Tyler enforced their contract and she had to do some serious risk taking.

Story cleared her throat.

Allegra turned. "Oh, I'm so sorry. Story, this is my sister,

Caprice. Caprice"—she faced her sister—"this is Story, my coworker."

Story shook Caprice's hand before turning back to Allegra. "Hey, if you want to take off for the rest of the day, I can cover you. Tyler went for a run, but it's super quiet right now, so I'm sure he won't mind."

Allegra chewed her bottom lip. It'd be nice to take the rest of the day off, but... "Are you sure he won't mind?"

Story grinned. "Nah, he won't mind. I think he has a soft spot for you." She winked and shrugged a slim shoulder. "I'll let him know what happened. He'd want you to spend some time with your sister."

Caprice threw an arm around Allegra's shoulders and smiled at Story. "You're the sweetest. But I know my sister, and I know she'll only have guilt if we take off."

Yep. Her sister knew her well.

"What time are you off?"

Allegra glanced at her watch. "It's only lunch. I'm not off until four o'clock."

"Perfect! I saw some cute shops down the way. I can look while you finish up your day."

"Um, that's four hours, you know."

Her sister grinned. "Exactly."

She squeezed Capri close. "Thanks, sis. I love you. And I'm so happy you're here."

"Ditto, chick. I'll be back in a few hours."

Allegra waved her off, grabbed her latté, and headed to her office. Her sister was here. So odd. She gnawed her bottom lip. What if something was wrong? Capri seemed pretty cheerful, but...was she *too* cheerful? Oh man. School. What if something was wrong with school? She knew the tuition payments for the semester had so far gone through her account okay, so it couldn't be that. It hurt to see that much money disappear from her bank account, but it was better than her sister starting life in debt with student loans. And she didn't mind ramen.

Much.

She shook her head and took a sip of the cooling coffee. Perfect. Just what she needed to get through the last few hours of her day.

"It's a travesty, you know."

It was Tyler's turn to jump. Allegra laughed from behind him, a light, tinkling sound. He squelched his grin before he turned to face her. "What is?"

"You left your coffee on the counter when you went for your run."

"Oh, that. Yeah. Don't tell anyone else, okay?" He winked. "This is Seattle. I might be banned from the city." He picked up a towel from his locker and wiped the sweat from his face and neck.

Allegra murmured something that he didn't quite catch.

"Sorry?"

"Oh." Pink tinged her cheeks. "I didn't say anything."

"You sure? I could have sworn I heard you say *yum*."

Her cheeks colored from pink to downright red. Uh-huh. That was exactly what she'd said. He tightened his mouth to keep from grinning. Funny how one person could bring so much laughter and smiles in such a short time, without even trying, it seemed. Not like the women he'd dated during his football days. All they'd done was hung off him, acting all sultry. He admitted he'd liked it back then, but Allegra, she was genuine, funny...and beautiful.

"Nope. Not at all. Gotta get back to work." She whipped around and stumbled over a chair in her way. He grabbed her elbow to steady her, but she pulled it from his grasp and kept going. Hiding in her office.

His cheeks lifted as his mouth started to stretch in a laugh, only to catch himself yawning. Apparently he'd stayed up too late. But no matter what he'd done last night, how busy he'd kept himself, he couldn't keep his mind off this beautiful employee of his.

Right. *Employee.*

With a groan, he tossed his towel across the room into the laundry hamper, grabbed a change of clothes from his locker, and hit up the bathroom to rinse himself off in the shower.

A cold shower.

―――⸙―――

The chirp of Tyler's phone indicated a new text message. Sliding his hand into his pocket, he grabbed his cell and pulled it out.

Bo: **Meet me at Market Diner, one hour?**

Huh. Tyler glanced at his watch: 1:00 p.m. He could make it there in an hour, and it'd be after the lunch rush.

Tyler: **Sure. See ya there.**

Bo hadn't been into the office in almost a week. He'd

taken out a couple of groups on daylong excursions and one group on a two-day trip, but otherwise was nowhere to be found. Something was going on with him.

Tyler's stomach rolled. Bo wasn't the kind of guy to be secretive, so it shouldn't be anything major. Unless this had something to do with Story. That little scene last week didn't sit well with him.

He shook his head. No doubt things were fine and the guy was just hungry and wanted company. Nothing new. Bo was always hungry.

Tyler worked for another thirty minutes before grabbing his jacket and heading to the front. "Hey, Story, I'm heading out to meet with Bo."

As soon as Bo's name left his mouth, Story averted her gaze and gave a quick nod. "Sure. Have fun."

"Thanks. I don't know if I'll be back again today. Can you tell Allegra where I went in case she needs anything?"

"Yep." She busied herself at a display of carabiner keychains near the checkout.

"See you tomorrow."

She didn't even glance up. "Bye."

He pushed open the door and walked out into a pressure cooker of heat. Spring temperatures in Seattle usually hovered around sixty-four degrees, but there were days like today when it reached much higher. And the humidity. His mom used to say it was "too muggy." He didn't understand that term growing up, but somehow, at almost thirty-two, he got it.

An electric trolley lumbered by as he decided to walk the

few blocks down to Pike Place Market. Cars moved slowly through the downtown area, especially so close to such a popular tourist attraction. And with the day so sunny day, there was plenty of activity, all a comfort to him. He saw high-powered suits chasing life on the constant go, reaching and achieving goals, not being afraid. He saw the down-and-outers, wishing for just a tenth of what those power suits had. And in the middle of it all, a retired veteran in his Korean War ball cap hawked *Real Change*, Seattle's weekly newspaper that served to help the city's low income and homeless.

If only he could get Allegra to see things his way. Why did she freak out each time he brought up doing something? Obviously she was afraid. He understood some people had genuine phobias, but she didn't claim that. She didn't even claim fear, really—it was more in the way she paled and withdrew when he brought up their agreement. Guilt pricked the back of his neck, but he shrugged it off. If she was really *that* scared—phobia scared—she wouldn't have taken the job.

Tyler almost stepped on an apple core in the middle of the sidewalk. He reached down, picked it up with two fingers, and tossed it in a nearby trash can. People who let fear run their emotions treated life like that apple: garbage. No thanks. Not him. He was making it his life's passion to not let others do that to themselves any longer.

Fear had no place in life.

And he wouldn't let Allegra run scared anymore. He nodded his head and smiled at the vet selling the copy of

Real Change.

"Can I interest you in a paper, sir?" The man's full white beard hung to his chest and quivered when he spoke.

Tyler dug in his pocket and withdrew a bill, handing it to the guy. "Thanks so much for your service, sir. I appreciate it."

The man took the fifty with a grin. "Thank you kindly. This will go a long way to help a lot of homeless."

Tyler nodded and moved on, clutching the paper by his side. His mind wandered back to Allegra and their upcoming paragliding trip. Honestly? Never mind paragliding on Saturday. There was no time like the present. He'd get everything ready tonight, and when she showed up at work tomorrow, he'd surprise her with it. That wouldn't leave any time for her to think about it. Just get up and go.

He rounded the corner and crossed the street in between traffic. *You rebel, you.* He grinned. *Jaywalking.*

Entering Pike Place, the odor of freshly caught fish wafted around him, causing him to inhale deeply. He welcomed the mix of fish and brine. A lot of people couldn't stand a fishy smell, but when it was fresh and the atmosphere suited it? Perfection.

He wound his way through the marketplace until he reached Market Diner. Stepping inside, he immediately spotted Bo sitting at a corner table. Tyler squeezed between a sitting patron and a waitress and sat down across from his friend.

"Hey, man. How've you been?"

Bo didn't look up from his work shredding a napkin. The

half-empty glass of Coke indicated he'd been sitting there for at least a few minutes already.

Tyler twisted his wrist and looked at the time. He wasn't late. "What's up?"

Bo's shoulders heaved as a sigh escaped. He finally looked Tyler in the eyes. "I have a job offer."

Chapter Seven

"...what?" His business partner had a job offer? "O-okay. Who did you have to turn down this week?" They'd each had job offers before and always turned them down. Quite a few colleges had called when they had announced their retirements, asking if they'd be interested in coaching, Tyler in football and Bo in hockey. He and Bo had said no. ESPN came calling. For Tyler, that opportunity had been tough to say no to, but the network had offered an announcer job only to him, not Bo. He knew Bo wouldn't have minded if Tyler had accepted it, but they'd wanted to launch their own adventure business. He and Bo had become brothers during high school. He couldn't imagine running this business without him. But Bo's mood made Tyler's blood run cold.

Bo's gaze dropped to his napkin. Or what was left of his napkin. "I accepted."

Tyler's stomach clenched. "Dude. This isn't funny."

His best friend pushed back in his chair and started

drumming his fingers on the table, looking everywhere but at Tyler. "I know this is sudden, and...I'm sorry. I just...things happened so fast, I didn't have a chance to talk it over with you, and they needed an answer right away. With me and—"

Tyler waited, biting his tongue, as Bo abruptly stopped talking.

"I just need a change of scenery, and this job—" He finally met Tyler's eyes. "It's an incredible opportunity. I'm gonna be coaching at my alma mater, Ty."

Tyler whistled low. "Okay. I admit that *is* an incredible opportunity. Boston College is what, number six in division one hockey? But what about Hawk's Flight?"

Bo scrubbed his face with his palms. "You can buy me out."

His mouth dropped. "What? No way am I buying you out. You put just as much into this business as I have." Tyler's mind flipped through the ramifications. He'd be down a guide, which would mean less excursions unless he could hire someone right away. But it was more than that. He'd be living this dream without his best friend.

Bo's hands raised in the air, frustration evident. "What do you want me to do? I can't pass this opportunity up."

The chance of a lifetime, but they'd both had more than their fair share of those. What made Boston different? Denver couldn't possibly have sweetened their deal more than Minnesota—ranked second and first—had last year, and Bo had turned them both down without batting an eye.

Edison's invention went off in his brain. Story. Bo was running. "Who are you running from?" Maybe if he framed it as a question, the man would own up.

Between clenched teeth, he answered, "I'm not running. I've been given an opportunity, and I'm taking it."

Still not talking about Story. Fine. "Well, I'm not buying you out. If you need to do this, then do it. I'll support you. But your half of the business is still your half. It'll be here for you if and when you need it."

Bo's shoulders drooped as he leaned forward and planted his elbows on the table. "Thanks, Ty. I..." He cleared his throat, still not meeting Tyler's gaze. "I appreciate it."

Tyler reached across the table and smacked Bo's arm. "Just don't make that team so good they beat Penn State, eh?"

Bo grinned. "You're going down, punk."

The waitress came and took their orders. After she left, Tyler sipped his water, watching Bo over the rim of the glass. He set the cup down and leaned back. "When do you start?"

"A month. I know it's quick, but they wanted me sooner. I had to make sure Allegra was settled in the job before I left her to the hound though." He pointed a finger at Tyler's chest. "That hound, of course, being you."

"Ha-ha. You're not nearly as funny as you think."

"Says you."

Bo told him all about the job over burgers and fries. The six-figure salary and added bonuses didn't appeal to Bo as much as working with up-and-coming kids who loved hockey for the game, not the money or fame. A few times, Tyler found himself a little envious of those kids. Growing up, all he'd wanted to do was play football, but his parents held him back, scared that the rough sport would trigger an asthma attack.

"Tyler, downfield. Run!" Tyler was off like a bolt of lightning, running down the field all while his eyes stayed on the pigskin in Russ's hand. He kept running as he watched his older cousin release the ball in Tyler's direction. He followed its arc as it sailed through the air. Tyler lifted his hands, forming a triangle with his pointer fingers and thumbs, ready to catch the ball and run to the end zone.

"Tyler Richmond, stop!"

The shriek of horror stopped Tyler in his tracks, the ball thudding to the ground beside him.

His mom, face pale and eyes wide, ran toward him from the sliding glass doors at the back of their house.

"Mom, I'm fine." But it was no use. She didn't stop until she reached him, her hands fluttering all around him.

"Are you okay? Are you breathing fine? Where's your inhaler?"

"I'm fine, Mom." Heat infused his neck and cheeks. Russ stood behind Tyler's mom and watched the embarrassing scene unfold, his eyes rolling heavenward.

"Auntie Michelle, he's okay. I've been keeping an eye on him."

At least Russ tried to help.

Tyler's mom ignored Russ and kept watching Tyler. She shook her head. "No. You're not doing this." She raised her arm and pointed a finger back toward their home. "Cynthia is inside playing school with her dolls. You can go play with her."

Was she serious? "Mom!" If ever he wanted the earth to

open up and swallow him whole, it was now.

"Get in the house. I don't want you overdoing it and having another asthma attack." *She jabbed her finger toward the house again. "Now."*

"Earth to Tyler."

His gaze focused on Bo standing beside the table, ready to leave. "Oh. My mind wandered. Sorry, man."

Bo clapped him on the back. "No worries. Listen"—his gaze bored into Tyler's—"thanks for everything." He held out his fist.

Tyler fisted his own hand and bumped Bo's. "I've got your back." He grinned. "Those kids won't know what hit them when you step onto that ice."

"Feel bad for them?"

"Of course."

Bo shook his head, his gray eyes twinkling. "What about me? I get a team of twenty-five college guys trying to keep their GPAs up when all their friends are out partying? Yeah." He paused a moment. "Maybe I should turn the job down."

Tyler laughed. "Nah, man. Those punks will be lucky to have you. It'll take a few hot seconds, but they'll learn you've got their best interest at heart."

His friend nodded. "Thanks."

They walked out of the restaurant and into the market. Summer was the busiest season in Seattle, but spring brought more than enough tourists to Pike Place. As he and Bo approached a vendor, a fishmonger tossed a salmon to the wrapper, who covered that fish in what seemed like less than a second. A sight Tyler would never grow tired of.

Stepping out of the market into a day with a bright-blue sky and hot sun beating down revived Tyler's spirit. There was always something about being downtown on a sunny day that made him feel like everything was right in the world. He felt that way more often out in the wilderness, but when he couldn't escape the city, this was his favorite place.

"See you tomorrow." Bo lifted his hand in goodbye and took off, heading for his car.

Tyler turned in the opposite direction, in no rush to go back to the shop. The sun glistened off the water as he strode along the quay. Seagulls soared overhead, no doubt hoping to catch some dinner. People—tourists and hometowners alike—rode bikes or walked past him, taking in their own perceptions of the city.

He had a lot to think about.

And more to pray about.

Allegra looked up from her locker when she heard the bell ring over the front door. Caprice was back. Allegra grinned, finished throwing her things in her bag, and slammed the locker closed.

"Hey, sis, I'll be right out."

"Don't hurry," Caprice called back.

Allegra tucked her light jacket over her arm, grabbed her travel mug from the counter, and rushed to the front of the shop. "So what did you end up doing for the afternoon?"

Something wasn't quite right. Capri didn't meet her gaze. "Capri?"

"Just took in the sights and sounds of Seattle. It's

beautiful here."

"Yeah. It is. But what's up?"

The bell rang overhead once more as the door opened behind Allegra. Great. Story was gone for the day, so she'd need to take care of this customer. "Hold that thought."

Allegra turned to greet the customer but instead came face to chest with Tyler. She looked up and grinned. "Phew! I thought you were a customer, and I was going to have to charge *you* overtime for staying past closing."

She loved it when he laughed. Loud, hard, and long. But this laugh didn't quite reach his eyes. Her grin faded. "Tyler? What's wrong?"

He looked over her shoulder and quirked a brow. "You have a customer. I can wait."

Oh! "No, I'm sorry." She turned and reached for Caprice. "Tyler, this is my sister, Caprice. Capri, this is—"

"Tyler Hawk!" Caprice reddened, fanning her face with her hand. Allegra had never seen her sister gush like this. Tension climbed Allegra's spine, and she clenched her jaw. Capri leaned in close to Tyler, flashing white teeth his way. Her hand reached out to him, seemingly of its own accord, and touched his muscled forearm...and stayed there.

She wanted to grab her little sister by the ear and throw her out of the shop. Caprice needed to leave Tyler alone. He was too old for her, and Capri had too much on her plate. Besides, he was Allegra's boss. And friend. She watched as Tyler grinned at something Caprice said. How could her sister flirt like that? She...whoa. Was she actually *jealous*? No. No way. Tyler was her employer.

A good-looking employer, but her employer nonetheless.

Allegra startled when she realized the conversation had died and Tyler and Capri were both staring at her.

"Well?" Caprice asked.

Allegra tucked a lock of hair behind her ear. "Uh…I'm sorry." She lifted her gaze to Tyler. "I got lost in thought. What was that?"

Laughter danced in his eyes, like he knew what she'd been thinking. At least he kept it to himself though. "Caprice invited me to join you ladies for dinner."

She speared her sister with a glare. Caprice was going to die. Spontaneous combustion. Or maybe a Jedi mind trick. If she concentrated hard enough and squeezed her fingers, maybe she could cut off Capri's air supply. Allegra swung her gaze back to Tyler.

"Uh, yeah. Of course. Join us."

Tyler watched her a moment, amusement lifting the ends of his mouth up in a smile. "I'd love to."

Allegra's stomach lurched. A night out with Tyler.

And her sister, of course.

"But I shouldn't."

And just like that, her stomach dropped. Was she actually disappointed?

Capri laid her hand on his arm. The brat.

"Of course you should."

"No, really. This is your first night in town to visit your sister, and it's no doubt a short visit. I don't want to intrude."

Caprice looked at her, her gaze pleading. While Allegra never cared about sports, Caprice followed college teams. A night out with an NFL star would be something her sister would absolutely love. Allegra eyed Tyler. The man probably had women throwing themselves at him all the time. Did she really want to spend an evening out with Tyler, watching women drool over the sight of him? No. But the raised eyebrows and huge eyes on Caprice's face were too much. Allegra sighed.

"Seriously, Tyler. It's okay." She gave an indulgent smile to Caprice. "I think you'd disappoint my sister if you didn't join us."

Tyler stepped close, his arm brushing hers, and quietly asked, "Would I disappoint *you?*"

She felt the vibration in the air as he spoke soft and low, for her ears only. The tantalizing scent of grapefruit, mandarin oranges, and the sea tickled her nose and weakened her knees. Her gaze flew to his, searching for and finding heat. Funny how she'd never noticed the depth of his eyes before. Like he was trying to share a secret with her, but she couldn't understand. Tyler's fingertips grazed down her arm, sending her stomach flipping in response.

This was a dangerous man.

Chapter Eight

Back off. BACK OFF! Red lights flashed in Tyler's mind. If the robot from *Lost in Space* were there, he'd be repeating "Warning, warning. Danger" in all his theatrical glory.

What was he thinking, flirting with an employee? She could file a sexual harassment lawsuit against him faster than a pass rusher blitzing the quarterback. Totally not something he wanted to handle, especially for an offhanded remark. Sure, Allegra was beautiful—more than any woman he'd seen in a long time—but she wasn't his type. She was wound up tighter than the Ace bandages his sports therapist had wrapped Tyler's ankle in before games. And that had left his toes blue. Allegra might have silky black hair that reminded him of a moonless night, and eyes that lit up more than the grandstand. Not to mention curves he'd like to wrap his arms around...

He shook his head to dislodge the trail of those thoughts.

He was already toeing a dangerous line. He needed to reel it back in. Besides, even though he was attracted to Allegra, it could never go further than that. Nothing meaningful could develop between them. Not only were they employer-employee, but more than that, there was nothing deep to connect them. They were oil and water, fire and ice, toothpaste and orange juice. He lived in the moment, and she no doubt had three-ring binders of one-, five-, and ten-year plans. The days when he let his physical needs drive his relationships were over. If there couldn't be a future with a woman, then there'd be no woman at all.

Nope. She wasn't for him.

He took a step back. She licked her lips, her ocean-blue eyes wide as she continued to stare at him. Two steps. "I mean, I wouldn't want to disappoint my employee." He cringed inwardly when he saw her pretty blush pale. *Wrong thing to say, man.* He never had any problems talking to women, but Allegra threw him out of whack. What was it with her? Or maybe it was him? Maybe his years of being single were playing a number.

The laughter left her eyes, and her gaze cooled and dropped to the floor. All due to him and his fumble.

"No." Though her voice was soft, it held a hard edge. "You wouldn't disappoint me."

Uh-oh. He never should have flirted with her. Apparently his flirting ticked her off. Or was it his backpedaling that did that?

Allegra looked at her sister as Caprice's gaze swung between the two of them. "I'm sure Tyler is busy. Let's just keep it to you and me tonight." She pasted on a smile as fake as a toupee.

"I'm not busy." And just like that, he threw his internal tug-of-war out the window.

He'd never understand himself.

Caprice jumped on his words. "Great!" She eyed Allegra before she spoke again. "I'm sure Allie wants to go home and freshen up. But we can meet you somewhere in an hour or so. What's a good place around here?"

Tyler almost laughed out loud when Allegra's eyes bugged out at her sister. But she didn't say anything.

"Have you been to Block 36, Allegra?"

"Uh, no. I can't say that I have."

"It's a great farm-to-table restaurant on North Thirty-Sixth. I can meet you there in"—he glanced at his watch—"about an hour and a half. Does that work?"

"Perfectly. We'll see you then!" Before Allegra could utter a word, they were out the door.

Tyler chuckled. This would be an interesting night.

"What were you thinking?" Allegra threw her handbag on the kitchen counter of her condo.

Caprice stared at her with innocent eyes. Yeah. Like she'd believe that angel act. Ha!

"Come on, Allegra. I saw the way you two looked at each other. You like him. And he likes you." A slow, sly grin covered her face.

"First off, this isn't high school. And second, he's my boss!"

"And?"

She huffed. Her sister could be so annoying. "Haven't you ever heard of workplace romances? And their failures? That usually result in being fired? No thanks."

"Oh, come on, Allie. Take a risk! He seems like a really nice guy. When was the last time you went out on a date?"

Allegra pulled her bottom lip in with her teeth. It had been a long time, but... "No, Capri. He's my boss. And yes, he's nice and funny and good looking, but—"

"Ha!" Caprice pointed her finger in glee. "You do like him."

Allegra felt a headache coming on. "Give it up. It's not happening."

Her sister gave her a side-eye and walked away, whistling an upbeat tune.

"It's not happening!" She rolled her eyes heavenward and shook her head. There was just no arguing with that girl.

After she showered and dressed, Allegra pushed Caprice out the door and down to the parking garage. Caprice hopped into the passenger side of Allegra's Pacifica as Allegra slid onto the driver's seat.

Allegra glanced at the clock on her GPS screen as pulled onto the street. "I can't believe we're running late."

"Psh. Only five minutes, Allie. Take a breath."

Allegra gritted her teeth. "You can't be *only five minutes* late when you start your internship, Capri. Being late is inexcusable and could cost you a good reference, if not your job." She heard a sigh next to her.

"I...I don't know if I'm going to accept the internship."

"I knew it! I knew something was wrong. Why wouldn't you take it? You said it yourself: it's *J. Wong*. I mean, hello? What's going on?"

Allegra let Caprice gather her thoughts as Allegra navigated the busy Seattle traffic. If she pushed, her sister would do the opposite. If she kept quiet and made a reasonable argument, she might have a fighting chance of convincing Capri to take the internship...despite the financial cost to herself.

Her mind whipped through budget calculations while Caprice tapped a finger on the console. It was going to be tight. Very tight. But she could give up her Netflix subscription and—*gasp!*—her Starbucks budget. That one would hurt. She had books she could read instead of binge-watching shows, but her Starbucks? Ouch.

"I worry about you."

She knew it. "Sis, I love you, and I absolutely love that you worry about me, but I'll be fine. I've already run the numbers"—kind of—"and it's doable. I don't want you to miss this opportunity."

There was another pause before Caprice spoke again. "Confession time."

Dread rolled Allegra's stomach. "What?"

"I didn't just come here to see you. I had an interview today."

Her stomach quit rolling and dropped instead. "An interview? Where?"

"Achung."

"Bless you."

Capri glared from the passenger seat. "Funny."

"I thought so." She tossed a grin at her sister. "Seriously, tell me about it, and tell me *why* when you already have an internship at a super-huge design house."

More silence. At this rate, they'd be at the restaurant before her sister told her anything more.

And sure enough, the signage came into view. Allegra pulled the car into a spot close to the doors and turned it off. She twisted her body to fully face Caprice. "If this has anything to do with my finances, I'm going to smack you." She softened her statement with a smile.

She watched as Caprice chewed her bottom lip. Apparently it was a family habit. "Kind of. But I also miss you. This will just be for the summer."

Allegra grabbed Caprice's hand and squeezed. "I miss you too. But think about it: What would be better for your career? Achung—whom I'm pretty sure no one has heard of—or J. Wong, a designer pretty much everyone knows, especially if they watch *Project Catwalk*."

Her sister giggled, a relief.

"Think about it. We'll talk more later, 'Kay?"

Caprice nodded as she climbed out of the car. Allegra held the restaurant door open for Caprice and followed her in.

Ready or not.

Chapter Nine

Tyler brushed some imaginary lint off the front of his shirt. The casual décor—wood beams overhead, butcher-block tables, and industrial metal—lent a hipster vibe that wasn't necessarily his taste but made for a warm atmosphere. Voices buzzed around his ears like a pesky fly. All he wanted was to see Allegra.

And that desire made him want to spill water all over himself again so he had an excuse to leave. The woman was becoming an obsession.

A thought hit him: an obsession he supposed he wouldn't be paragliding with tomorrow after all. He'd have to find out when her sister was leaving. Tyler stuffed the straw to his cola into his mouth and practically drained his glass.

"Wow, you're thirsty. I'll bring you another." The waitress he hadn't even noticed approach turned her back on him. Yep. Another cola would do him well. Or maybe something stronger. Nerves zapped his stomach like he was being electrocuted.

He glanced down at his phone. Allegra and her sister were five minutes late. Maybe he should call? She might have been smart and had second thoughts about coming. He slid his finger along the bottom of his phone and unlocked it, checking for a text message.

Only one appeared: *Just finding parking. Be there in a minute.*

His pulse picked up. She was actually here.

He licked his lips as the waitress sat a fresh glass in front of him and swooped up his empty one. "Thanks." He smiled.

She put a hand on her hip and cocked her head. "Hey...aren't you Tyler Hawk?"

Not now. Allegra was about to walk through the door, and the last thing he wanted her to see was him appearing to be flirting with their waitress. Not that she would care, but he did.

"Uh..." He couldn't very well lie. "Yeah."

Stars shone in her eyes. She pointed her chin over her shoulder. "Hey, guys!" A handful of customers, and a few employees behind the bar, looked up. "It's Tyler Hawk!"

Murmurs rose, and a guy at the table next to him whispered to a waitress, took a Sharpie from her hand, and leaned over. "Hey, man! Can I get you to sign my shirt?" He handed Tyler the Sharpie and pointed to the white number on the back of his shirt. Of course. A Seattle Seahawks jersey.

"Sure thing." Tyler scrawled his name and handed the marker back. "Thanks for being a fan." The guy held up a fist, and Tyler bumped it with his own.

The waitress stood silently by as a few others approached

Tyler. When they left, she crouched beside his table, angling herself so he could have a good view of her...ahem...assets. He made sure to keep eye contact with her, but she leaned closer.

Sweat broke out on his upper lip.

"I'm Lauren." She wobbled a bit and rested a hand on his thigh. To steady herself, or for other reasons? Either way, he was not okay with it. He shifted his legs, but she kept tracking him. Egad. Desperate women were definitely not attractive.

Lauren leaned her body toward him, now giving him an opportunity to have an indecent view. He glanced over to the door, keeping his gaze away from the woman. In his past life, he would have jumped at the opportunity she was offering him, but he was a changed man.

Still, temptation was just that for a reason.

Hot breath fanned his cheek. He turned his face only to feel the brush of lips across his.

And in his peripheral vision, he saw Allegra and her sister walk in.

Of course.

Yep. The sight in front of her was exactly how Allegra had imagined this night would turn out. Except she'd thought it would be after dinner. At least there was nothing in her stomach to throw up.

A little piece of her, however, wanted to run and hide under a blanket while she sobbed her heart out. Dramatic much?

Beside her, Capri gasped, her hand clasping her chest. Apparently drama also ran in the family.

"Allie, that woman! What is she doing?"

She eyed her sister. "What is the *woman* doing? Don't you mean, what is Tyler *allowing* her to do?" She glanced his way in time to see him push the lady off him.

Hmm. Maybe there was hope for him after all.

The woman stood to her full height. Blond, slim, with fabulous skin. Allegra looked down at her own curves. Nothing special there.

Caprice jabbed her in the arm. "Stop comparing."

It was like her sister was a mind reader.

"Come on." Capri grabbed Allegra's hand and pulled her along, weaving past tables and patrons until they stood beside Tyler's table. His admirer was still there, bottom lip sticking out as she watched Tyler.

Really? Allegra had never seen an adult pout before.

As she and Capri sat across from Tyler, the woman, apparently their waitress for the night—joy—faced them, eyeing her and Caprice up and down. She rolled her eyes at Allie but squinted in deeper examination at Caprice.

Dismissed. Again.

Except when the waitress lowered her gaze to look at Tyler, he was watching Allegra.

"Hi."

Chapter Ten

Hi. His eloquence never ceased to amaze him. A beautiful lady and her sister just walked in to have dinner with him, only to see the waitress throwing herself at him, and all he could say was *hi?* Brilliant.

Tyler let his gaze leave Allie's and rise to the waitress's. She was literally pouting. Bottom lip out and all. Did she think that was attractive? He glanced back at Allegra. Now *there* was an attractive woman. She oozed aloof right now, but over the course of the past few days, as he'd gotten to know her a little, he sensed she was anything but aloof. She came across as a balance of confidence and doubt, with a great dose of humor blended in, a combination he found all too appealing.

His heart rate picked up a step. Or three.

Hearing a throat clear, he turned to face the waitress but watched Allegra from the corner of his eye. She read her menu intently, as though trying to translate another language.

"Yeah?" A loud huff brought his full attention to the waitress.

"Your companions." She faced Allie and Caprice. "Drink?" Color-infused cheeks surrounded a sneer. This was a woman not used to being turned down apparently. Did he even dare let the sisters order from her? What if she spit in their drinks?

He narrowed his gaze as Allegra spoke up. "Um...Diet Coke."

He couldn't be sure, but he thought he heard a snort. The waitress was growing uglier by the second.

Caprice placed her drink request before the waitress stalked off. "She's charming."

He grinned. "Very."

Caprice's even, white teeth gleamed from behind full red lips. She was pretty in an exotic sort of way, but it was the older sister he had on his mind. Tyler squirmed. *And in my dreams.*

He let his mind wander while the sisters talked over the menu. Back in his football days, he'd had it all: fame, money, and women. He hadn't started out looking for girlfriends—they kind of fell into his lap as his fame grew. Once he realized what was happening, it became too much to resist. He ended up turning his back on his childhood faith and instead played in the fast lane when it came to the opposite sex.

Thankfully, he'd always protected himself and his girlfriends, so there were never kids or illnesses, but that didn't mean he didn't have serious regrets. He'd lost something he could never get back—and never give away again.

"Earth to Tyler." A hand waved in front of his face. He startled, only to notice the drinks already placed in front of them and the angry waitress waiting.

"Huh?"

Yep. Eloquent.

The annoyed waitress standing at their table sighed, like he'd just asked her to repeat listing all fifty states in alphabetical order—backward.

"Do you know what you want to eat?" She spoke slowly, like he was from another planet.

Allegra watched him like he might very well *be* an alien.

No offense to aliens everywhere.

"Oh." He placed his order, glad when the waitress stalked off.

"If you'd rather not hang out with us tonight, Tyler, it's completely understandable." Allie's husky voice reached across the table.

"What? Why would you think that?"

Her gaze slid in the direction of the waitress.

"Uh, no. Not on her life. No way, no how."

Caprice elbowed Allegra.

Caprice's elbow in her side wasn't the start of Allegra's discomfort. Back at her condo, Capri had gone through all of Allegra's clothes, making her try everything on until she walked out in skinny jeans, brown knee-high boots, and a wine-colored peplum shirt. The Queen Anne neckline perfectly framed her neck and face, drawing attention—in her opinion—away from her...flaws. Her copious flaws.

But right now, she wasn't worried about her many flaws. Just one. The one her jeans were digging into as she sat at the table.

Oh, the discomfort! She felt like she was an illusionist's assistant, being sawed in half.

It was ridiculous. She should have gone with her first choice—yoga pants. But nooo. Caprice wouldn't let her. Allegra had tried to argue that no one had ever been cut in half by yoga pants, but Capri didn't go for it.

Beside her, her sister cleared her throat. Allegra kept her gaze on the water sweating down the side of her glass.

"So, Tyler. What made you think to open your own adventure company?"

No response to Caprice's question. Allegra looked up to see Tyler contemplating her. She lifted a brow.

Wait...was he *blushing?* It was pretty cute, really.

But she'd be the one blushing soon if she couldn't adjust the waist of her jeans to sit higher. Who in their right minds thought midrise jeans would be a good idea? She missed the low rise of her younger years. At least they didn't try to kill her. Though she may have put on a slight bit of weight since she was fifteen.

She made sure Tyler wasn't watching—he was answering Capri—before she grasped the waist of her dumb skinny jeans and tugged up.

Didn't budge.

She squirmed a little in her seat, sitting higher and hopefully giving a little more room for her pants to move.

Hooking her thumbs under the band, she tried again.

Who would have thought adjusting her jeans would be so problematic?

She tried one more time. Tyler was still talking with Capri, so she took a chance and yanked.

Her thumb slipped, and her arm went rogue, hitting Caprice's bicep.

"Ohmygoodness! I'm so sorry." Could one die of mortification?

Yes.

Tyler's mouth gaped, his eyes as round as saucers, his gaze swinging back and forth between her and Capri. He sucked in one cheek, obviously trying hard to keep from laughing. It didn't work.

Allie forgot all about her jeans cutting into her when Tyler finally gave in to his mirth. His shoulders bounced as he cradled his forehead in his right hand, his left hand holding on tight to the table. She had to hand it to him—when the man laughed, he was all in.

It was rather attractive.

Within minutes, the waitress set their food in front of them. The mouthwatering aroma of the burger topped with cheese, ham, a sunny-side-up egg, mustard, and truffle mayo on the crispy bun reminded her that she hadn't eaten much at all today. Allegra's stomach growled, but thankfully the restaurant noise covered it up. She picked up a sweet potato fry that accompanied the burger and nibbled on it. Just the way she loved them: thin cut and crispy on the outside, while soft on the inside. Perfection.

Caprice kept the conversation flowing while they all ate, telling Tyler about the decision she had to make between Achung and J. Wong. He asked her some questions, but Allegra didn't hear any of them. She was way too focused on the man—her boss—sitting across from her. But considering the scene she'd walked in on when they'd first arrived at Block 36, she intended to ignore that jolt of electricity she felt whenever he was around. She had no time for a relationship. She needed to get Capri through college, and those electrical currents could derail that plan. As long as the power was on in her condo, that was all the electricity she needed in her life.

Right?

Thankfully, dinner ended without any more incidents. And miraculously, she wasn't entirely cut in half by her jeans, though she was proud of her stealthy ninja moves to undo the button and relax the band a little.

"Thanks for inviting me to come along with you two. It was a treat."

"It was fun." Capri's exuberance was normally something Allegra admired. When it showed up for her boss though...

"So, Caprice, how long are you in town for?"

Capri shrugged. "Just one full day tomorrow. I need to leave Wednesday to get back to school, and since I'm flying standby on a buddy pass, I should be there first thing in the morning to make sure I get out."

"Ah. Too bad." He turned to Allegra. "So you're taking

tomorrow off then, right?"

She hesitated. She hadn't been working there for long. She didn't want to take advantage. But this was her sister...

"It's okay, Allegra. You can skip work tomorrow. I won't fire you." He grinned, that little-boy charm setting off the butterflies in her stomach.

"Oh...thank you. I really appreciate it." Being on the opposite side of the country as her sister was rough. She would happily take whatever time she could get with Capri.

"See you Wednesday, Allegra." Tyler's eyes twinkled under the streetlights outside Block 36. She had half a mind to lean into him just so she could feel his arms wrap around her, but that would be crazy. She was trying to *not* be attracted to this man standing in front of her. Besides, that twinkle looked a little...mischievous? What was that about?

"Um, yeah. See you Wednesday."

They said their goodbyes, and she and Capri walked back to her car parked down the street.

Locking arms with her, Capri giggled. "He's interested, sis."

Joy shot through her like she'd dropped from the top of a roller coaster. "No."

Caprice snorted. "Deny what you will, Allie. You'll soon find out."

Chapter Eleven

An entire day together, and they still hadn't agreed her sister would accept the J. Wong offer, but Allegra was pretty sure Capri would go that way. And really, who turned down a famous designer in New York City, the mecca of fashion?

Allegra entered the shop, still thinking through her sister's choice.

"Ready?"

She jumped as Tyler came out of nowhere. "You scared me."

He laughed. The deep, rich chuckle fluttered her belly. She was beginning to yearn for that laugh, so much so she wanted to say or do almost anything to hear it again and again. T-r-o-u-b-l-e.

"Sorry. I didn't mean to. I thought you saw me."

"Uh, no. I didn't." She went through the door to the back and put her bag in the locker. Turning, she almost bumped into Tyler, he was standing so close. She lifted a brow. "Do you need something?"

A strange look flitted across his face. "You forgot, didn't you?"

Her skin tingled. "Ohmygoodness, what did I forget?"

He hesitated, and her stomach did somersaults.

"You and I are heading out today."

Allegra scrunched her nose. "Out? Where are we—" But wait... "I thought we weren't going until Saturday!"

"Oh, that." He ducked his head and smoothed the hair at the back of his neck. "I, uh, actually planned it for today instead. You know, so you wouldn't have much time to think about it."

Her heart picked up speed, doing its best to race toward death. Death that would surely follow her outing with Tyler. She'd managed to forget the impending doom with Caprice here, but she'd thought she had some time to get used to the idea. Tyler apparently had different ideas. This was it. Her first excursion.

Paragliding.

She'd better go update her will before they left.

He could pinpoint the exact moment she remembered. Her face paled, and her eyes started blinking faster than a strobe light. He better bring the portable defibrillator.

Feeling a twinge of sympathy, Tyler pulled her hand into his. "I've done this a million times, Allie." His use of her sister's nickname for her seemed to catch Allegra's attention and bring some color back to her face. "We'll fly tandem, so I'll be with you the entire time."

Her hand shook as she pushed it through her hair and looked away. "H-how long will this take? I mean, I-I have a lot of work to do. You know, maybe today isn't a good—"

"You're going, Allie, and it'll be fine. I promise."

"You can't promise that."

The hard edge to her words caught him off guard. "Okay." He drew out the word. "You're right. I can't. But in all the times I've been, nothing big has ever gone wrong." He grasped her chin and forced her to look at him. "I *can* promise I'll triple-check all the equipment and ensure everything is one hundred percent safe before we take off." He didn't want to blackmail her with the signed contract, but this woman needed to let loose a bit. Tyler had a heart for people living with fear. He really did. Kind of. Okay, he couldn't understand it. His parents lorded their fear of his asthma over him the entire time he'd lived under their roof, and it drove him crazy. He understood that having asthma was no joke, and he knew that many kids couldn't do the activities he did because their asthma just wouldn't let them. But he knew his own body, even back then, and knew when he could push it and when he needed to pull back. He wouldn't let fear stop him. And he made it his mission now to not let fear stop anyone else, including Allegra. He wanted her to experience the confidence that pushing through fear could bring. It was important to him, though he couldn't say why.

Her eyes welled, but before he could say anything more, she spoke. "Fine. What do I need to change into?"

She was dying.

They hadn't even parked at Tiger Mountain yet, but her heart pounded out of control, and ice clawed her spine. This was it. She knew it. She would never see or talk to her sister again. She should have called Caprice to say goodbye, but her sister would have just laughed at her and told her not to be so silly. But she wasn't being silly.

The grim reaper was knocking on her door, scythe in hand.

"There it is."

Could the man at least try to disguise the excitement in his voice? She'd never met someone so eager to see her die. One would think he'd just fire her if he hated her that much.

She followed Tyler's finger pointing off his steering wheel and saw a sign on the left that read *Paragliding Landing Field and Parking Lot*. So. They at least provided a landing field for the bodies about to drop like swatted flies. Nice. She wondered if her dead body would bounce when it hit the ground.

Her knee started bouncing as he pulled into a spot. Tyler turned the engine off and practically raced out of the car. She hadn't seen a person this excited since last Christmas. And that had been when her four-year-old cousin had unwrapped his Transforming Batbot. If she could harness a smidge of that enthusiasm, maybe she could convince Tyler she wasn't about to hurl all over him.

Slowly, she pulled on the door handle and, even more slowly, lifted one foot, then the other, out of the car.

"Hey, look! There's a group that's already taken flight."

Animation colored his voice. "Allie, seriously. Take a look. They're totally safe."

She refused to look at anything but the ground. "I'm good."

He laughed and tugged her hand. "Come on. You get some instruction time before we launch."

Launch. Like a rocket. Or the space shuttle *Challenger.* The one that exploded in the air. Her windpipe constricted as she imagined plummeting to earth like a piece of rocket debris.

It was a freak of nature, flying. Unless you were a bird. If God had wanted people to fly, He would have created them with wings, and the last time she checked, feathers weren't growing out of her back.

She followed Tyler like a lamb to the slaughter. She wanted so badly to run back to his car, but he'd think she was a wimp. But then…who cared what he thought? Did his opinion of her matter that much?

Yes. It does.

Drat. Since when had he become so important to her? Since Caprice put it in her head that they liked each other. *False, sister!* When you liked someone, you tried to protect her, not shove her off a sheer cliff. Which Tyler, practically giddy with anticipation, would do. The man was a murderer. One who took sadistic pleasure in torturing her before making her plummet to her demise.

Hmm. Maybe if she could kill him before he killed her…

"Are you coming?" His smile hitched up on one side, laughter flashing in his stupidly gorgeous eyes. He knew. He *knew* what she was thinking.

Time to buck up.

"I am." She lifted her chin and marched past him, only to hear a low chuckle follow her.

The punk.

A slight breeze cooled the mountain air as they walked toward the instruction area. She was thankful for her yoga pants and the sweater she carried to wear under her windbreaker. Too bad the delay of running back to her condo to change had been so short. She might have been able to stall long enough to cancel this outing. But alas.

"I guess it would be dumb to ask if you're excited, huh?"

The man wasn't even worth the effort of a glare. Allegra kept marching forward.

"You'll thank me after this is over. I bet you dinner out you'll end up loving it."

The *gall* of that man!

Dinner out? What was he thinking?

He stopped in his tracks as Allegra kept walking forward, her brown Merrell hiking boots—where had she even found those, considering her lack of love for the outdoors?—at complete odds with her black straight-leg yoga pants and pink *I love coffee, Jesus, and naps* short-sleeved T-shirt. At least she didn't seem to hear his offer. Maybe.

After some time spent on the training hill, Allegra pulled her sweater on over her T-shirt, then her windbreaker over that.

"Hey." He poked her shoulder. "Do you wanna hike the trail to the launch site rather than take the..."

Allegra's hands clenched at her sides. Wow. Tense.

"Okay. Um. The shuttle is faster."

They boarded the Tiger Shuttle that took them to Poo Poo Point, the launch site they'd be gliding off.

Allegra sat completely silent beside him, her hands tucked into opposite elbows. If he didn't know better, he'd think he was sitting beside a statue. He couldn't even hear a whisper of breath.

"Allegra?"

No response.

"Allegra, come on. You did great on the training hill."

She slid her gaze just enough to glare at him from the corners of her eyes. Well, it was something.

"You really did. You're going to do fantastic up there. And remember, you're tandem with me."

That statement got a huff as she turned back to look out her window.

He paused a moment, debating whether he should go there, but...no risk, no reward. "Why are you so afraid?" His words came out softly, almost a whisper.

Her back stiffened in response, but she didn't turn. He lifted his hand and let it hover over her shoulder before he withdrew it. No sense in comforting someone who so obviously didn't want to be comforted. Besides, he knew once she got over her hang-up, she'd love paragliding. She just needed some confidence.

The shuttle van braked, and the few other passengers

exited. A murmur of excitement electrified the air.

Tyler climbed out of the van and turned to help Allegra down. She wouldn't meet his eyes, but he still saw the tremble of her chin. His heart went out to her. But if he coddled her like his parents had him, she would never realize she had what it took to be great.

Chapter Twelve

Wow. It was colder at the top of the mountain than it'd been at the training field. Of course, anyone would know it got colder the higher up you went, but still. It had to be a good ten-degree drop. Allegra did her best not to pass out at the mere thought of *drop*. But her knees went weak when she turned and saw someone running down the hill and taking off into the sky.

Nope.

She whipped back around, intent on running to the shuttle before it left to go back down to the training field. Instead, she ran right into Tyler. This was becoming a nasty habit.

He grabbed her shoulders. "Not so fast, young grasshopper."

A nervous giggle escaped before she could stop it. "Whatever do you mean?" Man, she hated that her voice was so breathless. It must be the lack of oxygen at such a high altitude.

Tyler grinned. "I know exactly what you were trying to do. You're not getting out of this."

She glared up at him. "Contract-shmontract. I'm outta here."

"No can do. That baby is ironclad. Besides, you'll have fun." Challenge lit his eyes. "I double-dare you."

Did the man suddenly turn eight? "What?"

"I double-dare you. I know you'll have fun, but you can't turn down a double-dare. If you do, I'll…" He lifted his hand and rubbed his chin, the stubble scraping against his fingers. "I'll make you go skydiving instead."

Infuriating. Allegra swallowed past the lump in her throat and glanced over her shoulder in time to see another person run down the hill. Paragliding or skydiving? Either meant death. But at least this death would be quicker at a lower elevation than skydiving. "Fine."

"Let's do this." He handed her his phone and a short metal pole. "Put that in your front pocket." He pointed at the pole. "That pulls out and plugs into the phone. A selfie stick."

Leave it to the man to own a selfie stick.

"You'll want a selfie once we're in the sky."

"Not likely."

"Trust me."

Hmph. Right. Trust him. The man trying to kill her. She took the items and stuffed them in the pocket of her windbreaker.

Once Tyler hooked his own harness, he harnessed and attached Allegra to him. Her back warmed as the heat from his body radiated against her. She felt her body relax against him. *Inconceivable! No way am I going to let myself be attracted to someone who so obviously has no regard for my physical safety.* Despite her little pep talk, however, her knees turned to jelly when she felt his warm breath stir against the back of her neck. *Argh!*

He had her help lay out the canopy and double-check their attachment. When the wind caught the leading edge of the wing, Tyler motioned her into a run, and before she knew it, she and Tyler flew off the ground.

It wasn't the most comfortable position to be in either. The harness fit snug against her. She was sure to have some rashes to deal with later. Ugh. The gentle breeze she'd felt before they took off now flapped against the nylon fabric of the parachute. It was peaceful.

And once she actually opened her eyes, the scenery was incredible.

The view of her demise had never looked so pretty. The golden sun shone over the tops of the evergreens below her, and here and there she caught glimpses of watery diamonds sparkling in Lake Sammamish. The city of Issaquah sat in the distance, nestled among the trees and lake.

Behind her, she felt Tyler pull the controls, giving her different scenes as they turned.

"Want that selfie yet?" His deep voice brushed her ear.

Allegra clenched her jaw. *Insufferable!*

She had to admit though, it would be kind of cool. And Caprice would love to see that she followed through.

Grunting, she let go of one of the loops she was gripping

and reached into her pocket. Before she pulled the phone out, a thought struck. "What if I drop it?"

Tyler just laughed. "Then a bear is going to be getting lots of calls."

"Bears?" She didn't mean to shriek, but...

"We are above a mountain."

She ground her teeth and whipped that phone out so fast she was shocked she *didn't* drop it. She grabbed the selfie stick, attached it to the phone, then slid her thumb from the bottom of the screen up and opened the camera. Tapping the icon to turn the camera into selfie mode, she reached her arm out.

"Ready?"

"Always!"

She could see his grin on the screen and rolled her eyes. Pasting on a smile, she held up the stick, pressed the button on the handle, and caught her first outdoor adventure on camera, Tyler's grinning face and a bunch of treetops behind her own wide grin.

It never got old. Soaring high in the sky, looking out over Mount Rainier, so quiet and peaceful. That was why he loved paragliding *almost* more than any other sport, sailing far away from the rush, worry, and noise of the world.

Having Allegra strapped to him wasn't bad either.

The end of the flight always came too fast for him, whether his flight lasted fifteen minutes—as this one had—or hours, as previous solo flights had.

Tyler cleaned up and stowed away his equipment as he

watched Allegra sit on the ground, her hair messed from the helmet she'd worn during flight. His arms ached to reach out and hug her. She looked radiant. But he didn't want to push and have her think he was having an *I told you so* moment. So instead, he worked quietly and let her absorb what she had just experienced. He was confident this wouldn't be her only time paragliding.

As he walked past her, intent on putting the harness and other equipment in his Dodge Ram, he heard Allegra whisper. He didn't know if she was talking to herself or him though, so he kept moving.

"Tyler."

The strength in her voice this time stopped him in his tracks. He turned to face her. "Pretty amazing, huh?"

Allegra blinked, looked up at the launch site well above them, and back at him. "Yeah. I...I hate to say it, but...you were right."

Oohhh. He suppressed a grin. That admission had to physically pain her. "You're more adventurous than you know. I'm proud of you, Allie." He didn't wait to see her reaction but turned and continued to his truck.

Once he packed the gear up, Tyler collected Allegra's helmet and radio. "Ready to go?"

She looked over her shoulder. Tiger Mountain was one of his favorite launch sites. He hoped she'd be back.

Maybe even with him.

He had to get it through his brain that she wasn't his type. He didn't do safe. But his heart picked up speed just remembering her courage in facing this fear. If he could figure out why she was so scared—it went deeper than a fear of heights or adrenaline rushes, clearly—maybe...*maybe*...something could happen with them.

His stomach swelled with nausea. Never mind that she wasn't his type. With his past, no way would she touch him with a ten-foot pole.

Chapter Thirteen

Allegra stirred the ramen noodles in the pot one last time. She removed it from the burner of her stove—she chuckled at the memory of her argument with Caprice about it being better cooked in the microwave—and opened the seasoning packet, pouring it in.

She'd be lucky if her doctor didn't scold her about her blood pressure because of so much stinkin' sodium. So lucky, she might even go buy a lottery ticket.

As she finished pouring the last bit into her bowl, her cell rang from the living room. Carrying her dish, she walked to the gray couch, set the bowl on her reclaimed-barn wood coffee table, and picked up the phone. Tyler?

She leaned against a silver-sequined throw pillow—an uncharacteristic splurge but one she couldn't resist—and slid her finger on the screen. "Hi, Tyler. What can I do for you?"

"Hey." His deep voice came through the speaker. "Nothing, actually. I just wanted to make sure you're doing okay after your first excursion today."

She heard the smile in his voice and couldn't help but reciprocate.

"I'm good." Allegra sat down in the corner of the couch and pulled her knees up. "Thanks for checking up on me though."

"Anytime."

An awkward silence followed. Had hearing his low, husky voice through the phone immobilize her brain cells? It seemed like Tyler's brain wasn't functioning, either.

"Well, I should go. I don't want to interrupt anything."

Interrupt ramen? Allegra rolled her eyes. "Thanks again for calling. I appreciate it."

"See you at work tomorrow."

"Bye." She tapped End and laid her phone on the glass-and-chrome side table she'd picked up for cheap at the thrift store. She hated the table—and its mismatched status—but it served its purpose. One day she'd be able to afford one that went with her coffee table.

"Well, that wasn't uncomfortable or anything."

She should really get a cat so she had someone else to talk to other than herself. But that'd be breaking her self-imposed rule of no pets. No way she wanted to wind up a ninety-year-old cat lady with fourteen felines running around.

Her phone rang again. Sheesh. Though maybe if people kept calling and interrupting her dinner, she'd lose weight.

She picked up the phone again. "Hey, sis. Whatcha up to?"

"Ohmygoodness. Allie, you *did it*!"

Allegra laughed. Obviously her sister got the selfie Allegra had texted to her. "I did."

"And? How was it? Was it super romantic?"

"Caprice!" Thank goodness her sister was back at school. She'd do everything in her power to get Allegra and Tyler together if she were in Seattle. "He's my boss." *Not to mention high risk.* "It's not happening. As for paragliding...I have to admit, I kinda liked it. Once I opened my eyes."

"So you'd do it again?"

"Hardly." Allegra laughed. "I *kind* of liked it. I can say I've done it. And lived. Why would I put myself at risk again? The more times you do something dangerous, the higher the chances you have of something happening."

A huff sounded. "Honestly, Allie. Just because Mom and Dad died while—"

"I don't want to talk about it. They made their choices. Now it's you and me, and I'm *not* putting myself at risk."

Caprice stayed quiet.

"I have too much to live for, sis," Allegra said quietly. "I refuse to do anything more than what I absolutely have to in order to keep this job."

"You're missing out on *life,* Allie. 'There is nothing better for a person than that he should eat and drink and find enjoyment in his toil. This also, I saw, is from the hand of God.' Straight from the Bible, dear sister. Mic drop."

Allegra couldn't help the chuckle that escaped her lips. "Mic drop? Oh dear."

"You're missing the point. Intentionally, I might add. God wants us to be thankful for and enjoy what He gives us. He's given you this job, which involves enjoying His creation. So it's in a different way than most. Maybe He wants you to get over your anger with Mom and Dad."

"They made a choice. They chose to put their adrenaline rushes ahead of their concern for us. Am I angry? Yeah, I am. What parent does that?"

"Allie. They didn't choose to die. They loved us, and you know it. It was an accident."

"A preventable one." Allegra pinched the bridge of her nose. "Look. I don't want to argue. Let me do my job and live my life the way I know I should."

"But what if your way is wrong?"

Allegra took a deep breath. If she spoke without thinking, she'd hurt her sister, and that was the last thing she wanted to do. "That's between me and God. He'll let me know if I'm in the wrong."

Caprice's quiet voice echoed in Allegra's ear. "What if He's using me to tell you?"

The beep of Tyler's alarm finally brought him out of a deep sleep. He stretched where he lay on his bed, then rolled over to pick up his phone and check his email.

So many emails.

Scrolling through them, he paused at one from Peter, a man on the board of directors for Tyler's charity. When he'd first joined the NFL, he started a foundation to help kids with asthma learn how to control their condition while playing sports. Growing up, his parents had kept him from doing things he so desperately wanted to do. It wasn't until a coach in junior high took him under his wing and taught him he could be more than his asthma that he fell in love with the sport of football.

He opened and read the email. A grin tugged at his lips. Yeah. He loved this idea.

He shot off a quick reply.

Another day of warm sun shone down on the city of Seattle. He could get used to this weather. He reminded himself that this was Seattle. Rain would inevitably come. Ah well. He'd enjoy today, for sure. Maybe leave work a little early and go for a long bike ride. Better yet, kayaking in Elliott Bay. That sounded perfect.

He shoved the door to the shop and entered under the jingling bell. "Hey all," he called.

Story came out from the back with a halfhearted smile.

So Bo had told her about the job offer. Whatever was going on with these two, it was pretty obvious Story's heart was, if not broken, at least pretty bruised. He reached out his arm and grabbed her in a side hug. "You talked to Bo."

Her eyes welled as she looked at him. "Yeah. It'll be good for him, no doubt."

"What about you?"

"What about me? There's nothing between us, Tyler." She shrugged out of his hold, walked to the pamphlets, and began straightening them. "This isn't an opportunity he can lose. He'll have a great life."

"Story..."

She waved him off. "I'm fine, Ty." She turned back to face

him, any trace of tears gone. "Get to work. He copied me on that email from Peter. Are you going to be putting me and Allegra to work too?"

Tyler laughed. "But of course. I need all hands on deck in order to pull this off so quickly." He winked and left her to continue organizing.

In the back room, he glanced into Allegra's office to find her sitting behind her desk, tapping away at her keyboard. The short-sleeved burgundy shirt she wore looked good against her fair complexion. He knocked on her open door.

Allegra glanced up. "Good morning." A smile lit her tired eyes.

"Morning. You okay? You look like you didn't sleep all that well." He grinned. "Adrenaline from yesterday?"

She rolled her eyes. "For your information, no, I didn't sleep well, but no, it wasn't from adrenaline. Nerd."

"Ha!" A tease from her. Go figure. "Hey, let's go grab a coffee? I need to get out of here and have some fresh air."

She turned the rest of her body away from her computer and faced him directly. "Um…"

"It'll be quick, I promise."

"You don't have to ask me twice."

"Allegra?" He waited for her to look at him. "I just did. Well, kinda."

She laughed as she grabbed a small purse-looking thing and hung it from her wrist. He'd seen those before but couldn't remember what they were called.

"After you." He motioned her through the door.

Outside, he steered her to the left and down a block,

enjoying the silence between them. Up ahead was a coffee bar. They lined up on the sidewalk, waiting to order at the window. Once he had his black coffee and Allegra had some sort of sweet concoction that passed for coffee these days, he turned them into Westlake Park. The concrete park hosted outdoor lunch-hour concerts, a giant chess board, and a fountain waterfall feature. It was a lively place, and though it was missing some greenery, Tyler loved it.

He moved them forward to a bench where they both sat facing the fountain.

"How've you been feeling about your job here?" He didn't think she'd refuse to work the fundraiser, but it never hurt to tread softly.

She gave him a side-eye. "Have I done something wrong here?"

"What?" He jerked his gaze to her. "No. Why would you ask that?"

"Well, you take me out of the office, are completely silent on our way here, and start out with that question?" She waved a hand around her.

He bumped her shoulder with his. "Nah. I seriously just wanted to get out. And get coffee. But I also needed to speak with you." A little one-on-one outside the office was like the proverbial cherry on top.

"Uh-huh." Back to the side-eye.

"I got an email from Bo last night, a forward. Peter, one of the men on the board of directors for my foundation, emailed about funds being a little low. We need to hold a fundraiser. The quickest way to get funding is through those who have money, and well, they like galas."

Allegra quirked a brow. "Go on."

"I'm going to need everyone's help in this. The foundation will take care of ticket sales, but it doesn't have many employees, and holding a gala in a month or two will take a lot of work and planning on their parts. I was wondering if you might be willing to take responsibility for a silent auction?"

She twisted to better face him. "Me? But I've never done an auction before. What all will I have to do?"

"Basically, gather donations. It's short notice, but I think you'll find most businesses pretty generous, especially when you mention my name."

Allegra frowned at him.

"I don't say that from ego, but let's be honest—people do recognize my name." She nodded, so Tyler continued. "Anyway, gather donations, then set a minimum bid that's a bit below their value. My usual donors have big wallets and even bigger hearts, so they always go well above the value of the auction prizes. The night of the gala, you'll need to monitor the tables before the dinner. Once the dinner is finished and everyone is dancing, you'll figure out the winners. I'll start announcing them a little while later." Tyler waggled his brows. "You'll have time for a dance, so save one for me."

Allegra rolled her eyes and smiled but didn't make any promises.

Shoot.

"Once the winners start being announced, I'll need you

back at the tables to collect payment as they claim their prizes. Most will pay by credit card, though one or two might pay with check or cash. Just save it all and put it in a deposit bag I'll get you, and give it to me or Peter at the end of the night."

Allegra chewed her bottom lip. "It sounds simple enough." She watched him for a moment, then grinned. "Will I need to wear an evening gown?"

Tyler's breath hitched as he pictured her in a long evening gown that outlined her curves. His mouth dried. "Um, yeah. Of course," he croaked.

He was positive she knew exactly what he was thinking. She tapped her fingers against her mouth and cast her eyes back toward the fountain, its bubbling a soft background music to the sounds of the city. "Sure. I'll do it. But I better get back to work." She faced him once more. "I have a slave driver of a boss."

Tyler laughed and stood. "Then get at it. And Allegra…" He offered his hand to help her up off the bench and waited for her to meet his gaze. "Thanks. I really appreciate it."

She smiled, fatigue no longer evident in her eyes. "My pleasure."

His heart thudded against his chest. She was so beautiful. Inside and out.

Chapter Fourteen

Allegra tossed ideas for the silent auction around in her mind as they made their way back to the store. When they arrived, she headed straight to her office. She had a lot to do if they were going to pull this gala off in a short time.

When lunch rolled around though, she found that the latté she'd had with Tyler had worn off, and she needed food. Stat. She grabbed her wristlet and wandered into the storefront, where she found Tyler and Story rearranging scary-looking equipment used for...torture? Though she was sure Tyler would tell her it was for rock climbing or something.

"Hey, I'm going out to grab some lunch."

Story looked up. "Is it really lunchtime? No wonder my stomach's growling."

Her laugh filled the few empty spaces in the store. It made Allegra like her all the more.

Speaking of, maybe... "Do you want to join me?"

"Oh! That'd be great!"

Story turned to Tyler, who was watching Allegra with what looked like approval in his eyes. That approval flipped her stomach on its side.

And not a small amount of joy either. *Get. A. Grip, woman. Off limits. High risk. N-O.*

Better to keep her focus on Story.

"Tyler?" Story followed Tyler's gaze back to Allegra.

Whoops. Caught. The man smirked at Allegra before he finally answered Story.

"Of course. I can finish this up pretty quick."

"Thanks." With one final glance at Tyler, Story walked past Allegra with a wink. "Just going to grab my bag."

She found herself alone with Tyler. Again. But this time, there were no real distractions, like a water fountain. She looked around, trying to find something to talk about.

Thankfully, Tyler found his voice first. "I'm glad you two are getting to hang out."

Oookay. "Yeah. It's great." Did he think she didn't have any other friends? Maybe Story thought the same thing and was taking pity on her.

"Story hasn't been herself in a while. And she never talks about doing things with friends." He ducked his head. "And I've crossed that line to gossip. Sorry. Even guys aren't immune to it."

Allegra laughed, partly relieved that maybe it wasn't pity and partly because the guy looked like a cute five-year-old when he was embarrassed.

"No problem. I like her." Dare she take a risk and tell him

the truth? *I feel like I'm walking on the wild side. What's happening to me?* But... "I can admit that I don't have many friends outside my sister, either. It's harder than it looks to make friends, I think."

Tyler's forehead creased as he bunched his brows together. He opened his mouth to say something, but Story came back out.

"Sorry I took so long. Allie, do you mind if we go somewhere specific? The food isn't great, but I feel a need to"—Story glanced at Tyler—"well, just...do you mind if I choose where we go?"

"Nope, not at all."

Story grinned. "Thanks."

"An ice rink?" Allegra gaped at the Seattle Ice Arena looming over them. "You're not going to make me skate, are you?"

Story had the nerve to laugh. Laugh!

"I was kind of hoping you would. But if you just want to grab a hot dog or nachos and sit in the stands, that's okay."

Allegra shook her head. "You're unbelievable." She rolled her eyes, then laughed. "I think I'll be just fine in the stands, if that's really okay with you. Tyler is providing enough excitement to last a lifetime." *No double meaning meant at all, Story. Move along.* She couldn't believe she mentioned Tyler. Good gravy.

Story walked forward with a glance over her shoulder. "I bet he is."

And again with that laughter.

Sheesh.

When they entered the rink, Story was greeted by quite a few people. Did she live here or something? "Do you come here often?"

Her friend looked up from tying a skate. "Haven't I mentioned it?"

"Mentioned what?"

"I coach figure skaters part time."

"What?" That was news to her. She would have remembered something like that.

"Yeah." She finished off the double knot and moved to put the second boot on. "I grew up figure skating—even won a junior national championship."

"Get out! That's crazy!"

Story laughed. "It was a while ago."

"Did you ever get to the Olympics?"

A shadow as dark as her leggings crossed her face. "No." No further explanation. She finished tying her second skate, stood, and nodded toward the counter. "Let me pay for my ice time while you grab some food if you'd like."

Allegra carried her nachos and Diet Coke and followed Story into the rink. Cold air blasted her face. Um…next time, she'd bring a blanket. And maybe a parka? Sheesh. Obviously jeans, heels, and an off-white henley with a belted beige cardigan wouldn't keep her warm.

"So you said you coach part time now?"

Story nodded. "I'm gathering student athletes to coach, but I'm being picky. I want to train the best, but I also know I need to prove my value as a coach, so it's coming along slowly. I just have a couple of students, but it'll come in due time." Story's gaze moved over the ice, as if seeing a past program in her mind's eye. "In the meantime, skating gives me the opportunity to forget the problems and concentrate on what's good and beautiful in my life."

Problems like Bo, maybe?

Story leaned against the boards and removed plastic things from the blades. Guards, Allegra thought.

"Anyway, I like to keep up with my own skating. There's nothing like feeling the rush of air whiz by you as you pick up speed and launch into a jump."

And to prove it, Story took off on the ice, her dark-blond ponytail whipping behind her, before Allegra could say another word. But the grin on Story's face as she sped past, dug in her toe pick, and swung herself into the air said it all.

The woman felt the freedom of a bird on the ice. Oh, how Allegra wished she could find something to give her that same rush.

Without her feet leaving the ground.

Chapter Fifteen

Allegra walked down the next aisle of Read Between the Lines, sipping on the chocolate latté she'd picked up at the store's coffee bar. The wood floors creaked beneath her feet as she stopped in front of the shelves dedicated to Northwest authors.

With more work on her desk than before, Allegra hardly had time for reading. Along with her regular duties at work, gathering donations for the gala and researching how to run a smooth silent auction took up most of her time. She needed a sanity break, and what better than a bookstore? Black iron rails topped with rustic wood drew her up the stairs, where she found a section dedicated to fashion. Huh. Now that she thought about it, it'd been almost two weeks since she'd talked to her sister.

Digging through her purse, she found her cell and tapped on Caprice's name. She was just about to end the call when her sister's breathless voice answered.

"Allie!"

"Hey, I didn't think I'd catch you. Am I interrupting?"

Capri giggled. "Nah, not at all. I was just doing an exercise video on my computer."

Guilt nipped at Allegra. She looked at the books in front of her and the extra-large latté in her other hand. Whoops. "Oh, yeah. Um, me too."

Her sister laughed. "Sure, Allie."

It was so good to hear Capri's voice. She sounded happy. "How are you? What have you been up to? Have you made your decision yet?"

"Sheesh, woman! One question at a time please. I'm good—busy though. I had finals, which is why you didn't hear from me for a while."

"Oh right. I forgot all about that. How'd you do?"

Another laugh. "At least that was one question, but before I get to that, let me answer the other two. I've since been working—"

"Working?" Allegra walked back down to the main floor of the bookstore. "I hope you mean for J. Wong and not some low-paying job."

"Good grief, Allie. I'm an intern. Of course it's low paying. But to answer your other question, which I was about to do before you so rudely interrupted"—another smile through the phone—"I did in fact make a choice, and I am in fact working at J. Wong. Or at least working on getting to New York. I'm trying to find an apartment right now."

Allegra lifted her eyes heavenward and mouthed *Thank You*. "That's great, sis. I'm so proud of you. So tell me all about it."

She left the store and climbed into her car that was parked almost directly out front—a miracle in downtown Seattle. As she drove the few minutes back home, she listened while Caprice spoke at length about what her duties would be, where she was hoping to find some roommates, and all the other things that came with moving to a huge city.

"Do you know how much money you'll need?" Allegra pushed her key into her door lock.

"Allie, I don't—"

"Just tell me, Capri."

The line was silent for a moment before Capri gave her a figure.

Allegra swallowed hard before she responded. "Okay. I'll wire that to you tomorrow." It was going to wipe out her meager savings, but there was no way she'd tell her sister that. She dropped her bag on the kitchen counter.

"Sis, are you sure? Because honestly, I'm sure I can scrape enough together. You've been doing so much for me. Let me do this."

"That's enough of that talk."

Allegra sniffed the air. The faint scent of vanilla wafted from her kitchen. Oh! She'd forgotten about the cookies Story made for her today. Her mouth watered the closer she got to the plate on her counter. Capri was winding down and mentioned Tyler—

Nope. "Oh, I have to take care of these cookies!" Allegra told Capri. "I'll call you in a day or two. Let me know if you find an apartment!" Hey, a lame excuse was better than no excuse, and she so didn't want to talk about Tyler.

She tapped the phone off and lifted the plastic wrap and snatched a cookie. Remembering Capri's workout and her own not-so-subtle lie, she walked around her coffee table five times before plopping back down on her sofa and taking a bite of the chewy sweet. Mmm. She just might need to grab another one.

She repeated her little "exercise" and sat back down, taking a big bite just as her cell rang. *For heaven's sake.* Ignoring the call, she slowly chewed, took a sip of her coffee, and picked up her book.

A perfect night.

"She isn't answering her phone." Photos of Bo with the Stanley Cup—too bad it wasn't as part of the winning team, just a tour—and Bo with old teammates, coaches, and other NHL players plastered the walls and shelves on either side of the fireplace as Tyler paced in his friend's living room.

Bo looked up from the laptop in front of him. "Try again? We need to get this figured out."

Tyler tapped Allegra's name on his phone again. His call went unanswered. "Maybe she's asleep."

"It's only eight o'clock."

"Yeah, but I've been having her run around a lot the past couple of weeks. She isn't on work hours, so she doesn't actually *have* to answer my call." Tyler sat on Bo's black pleather sofa, trying to decide what to do. When he'd been called an hour ago with a problem with one of the donations Allegra had gathered, he didn't think it would be a big issue to sort out.

"Maybe I should run over there."

Bo lifted a brow. "You know where she lives?"

Tyler blew out a puff of air. "No." Only a little white lie. "But her address is in the employee files at the shop." He stood and walked the length of the living room. "It isn't like her not to answer. She seems so...diligent. And on top of things. I can't believe this slipped past her."

"Well, it did." Bo stood and walked to an open box. Staring down, he mumbled something under his breath.

"What was that?"

He sighed. "Story gave me a book a while back. Loaned it to me, I think, though she's never asked for it back. I haven't read it yet. Should I give it back to her?"

Momentarily distracted, Tyler peered over Bo's shoulder. *Diversify: Build the Life God Wants for You.* "I don't know, man. Do you want to read it?"

Bo straightened and looked out a window. "Yeah. I might."

"Then knowing Story, she won't mind if you take it with you."

"Truth." Bo turned. "So what are we going to do about those programs? They need to be sent to the printer tonight if we're going to have them in time for the gala, but—"

Tyler's phone chimed. He pulled it out of his pocket, relieved when he saw the caller ID. "Allie, thanks for calling back."

"I'm sorry I didn't answer. I was just...well, I'm sorry."

"Totally okay." He ignored Bo's scowl, turning to walk

toward the kitchen. On the table was a list of companies and people with matching donations. "I need to check on something. I have a list of the donations for the auction—thanks for all your hard work, by the way—but one of the donations is missing the donor name. We need to send the programs to the printer tonight."

"What's the donation?"

Tyler picked the sheet up and studied it. "A small kitchen appliance package. That's all it says."

Silence greeted him on the other end.

"Allegra?"

"Yeah, I'm here. I, um...I do remember that package. It was a very high-end cappuccino maker, KitchenAid mixer, and a few other things."

"Those are great. Do you remember who donated them? Or do you have that in your office at the store? I can always run down there and get it."

"No! Don't worry about it. I'll go."

"It's no skin off my nose."

"Nope, I'm already out the door. Talk to you soon."

She hung up before he could thank her.

"What'd she say?" Bo stood behind him, Story's book in his hand.

Tyler slid his hand over his hair and down the back of his neck. "She's already on her way to the shop to look it up."

She'd sounded nervous though. Hmm.

Chapter Sixteen

I'm going to lose my job! Allegra had already gone through the few papers on her desk and was now riffling through her drawers. She knew she'd put the list in her office, but for the life of her, she couldn't remember if she ever wrote down who that donation was from.

Tyler wouldn't be too thrilled if she didn't have that name.

Sweat beaded along her hairline. She swiped it away with her forearm and kept searching. It had to be there somewhere. She knelt down to go through the bottom drawer where she kept some folders. The files she was currently working on stood in a holder on her desk. The ones in this drawer were frequent but not constant. She knew the folder couldn't be in her filing cabinet though—those files had either been closed completely or were not needed nearly as often.

Think, think!

She sat back on her heels and wiped her forehead again. This wasn't going to go down well.

"Allegra?"

She startled and fell back on her behind. No. *No!* What was Tyler doing here? She told him she'd come look herself. Where was that paper? She frantically reached into the drawer and started pulling and dumping the files. She could clean it up later.

Yes! The sheet with both typed and handwritten notes fell out of an accounts receivable folder. What it was doing there, she had no idea, but right now, who cared? She grabbed it and called out. "In my office."

Oh. No. She looked a hot mess. Allegra ran her hands over her hair, smoothing it as best she could. Strands had fallen out of her ponytail during her search. She looked down at her baggy T-shirt and holey sweatpants. When Tyler had called, she didn't give a thought to what she was wearing before she walked out the door. There was nothing she could do about it now, but sheesh.

Tyler started talking before he reached her office. "I know you said you'd come down yourself, but we're in a rush to send the program to the printers tonight, so I thought I'd meet you here and email—" He stopped in the doorway, his gaze taking in first her office floor, then her pants, shirt, and finally her hair and face. He pulled his lips into his mouth, clearly trying hard not to laugh. "Uh, did we have a break-in?"

"No!" Allegra took a deep breath. "Everything's fine. I just…I thought I had misplaced the donor sheet."

Tyler grinned. "You didn't check your computer first?"

"I had some penned notes that aren't on my computer yet." If she hadn't been so lazy at quitting time, she would have stayed to transcribe them. But nooo.

"No prob. So you have the donor name, right?"

Allegra looked down at the paper in her hand. "Yeah, it's right—oh." She looked back up at Tyler, her stomach rolling.

Tyler stilled. "What?"

Dare she tell him? *Duh.* She had to tell him. He was standing right in front of her. But her job. Caprice's internship. She may be overreacting, but if the program had to go to the printer tonight—she glanced at the clock; it was already 11:00 p.m.—they were running out of time, and she couldn't start making phone calls at this late hour. She lifted the sheet in her shaking hand. "I...I have the donation written down, but..."

His eyes narrowed. "But?"

She was going to be sick. "But not the donor."

He couldn't have heard right. "Pardon me?"

Allegra's eyes rounded, like she was trying to dry her eyes of any tears that might be threatening to fall. "Tyler, I'm sorry. I don't know what I was thinking. I was talking on the phone with the donor, and I could have sworn I wrote the company name down, but it's not here."

Those tears flowed freely down her cheeks by the time she was finished. So not like her. None of this was like her.

Tyler stepped forward and hooked his hands over her

shoulders. He waited a moment to steady his tone. "You say you think you wrote it down. It isn't on this paper?"

Allegra sniffled. "No." She thrust the page into his hand. "I swore I wrote it down. I'm so, so, so sorry, Tyler." She quieted when he squeezed her shoulders.

"Maybe you did write it down, just not on this." At least, he hoped so. "Let's pick everything up off the floor, and we can go through it all, the two of us. Okay?"

She plucked a tissue out of the box on the corner of her desk and nodded. "Okay."

For the next forty minutes, they picked up and carefully read every single piece of paper that had been strewn on the floor and her desk. With no luck. Tyler rubbed his face, trying to think.

"I'm sure I did, Ty."

His heart picked up its pace at her use of his nickname. He eyed her. "Is there a possibility you didn't?"

She didn't meet his gaze. So not a good sign. "Well...I guess."

He couldn't stop the sigh before it escaped. Allegra's shoulders dropped. "Tyler, I'm so sorry."

As much as he wanted to comfort her right now—and it annoyed him that he *did* want to—they needed to find the name. It was almost midnight, and though the print shop wouldn't be open until 8:00 a.m., he would like to find it so he could get some sleep. "Let's keep looking. Maybe it's in your file cabinet." He paused. "You know what? Maybe we should pray."

Allegra's gaze flew to his. "You mean...pray-pray?

Together? To find something?"

He snorted. "We haven't had any luck on our own, have we?"

His heart skipped a beat at her small smile.

"No." She reached a hand to him. "Okay."

Tyler grasped her hand—only to have the touch sting and exhilarate him like he'd just caught a twenty-yard driveline pass. He almost dropped her hand but managed to hold on. *No hardship there.* He hesitated. He hadn't prayed in a long time. *Better late than never, God? I hope so.* "Dear Lord, we know this is a small thing in the grand scheme, but can You please help us find the paper we've been looking for? We need it tonight and would love Your guidance." He lifted his head and watched Allegra for a second before he continued. "And, God...please release any feelings of guilt. In Your name, amen."

A soft "amen" followed his. Allegra blinked back more tears before she whispered, "Thanks."

They both stood and began pulling out files one by one from her filing cabinet. An hour later and into the *I*s, Allegra gasped. "I found it!"

"What?" As much as he knew God could answer his prayer, Tyler didn't know if He really would. "Thank God." His body went weak with the release of tension.

Allegra spun into his arms. "I'm so sorry, Tyler."

Whoa. Tyler wrapped his arms around Allegra and rested her head against his chest. "Sh. It's okay."

"No, it isn't! I almost lost a donor for your foundation. That was *my* fault. *Mine.* I don't know what got into me or how that happened, and I'm just...I'm so sorry."

Tyler gently pushed Allegra's head back and looked her in the eyes. "Honey, it's fine. It's over and done with. You found it—thanks to God—and we can get everything done in time. Okay? All's forgiven."

She nodded. "Thank you."

"You're welcome. Now"—he stepped away and looked at the donor list—"let's get this file sent."

Chapter Seventeen

Allegra parked her car and leaned her head against the headrest. Her emotions still rang through her body from last night. A combination of feeling like a fool, leftover fear, and relief kept her up the rest of the night. She leaned forward to study herself in the rearview mirror. Bloodshot eyes had greeted her in the mirror first thing this morning. Thank goodness for Visine. Still puffy eyed and also pale faced, she looked like death. She rummaged through her handbag and found her mascara, blush, and lip gloss. Maybe if she added more of each, she wouldn't scare the customers away.

A knock on the window startled her, shaking her hand and smearing mascara down her cheek.

Clutching her chest, she peered out her window to see Tyler standing there, the sun making his hair look like gold. Allegra lowered her window. "Thanks." She pointed to her eyes before she went back to her purse and found a makeup remover sheet.

Tyler laughed. "Sorry about that. Hey"—he reached in and tapped her cheek—"you have something right here."

Allegra narrowed her eyes. "You're not funny, boss-man."

He waggled his brows. "I'm hilarious. But I digress." His look turned serious. "You doing okay? I called the printer to make sure everything went through fine, and it did. No harm, no foul."

She smiled. "Yeah, I'm okay." It was only a little lie. "But still, I'm sorry. That shouldn't have happened."

"Over and done with. Got that?"

"Got it. And thanks."

Tyler opened the door for her and waited as she raised the window and gathered her things. She stepped out of the car, thankful she wore her denim jacket when the chilled morning air touched her. The yellow maxi skirt she wore fluttered around her legs in the light breeze. Allegra smiled. It was one of her favorite outfits, and she always felt the most comfortable in it.

They walked in silence to the shop where Tyler again opened the door for her. As she stepped across the threshold, he stopped her.

"You know, I think after last night's stress, we need a day out of the office."

Allegra's breath hitched. "W...what do you have in mind?" The glimmer in Tyler's eyes put her insides on ice. "Tyler?"

A slow smile stretched across his face. "Well, I was thinking you did so well with paragliding..."

Oh. No.

Not again. No, no, no. What on earth could he have

up his sleeve on short notice? *Seriously!*

"I think it's time to try your hand—and feet and grip—at rock climbing."

She hoped he was quick on his feet, because she was about to pass out.

Could she get any paler? He didn't think so, but he was wrong.

"Rock climbing? Are you crazy?"

Tyler couldn't help himself. He laughed. He was doing more and more of that since meeting her, and he liked it. "I'm not going to take you to climb Mount Everest today. I promise."

"But where? Where would you take me? I've never done anything even remotely like rock climbing before. No. No, I can't do this. No, no, no." Allegra stepped back, shaking her head.

"Allie." He spoke as if she were a frightened rabbit. "A climbing gym. I wouldn't take you outdoors until I knew you were capable. I wouldn't risk you." He grinned. "You're too good at your job for me to lose you."

She licked her lips. "A climbing gym? Like, inside? Where I won't drop to my death against craggy rocks jutting out the side of a mountain?"

Tyler jammed his hands into his pockets to keep from hugging her. *Employee. Boundaries. Stop forgetting, hot shot.* "A climbing gym. Indoors. With instruction before you even get harnessed." He stuck out his hand. "Deal?"

She watched him for a moment, as if debating whether or

not she could trust him. He'd hoped after their paragliding day that she would open up and be more comfortable. Apparently not, but that didn't mean he'd stop trying.

Tyler withdrew his hand. "Allie. I won't make you climb until I know you're ready. I have every confidence you'll learn quickly, but I promise I won't rush you."

Her eyes dampened, but no tears escaped. "Okay."

Tyler's pulse skittered. She didn't sound excited or even confident, but it was progress. "I'll go let Story know. We'll probably only be gone a few hours, if that."

Tyler insisted Allegra pick out some yoga pants and a T-shirt at the store—he didn't trust her to come back out of her place if he took her home to get her own clothes. When they arrived at Peak Project. Tyler showed his membership card and paid for Allegra's admission and gear rental before taking her to the locker rooms so she could change. He looked over his shoulder. Whew. She hadn't snuck out while he wasn't looking. Tyler gave her props for still following him. He stopped and faced her. "I just had a thought. Would you feel more comfortable getting trained by a climbing coach rather than me?"

Her hesitation answered his question. "You won't hurt my feelings, Allie. Why don't I go get one for you? I want you to try top-roping—using a belay partner, me. I think you'd like that, and no doubt feel more comfortable having a partner on the other end of things."

She nodded, cheeks puffed out.

Tyler returned to the front, paid, and walked back to

where Allegra stood, staring at the other climbers in the gym. There were some grunts here and there, and hollers for *on belay* and *lower* among other commands she would eventually learn. A few other climbers were on their own, using an autobelay.

Tyler turned to Allegra. "I have the coach. We need to start by getting you belay certified." He nodded toward a separate area of the gym where the instructor waited. "Ready?"

Allie nodded, leading the way. She kept silent, her face still pale. Tyler drew his brows together. What was she so afraid of? Climbing in a gym wasn't nearly as risky as climbing outdoors, but she was acting like she was walking to her death. He couldn't understand people who hated adrenaline and risk as much as she seemed to. He shook his head. There was no reasoning with those kinds of people sometimes, but he couldn't help himself with Allegra. He wanted so badly for her to enjoy doing the things he did and taking risks—life was boring without all these adrenaline rushes. He pushed aside the question that begged to be answered: *Why* did he need her to love what he loved?

Chapter Eighteen

Allegra pulled on her hair to tighten her ponytail and plucked at the bright-pink body-hugging dry-wick tank top. Why was Tyler being so pushy?

That question haunted Allegra throughout the belay certification. As she tied figure-eight and fisherman's knots, she wondered why she was *allowing* Tyler to be so pushy. Yes, she needed this job, but she was beginning to think he wouldn't fire her if she refused. However, her hyped-up sense of responsibility to not break a promise messed with her. She couldn't break her contract, despite wanting to. She'd made a promise, both to Tyler and, more importantly, to Caprice.

Allegra shook her head. She needed to pay closer attention if she wanted to keep her body intact.

"Are you a righty or a lefty?" Gabe, their instructor, asked.

Allegra lifted her right hand. "Righty."

"Okay." Gabe lifted the belay device. "You're always going to keep your right hand in break position—home base, if you will, below the device. Most importantly, don't let go." He eyed her. "I mean it. Don't let go."

Allegra swallowed hard. So not only would her life be in danger while climbing, *she* held another person's life in her right hand?

Gabe continued. "When your partner is ascending the wall, they're creating slack. Your job"—he pointed to Allegra—"is to pull that slack through to catch them. So if Tyler's climbing, you're going to pull the slack from his side by pulling with your left hand, and at the same time, you're pulling the slack up with your right hand. Then you'll come back to the break position." Gabe demonstrated the action. "I need to stress again—never let go of the rope with your right hand."

Allegra nodded. After a few turns practicing what Gabe had just taught her, she gave it back to him. "Got it."

Gabe nodded. "You're ready to go. Congrats."

She didn't think this was something to congratulate. She was about to plummet to her death—or cause Tyler's death.

Gabe and Tyler helped Allegra into the harness so she could climb first. As Tyler went back to get his own equipment, Gabe spoke while he double-checked everything. "You're going to use your core. If you don't already have core strength, you'll build it up fast here. Don't try to use your arm strength. Use your legs to propel you. This isn't easy, but keep at it, and you'll eventually get higher and higher."

Allegra looked up, mouth dropping at the sheer height of the rock wall facing her. Butterflies flew in her stomach at sonic speed.

I can't do this.

But she had to. Her job—her sister—depended on this accomplishment.

A cold sweat broke out on her upper lip. The voices around her faded as she gazed at the top of the wall, where her destination sat like a king looking down on his lowly subjects. Her breath hitched, and she choked down some bile.

Trust God. He'll keep me safe. Wouldn't He? Others climbed and survived. But then, others didn't.

Like her parents.

Allegra's vision blurred. Her parents. The two people in the world who should have been there to protect and care for her and Caprice, who instead found the rush of adrenaline more important. And it cost them their lives.

It cost Allegra her trust, both in people, and to be brutally honest, in God.

Shaking her head, she turned. Her gaze collided with Tyler's, a question in his eyes. More flapping in her stomach, but this time, the butterflies were a different variety. Not fear. Argh! *He's your boss. He's a* risk taker, *Allegra!* Off limits. No touching.

But oh, he did take her mind off what she was about to do. That chest screamed for a touch. And those lips, they begged for a—

Nope.

Allegra watched as one side of his lush mouth curved up, a glint in his green eyes. Oh sweet heaven.

She was in trouble. With a capital *T.*

The color crawling up Allegra's neck was a charming pink. Tyler grinned. She might be his employee and a scaredy-cat, but she was still a woman. And he was still a man.

A man who appreciated beauty.

Tyler snatched his harness and strolled to Allegra, his climbing shoes puffing air with each step. He couldn't wait until they warmed up. He spoke when he reached her. "Hey, you okay?"

Allegra's eyes widened as she looked up at him, and he saw a shimmer of tears. Tyler's stomach dropped. He reached up a hand and gently brushed her cheek. "Allie...I never meant for any of this to scare you."

She took a step back, leaving his hand hovering in midair. He lowered it.

"If you're worried you'll lose your job if you don't do this, you won't. You've become too valuable to me." His coughed and sputtered. "Uh, I mean, the company. You've become too valuable to the company. Your work. You're good at it."

Allegra's teeth caught her bottom lip, but she stayed silent. Tyler groaned. He took a step closer to her. "I mean it, Allegra. You don't have to do this, and you don't need to worry about your job."

Her voice caught on a gasp. "My parents. They died."

Tyler frowned. "You haven't mentioned that before." He watched as her gaze rose to the ceiling and her blinks quickened.

"No, I mean they died...doing this."

He tried swallowing, but it was no use getting around the

lump in his throat. "Oh, honey." How many kinds of fool could he call himself? He'd practically forced this on her. He'd known for a long while that there was more to her fears than just a lack of adventurous spirit, but in his selfishness, he chose to ignore his conscience and push her. For what? Did he honestly do it for her sake...or his? Was he that desperate to turn her into his "type"? What was *her* type? If they'd met while he was still in his former fast-lane lifestyle, would he have appreciated it if she'd pushed him into being someone he wasn't before he was ready?

Probably not.

Tyler reached out a hand. "Get out of that harness. We can go for a bike ride instead."

Allegra shook her head, frowning. "No." She lifted her chin. "If there's one thing I've learned working with you, it's that there's no time for fear." She offered up a small smile. "God doesn't leave room for it in the Bible, does He?"

His heart thumped double time. "No. He doesn't." Tyler grinned, eliciting a bigger smile from this beautiful, brave woman. He couldn't be more proud if she were his own girl—

Oh man. He was a goner.

Chapter Nineteen

Deep breaths. I can do this.

Allegra stood at the base of the rock wall, fingers in position. She closed her eyes only to see an image of her mom in this same position at an indoor gym six years ago. She used to go with her parents when they climbed, just to watch the sheer joy on their faces that she didn't ever remember seeing when they looked at her. The memory was bittersweet.

The day her parents died, Caprice was at high school and Allegra was home after her shift at a local coffee shop. She'd just graduated college but had taken the part-time job until she could find an accounting position. When the police knocked on her door, she knew.

Her stomach lurched at the memory. *Shake this off. Before you're too emotional to try this climb.* Her mother always told her climbing required concentration. *So concentrate.*

She looked back up at the footholds on the wall. Gabe had

told her to seek them out and plan her route before starting the climb, and it made sense. Better that she knew where to go next than hang in the balance on her harness.

A harness that seemed awfully wimpy.

"Get going, Allie." Behind her, Tyler chuckled. The punk.

"Climbing," she called over her shoulder.

"Climb on," Tyler answered.

Allegra gripped the rock, placed her foot, and pushed up.

She was on the wall. Half a foot off the ground, but still on the wall. She groaned. What was she doing? But she was up now. Shutting off her internal voice, she concentrated on where to grip next, where to put her foot, and pushed upward.

Her stomach blazed. Muscles she never knew she had burned like a raging bonfire. Allegra clenched her teeth, but it was no use. Her hands were clammy and her body tired.

Weak is more like it. Oh man, what was the command she was supposed to use when she was done? She was about to lose her grip completely and fall if she...oh!

"Take!"

Allegra felt the change in the rope as Tyler took on her weight—the poor man—on her rope and began to lower her down. She looked up, expecting to see she'd at least almost reached the top. Uh...wow. Had she even make it halfway?

The floor came up under her feet, and she was finally on solid ground again. Her knees buckled, but Tyler was there in an instant, his arms full of corded muscles surrounding her in a hug. The warmth from his body and the unexpected kiss on the top of her head did funny things to her. And then it happened.

She cried.

For the first time since their deaths, Allegra Isabel Spencer shed tears over her parents. Of relief, of anger, of grief.

Crying women weren't usually his thing. But Allegra...Tyler couldn't deny how she felt in his arms. Right. Good.

Safe.

His gut churned as spikes of adrenaline needled his body. He immediately released his hold on her and stepped away. *Safe* wasn't a word in his vocabulary. He avoided safe at all costs. The last thing he wanted was a life full of safe, a life his parents made him live growing up. He never wanted to feel that inferior and helpless again.

Allegra looked up at him, eyes bright, like they were filled with stars. Stars he may have just put there.

Or maybe it was the adrenaline rush she was experiencing after conquering an incredible—and well-deserved, he had to admit—fear. If his parents had died rock climbing, he didn't know if he could push through and do it.

Maybe she wasn't so safe after all. Tyler reached out and squeezed her shoulder, his fingers tingling in response. "You did really great, Allie. I'm proud of you." He couldn't help it. He pulled her back into a hug. "Really proud."

"Thanks for pushing. I didn't get nearly as high as I thought I did though."

Tyler laughed. "You got higher than I did my first time."

He felt her startle before she stepped out of his hold. "Are you serious?"

"Very." He laughed then. "Mind you, I was twelve." Tyler winked and ducked from her oncoming fist.

"Punk!"

The zips of rope and voices calling out commands faded. Tyler stared at her smiling lips and wondered just how soft they were. He reached a finger and gently touched her mouth. "You're so beautiful." His stomach flipped, like he just took a running leap off a cliff above the ocean and was suspended for that one millisecond before falling.

And he *was* falling.

Cupping her face, he drew her to him like a magnet. His mouth was inches from hers. "So beautiful." His voice lowered. "Courageous." Closer. "Smart." Her lips parted. "Tempting."

Warmth flooded his body. Then finally... Finally, his lips grazed hers, softer than they'd promised. He more felt rather than heard a small gasp right before she melted into him.

He was home.

Tyler moved them around the corner into an alcove, away from prying eyes. He tilted his head, moving his body even close to hers, his hands sliding to the back of her neck and up into her hair. She shuddered and parted her lips, a tiny mew coming from her throat. He moved his mouth along her jaw, kissing her neck just below her left ear before he pulled back. If he wasn't careful, he'd find himself back in his football days, not caring about anything or anyone other than his own needs.

Allegra was worth way more than that. Worth more than him.

Dotting her neck with one last kiss, he pulled back but didn't let go. "Wow."

Her flushed skin told him she definitely felt that kiss like he had. He grinned.

"Yeah," she whispered. "Wow." She looked up at him, her eyes glazed with leftover passion.

She was definitely not safe.

Chapter Twenty

Wow. Wow, wow, wow. That kiss still tingled. Never had Allegra felt such sweet passion. She and Tyler had left the gym in a rather dazed silence and made their way back to Hawk's Flight. When they walked through the door, Story gave them an odd look but didn't say anything. Tyler stayed beside Allegra as she walked to her office, but stopped at her door.

"Thank you, Ty. I never would have done that without you." The warmth in his eyes melted her soul. "I *couldn't* have done it without you."

Ants tickled her stomach as she watched his eyes darken, his gaze sliding from hers to her mouth. Feeling confident after all the risks she'd taken today, she moved closer and did what she'd been longing to do for longer than she cared to admit—she laid a hand on his chest and looked up. "I wouldn't have wanted to do anything like that with anyone other than you."

And perhaps sharing that with him was the riskiest thing

she'd done all day.

Tyler opened his mouth, but no sound came out. Allegra stood up on her tiptoes and leaned to the side to lay a kiss on his cheek. Instead, he turned his head so their lips met. Any remaining tension released from her body, and her bones turned to liquid. Tyler inched back to look at her. "I wish I didn't have to go," he whispered. "I have a client meeting."

She nodded, disappointment sagging her shoulders. Until he brushed her lips again. "Will you be back before the end of the day?"

Tyler shook his head. "I doubt it. But I'll call you later."

"Okay."

One more lingering kiss and he was gone.

Allegra sat at her desk and stared at the dark computer screen. Wow. Today caught her totally off guard. She knew there'd been attraction between the two of them, but they were so different.

Yeah. Like employer and employee. Like safe and daring.

It had been ingrained in her throughout her education and work experience at the accounting firm that office relationships were a big no-no. Which was a pretty good cover, if she said so herself, for avoiding a man who was so extremely high risk. But where did that leave her and Tyler? She couldn't deny she liked him. A lot. And his kisses...

Allegra shook her head. She was being paid right now to work, not to daydream.

What was he thinking?

Tyler finished stowing the kayaks on his truck, hopped in,

and headed to Elliott Bay. He couldn't believe he'd kissed Allegra. Multiple times.

And what kisses they were.

He grinned at the memory. He didn't think he'd ever experienced a thunderbolt like that before. But that also left him in a quandary. Everything in him rebelled at the thought of a relationship with Allie, despite his obvious attraction to her. She was beautiful, kind, funny, intelligent...and safe. Yes, she'd taken risks today, big risks, but in the end, she was still safe. She didn't like risk, didn't like adrenaline.

It was hard for Tyler to understand why some people wouldn't want to push beyond themselves to experience everything God created. It was why he owned Hawk's Flight. He wanted to encourage people to let go of their safety nets and experience thrills that would challenge their boundaries.

Despite her effort, he didn't think Allegra was experiencing thrills in the way he intended. She'd just come off a major victory, and he wouldn't take that away from her, but if he were to walk into work tomorrow and offer a skydiving excursion, he was confident she'd say no.

Well, maybe not. They did have a contract, after all. But she'd likely pass out. Then go. And he'd have to see her tremble and cry again...and *that* would break him.

Cracks of weakness were breaking open, and he didn't like it. Allegra tore through every wall he'd built up over the years as he proved again and again that he could do whatever he intended. His parents kept him from sports and even just running around with his friends when he was younger because of his asthma. He'd proven them wrong when he and the middle school coach confronted them and he played on the school team. He'd had some attacks, but his coach taught him to sit upright instead of bending or lying down. He'd proven his parents wrong each year following that confrontation until he graduated high school and then college, where he'd grown to love coffee, which was good since a hot caffeinated drink helped to open his airways. He'd proven his parents wrong when he entered the NFL draft and was picked second round. He had to admit that entering the NFL had made him nervous. It was a whole different game than high school and college ball. One attack in particular almost scared him out of playing, but his middle school coach, whom he'd kept in touch with, talked him down and pointed him in the direction of a great pulmonologist. That coach and the doc had gotten him through training camps, practices, and games and taught him that he couldn't allow circumstances and people to hold him back. People like his parents, whom he'd proven wrong again when he played for the Seattle Seahawks and brought home a Super Bowl ring.

Now he was proving them wrong with each excursion he led for clients. Skydiving, paragliding, rock climbing, bungee jumping, heli-skiing...

Tyler parked his truck at Seacrest Park, where he was meeting his clients. He looked at his watch. Twenty minutes. Just enough time to get the paperwork in order and portage the kayaks to the meeting point. He pulled out the sheets the Powells had signed and checked them over one last time before he exited his truck. He looked out across the water to the downtown Seattle skyline. The sun glinted off the thousands of windows, the Space Needle standing guard over them all. A view that was beyond words. Just like Allegra.

What was he going to do about her?

Chapter Twenty-One

"What am I doing?" Allegra blew out hard, disturbing the wisps of hair that had fallen out of her ponytail. "Sitting by the phone like a tween, that's what I'm doing."

Determined to not waste any more time waiting for Tyler to call, Allegra twisted her laptop to face the open side of her living room and hopped off her couch. No time like the present to start exercising. She found the website and spent the next forty minutes lamenting her lack of muscles. Maybe she shouldn't have let her gym membership lapse so she could send that money to Capri for school. Did that forty dollars a month *really* help her sister? Allegra squeezed in a breath between a crunch.

She was going to die. And of course, now that she was sweaty and out of breath, Tyler would probably call.

A half hour went by without her prediction coming true. Fine. She took a shower, then spent the better part of ten minutes towel drying her hair while pacing her condo.

Still no call.

Grabbing her car keys, she decided to go for a latté. After all that exercise, surely she deserved a reward. As she passed the mirror by her front door, she spotted the width of her hips.

Never mind that latté. Maybe she'd go for a walk. Hmm. Or maybe she'd walk while drinking her latté.

She shoved her phone into the back pocket of her jeans—in case of an emergency, of course—tied her tennis shoes, and marched out the door.

The sound of evening traffic littered the neighborhood. The oranges, purples, and pinks mixed with the azure sky and reflected off the water in the distance. She had to admit it: Seattle was her favorite city.

As she walked, Allegra kept her eyes on the distant water, wondering if Tyler was still out there with his clients. Maybe that was why he hadn't called yet.

She hoped.

Who was she kidding? He was an NFL player, a small-business owner, an adrenaline junkie. He was gorgeous, wealthy, and fun. And no doubt had a line of women waiting to entice him. What in the world would he see in her? She was a ramen-eating, latté-drinking, curvy woman who hardly had any money because she was paying her sister's tuition.

More than that, she was a scared little girl.

Her brutal self-assessment stopped her in her tracks. Allegra peered up at the sky. It was true. She was scared, still wishing she had the love of her mother and father. She was scared of risk, scared of relationships. Scared of letting go.

Fear. Was that why she insisted on paying Capri's tuition despite her sister arguing against it?

It was time for a change. The evening air carried the scent of Seattle. The faint brine from the ocean mixed with exhaust and a spring shower. Change. The city was always changing, so why not her? She wrapped her arms around her stomach and held on.

Allegra walked into Bean There and ordered her favorite Kit Kat latté. She sipped some of the creamy foam off, relishing the sweet flavor of her comfort food. She opened the door, and the sounds of the city tickled her ears. She turned back toward home. What kinds of changes could she make? She needed her job—she couldn't stop paying Caprice's tuition, despite her sister's arguments. Maybe she *was* scared of letting her sister go, but she refused to allow Capri to get caught up in student loans. That was no way to start a life—she knew from experience. Besides, with the gala happening so soon, she couldn't quit now. But that was all about letting go, wasn't it? Trusting God.

Why is it so hard to trust You, God?

The answer was as clear as purified water. Fear. She was scared of letting God take care of everything and everyone around her when He hadn't taken care of her parents. Oh, she knew it wasn't true. Her parents made their own choices, and they paid for it with their lives, leaving her and her sister scrambling to make it on their own.

Allegra was back in her condo before she had any answers. And still no call from Tyler.

Allegra did something she hadn't done in ages. She got

down on her knees, like she had as a little girl. Her parents had ensured she and Caprice had a religious upbringing, but it was never really part of her daily life. She still went to church...when she didn't sleep in. Which was almost always. But the occasional Sunday found her sitting in a pew. She just didn't connect. Everyone else seemed so happy, and it bothered her that she didn't have that.

Allegra rested her elbows on her coral, teal, and cream duvet, clasped her hands, and bent her head. She didn't know quite how to do it, but it was time to rely on God again. And it began with asking Him for help.

He was a complete and utter jerk.

Tyler sat in his truck in the nearby parking lot, procrastinating. He hadn't called Allegra the night before, hadn't even bothered to text her. The last thing he wanted to do right now was go in and face her.

Coward. But he had to go to work. The gala was coming up quick. Between that and Bo's move, the next couple of weeks would fly by. He wasn't looking forward to his best friend leaving the city, but he would rather be facing that right now than Allegra.

No pain, no gain. Time to get to work.

Hawk's Flight was as silent as a tomb when Tyler entered. Where was everyone? "Story?" He didn't have the guts to call out for Allie. *Jerk. And coward.*

Tyler walked past the rock-climbing gear, feeling lower than an ant on a sidewalk as he remembered his kisses with Allie. He gave himself another mental kick and entered the back room, his stomach rolling at the thought of facing the most beautiful woman—the one he'd no doubt hurt badly.

He called out once again. "Hello?"

A rustle of papers coming from Allegra's office alerted him to her presence. Time to man up.

He walked to the doorway and rapped his knuckles on the frame.

She glanced up but didn't meet his gaze. "Hi. I've been going over the donations list, and it looks like your foundation has procured quite a bit. I'll email the list to you, and you can decide how best to organize it. Or I can do that, if you'd like. Either way." She looked back at her computer screen. "Oh, and the Johansen account has been paid in full."

"Allie."

"I'm compiling the monthly reports for you to look over when you have a moment. I'll email those to you too."

"Allie."

Allegra sighed and finally looked at him. "I get it. You thought it over and regret it. I live with a safety net. You don't even know what a safety net is. No big deal. I won't let it happen again, okay? Besides, I'm your employee. You're my employer. I won't press charges or go to the press, if that's what you're worried about."

The thought hadn't even crossed his mind. "I...I appreciate that. But that's not what I was going to say."

"Mm. An apology. Well, if you're going to apologize to me, then I should be apologizing to you too. I'm sorry. I let myself lose control, something I *don't* normally do." Her hands shook as she reached for her mouse. "It won't happen again."

His heart thundered in his chest. "Allegra, stop. Please."

She let go of the mouse but didn't turn to face him. He wished she would so he could look her in the eyes and see what she was thinking. "I'm sorry I didn't call. I'm not sorry I kissed you though."

Allegra's shoulders stiffened.

"It was probably the best afternoon—full of the best kisses—I've had. But yeah..." He braced himself. "It can't happen again. Like you said, I'm your boss. And I just...I can't."

She nodded her head once. "Are we finished? I have a lot of work to do."

Class-act heel. He'd no doubt regret this down the road, but he was pretty sure he'd regret it if he let whatever happened yesterday to continue. Right?

"Yeah. And again"—he swallowed hard, his blood pounding through his veins like he was about to jump off a cliff—"I'm sorry."

Tyler stood in place for another moment. Allegra tapped away at her keyboard, though he was pretty certain she wasn't seeing what she was typing.

He risked one last word. "You truly are beautiful." Tyler turned on his heel and walked out of her office. He clutched his chest, the pain making him wonder if he was having a heart attack. Which would be far better than hurting Allegra.

Chapter Twenty-Two

Allegra leaned over the box of...she didn't know what. "Story, what are these?"

"AADs."

"What?" She glanced up from her crouched position to look at her friend before studying the contents of the cardboard box. Inside were several black rectangles with two cords leading to a smaller rectangle with an LED screen.

"Automatic activation devices. They make sure your descent speed matches what it should be, then detects whether you've opened your chute properly. If you haven't, it releases your auxiliary chute." Story looked up from the box she was stocking. "You know, skydiving. Especially necessary for night jumps, when you can't see how close to the ground you're getting. That little thing saves lives."

Allegra's stomach dropped. *No way, no how.* It would never be saving her life because there was no way she'd let herself depend on such a tiny thing. Her feet belonged firmly planted on the ground.

She sat down on the floor, reached into the box, and stocked the bottom shelf with the death devices.

The atmosphere in Hawk's Flight over the past two weeks felt like a rubber band stretched to its limit. Between her breakup—if it could even be called that—with Tyler, and whatever happened between Bo and Story, along with Bo's impending move and the upcoming gala, the stress level and tomb-like silence of the place was oppressive. Thankfully, Tyler had been out almost daily, taking clients on excursions. Allegra assumed Bo was out of the office packing up his home and making the arrangements to move across the country. And Story…Allegra watched her walk into the back without a word. She didn't know what was going through her friend's mind, but she definitely wasn't herself.

Hawk's Flight seemed to be falling apart at the seams, at least emotionally. Thankfully, business was brisk, especially entering summer. If she had to say anything about Tyler, it would be that he really was a great businessman.

Thank goodness. Allegra stood and stretched her arms to the ceiling—where she conveniently avoided looking at the raft overhead—twisted from one side to the other to stretch her back, then her neck, following the same motions. She reached into her back pocket to pull out the printed email Caprice had sent her outlining which classes she was signing up for when she registered for fall in a few weeks. Allegra calculated the cost, then figured what she would need to set aside to pay that bill. Though Capri had insisted she buy her own groceries and pay her portion of the rent, the amount Allegra needed to save for tuition payments starting again in

September was still exorbitant.

A gurgle sounded from the back room, grabbing Allegra's attention. It sounded like the espresso machine. Deciding she needed a break, she grabbed her water bottle—she was determined to get healthy—and followed the direction Story had gone.

Story stood at the espresso machine, making herself a coffee. "Hey."

Allegra walked up beside her and bumped her shoulder. "How are you?" When Story turned to face her, Allegra saw tear tracks down her cheeks. "Oh, friend! What's wrong?"

"What am I going to do without him?" Story's quiet response broke Allegra's heart.

"What's gone on between you two?"

Story shrugged and looked away. "Nothing, really."

"Don't give me that. It's obvious you two like each other, and even more obvious something happened to stop a relationship."

A derisive laugh escaped Story. "Yeah, you could say that."

Story didn't offer any more information. It was really none of Allegra's business. Maybe one day she'd get the whole story. Allegra glanced down at her watch. Until then... "Hey, do you want to go get some dinner together? I'm tired of eating ramen."

A soft smile lit Story's face. "That actually sounds good. Yeah. What were you thinking?"

"Well, it'd be a splurge for me, but I've been dying for some sushi."

Her friend's eyes brightened. "Yes! Let's get out of here."

They worked together to get the shop closed up for the night and then left to find their sushi. If she couldn't—wouldn't—spend time with Tyler anymore, she at least had a friend. It'd been a long time.

She and Story entered Wasabi, its electric blue lights and black tabletops contrasting against the chrome table legs and accents on the walls. Top 40 music played quietly in the background—loud enough to be heard but not to overshadow the buzz of conversations at the tables around them. Their table sat next to large windows that framed a golden view of Elliott Bay. Definitely a vibe that didn't match their moods, but maybe it would do them some good.

After ordering lemon water and blueberry bubble tea, Story watched Allegra for a moment before she spoke. "So what happened between you and Tyler?"

"Hey. I thought we were going to talk about you and Bo."

Story waved a hand in front of her face. "Nothing to tell. Not anymore. You and Ty, however..." She raised a brow in question. "Speak."

"Woof."

Story's laughter tinkled through the small restaurant. "I deserved that. I'm sorry. But seriously"—she smothered the grin on her face—"what happened? You two seemed to really like each other. Now, it's like walking into a freezer every time you two are in the same room."

Allegra wove some hair between her fingers, wondering if she should tell Story the truth. But it wasn't as if anything more had happened. She and Tyler were barely speaking. "He kissed me." She waited for the shock to show on Story's face. It didn't. "The day he took me to the indoor rock-climbing gym. I—*we*—both got carried away. He kissed me at the gym, and I kissed him when we got back to the shop that evening." She stopped there.

"And?"

Allegra sighed. "He promised me he'd call that night. He didn't." She picked up a napkin and began tearing it in little pieces. "I waited by the phone like a lovestruck puppy for a few hours, then went for a walk." She grinned at Story, sitting across from her. "To Bean There for my latté. He still hadn't called by the time I went to bed. He showed up at work the next morning and told me he regretted it all, he was sorry, and it couldn't happen again."

Story reached across the table and patted Allegra's hand. "I'm sorry."

"No, it's okay. He was right. It shouldn't have happened." She stopped while the waitress set their drinks in front of them." In all reality, she *wasn't* okay. He'd hurt her. She'd taken a risk, and it felt like he'd shoved it back in her face.

Her gut caved in on itself. She'd been a fool.

"Have you decided on your meals?"

Story ordered a spicy tempura shrimp roll topped with pineapple and coconut, while Allegra ordered her favorite standby, salmon nigiri. The waitress finished their order, then left.

Allegra picked up the conversation. "I lost control. I knew better than to try to start something with my employer."

"Allie."

Allegra looked up to meet Story's gaze.

"I don't think that's *losing control*. I've been watching you two, and you both really like one another. And that's okay."

The waitress returned with their sushi, and Allegra dug into her nigiri, buying herself a moment before she responded. She placed her chopsticks between her fingers, picked up a piece of sushi, and dipped it in some wasabi and soy sauce before she popped it in her mouth. The fresh salmon and rice were mild, but she loved mild.

Of course. Mild was safe. She rolled her eyes. She'd taken a walk on the dangerous side by kissing Tyler, and she'd fallen hard. She may not have died, but a piece of her felt like she had.

Time to pick up where Story left off. "No, it isn't okay. But I'll live, Story. Really." She offered a smile and tried to shake off her melancholy. "So..." Dare she ask? "What's with you and Bo?"

Could a grunt be considered an ample answer? Story seemed to think so because that was all she offered Allegra before stuffing her mouth with her own roll. Maybe if she waited long enough...

"Fine." Story lifted her lemon water to her lips and took a long swallow before she set her gaze back on Allegra. "Bo and I have a history."

"Duh."

"Cute."

"Come on, Story. 'Fess up."

"Can we just leave it to say that we tried a relationship, garbage happened, and it ended? And now he's leaving."

Allegra reached across the table to squeeze Story's hand before she took another sip of her bubble tea. Seriously, the stuff was sooo good. She chewed on a "bubble" and swallowed.

"So you still have feelings for him?"

She watched as her friend leaned back against her seat, closed her eyes, and sighed. "I don't know. Yes. I think."

Allegra sucked on the giant straw—wide enough to accommodate the chewy bubbles in her tea—and drank...until a bubble shot out of the straw and lodged in her throat. She coughed, trying to move it, but the stubborn sphere wouldn't budge.

"Allegra? You okay?"

She grunted. Huh...maybe a grunt *could* be considered response enough.

Story shot from her chair and rushed to Allegra's side. And smacked her. Hard. On the back.

Then did it again.

Was the woman trying to beat her to death?

Just as she tried coughing again, Story threw her arms around Allegra and squeezed.

Now was *not* the time for a hug. She'd need to talk to her friend about personal space too.

But the bubble moved! Then spewed straight from her mouth and plunked itself with a small splash into Story's lemon water.

Allegra pinched her lips together, trying so hard not to laugh. It didn't work.

She and Story cracked up, their laughter drawing the

attention of diners nearby. Story moved back to her seat just as the waitress brought another water. Very astute of her. Allegra would have to remember to give her a large tip.

"Anyway, let's make tonight about *us,* not the guys. We both need some fun."

Story raised her fresh lemon water. "I'll drink to that."

Allegra lifted her bubble tea—she'd have to be careful of those chewy things—and seconded that toast. "A girls' night."

Chapter Twenty-Three

"You ready, man?"

Tyler looked up from his phone to see Bo walking toward him. "As ready as I can be." He looked around the Garden Room at the Fairmont Olympic Hotel. The floor-to-ceiling glass looking out over the garden with city buildings beyond it made a statement when one first walked in, with six tall, thin trees spaced evenly among the windows. The parquet dance floor—with more potted plants around it—stood ready at the back of the grand space, waiting for the foundation's guests to use it for a night of enjoyment. At the far end, up on a raised floor, stood a beautiful grand piano, and beyond that, a wall of honey oak paneling. Tables were spread throughout the space, elegant ladder-back chairs framing the white tablecloths. The three stairs leading up to the wall of glass were girded on each side by a thick brass rail and boxes of green plants with yellow flowers. For a moment, he pictured Allegra walking up those stairs in a white wedding gown, coming to meet her groom.

His heart ached.

"Earth to Tyler."

His attention swung from his thoughts—thank goodness—back to Bo. He eyed him for a moment. "I can't believe you're really leaving me. Tomorrow."

Bo started to say something, stopped, and shrugged. A silent apology.

Tyler clapped his friend on his shoulder. "I'm gonna miss you, buddy."

Bo smiled. "Ditto."

And that was as mushy as they were gonna get.

Bo walked off to speak with the event coordinator. Tyler did his best to avoid checking on the silent auction set up in the hotel's mezzanine, where Allegra was likely to be right now. He didn't know if his heart could take seeing her decked out, working hard to raise money for his foundation. Her help over the past number of weeks in organizing and collecting the donations was invaluable. There was no way he could have done it without her.

As he moved throughout the space, he prayed. His foundation was in need of an influx of cash, but it wouldn't happen without God. He was coming to recognize that *nothing* could happen without God.

Please bless this event, Lord. Tyler bit his lip. *And help me to get back to normal with Allegra—pre-kiss normal—and learn to live without her.*

Allegra smoothed the front of her black evening gown. She and Caprice had Skyped one another and surfed the internet, looking for the perfect dress that could fit in her budget. They finally found this one. She'd been apprehensive about it, but she had to admit, she felt pretty in the off-the-shoulder column dress. The elbow-length sleeves covered her upper arms—something she really appreciated—while the rest of the dress hugged her curves until it loosened just below her hips. Capri had convinced her to buy a chunky gold-and-turquoise necklace to lie just above the portrait neckline, and matching earrings, and gold bangle bracelets. She finished the look by sweeping all her hair back and into a low, loose bun. Wisps framed her face. She brushed them back and put on a bright smile as two guests entered the mezzanine.

After helping the gentleman and his wife place bids on two auction items, she left one of the foundation employees in charge so she could walk down the hall and peek into the Garden Room.

The stunning room sparkled with brass and early-evening sunlight shining in. The plants and elegant table settings added to the luxurious but cozy atmosphere.

"Pretty, isn't it?"

Allegra grabbed at her chest and spun at Tyler's rich voice behind her. "Uh...yes. It's gorgeous." She slid her gaze to watch as more guests walked past.

"You've done a great job with the silent auction area, Allie."

"Mm. Thanks." She turned back to him. "I didn't do it by myself though. I had a lot of help. Story especially."

Tyler nodded. "Is she here yet?"

"No." Allegra frowned. "I don't think she'll come until it's already started. She said she had something going on, so she left after she helped me set up the tables out there."

"Ah."

Allegra licked her lips, trying to think of something to say. When she looked back at Tyler, he was watching her mouth. Her stomach fluttered. She wished so badly he wouldn't do that. Tyler had told her he couldn't do this right now, but he didn't make it easy with his mixed signals when he was staring at her, heat in his eyes.

No doubt that same heat was reflected in her own gaze. *Tame yourself, Allegra.*

"I better get back to the auction. I left Sandra in charge but told her I'd be right back. So I…" Allegra swallowed. "I better go."

Tyler's gaze lowered to the ground. "Yeah."

She moved to walk around him, when he held a hand to her arm. "Allie."

She turned, her belly knotted.

"In case I forget to tell you later, you look beautiful."

Her voice trembled. "Thank you." She tried pasting on a smile. "You don't look so bad yourself."

Walking away from Tyler in that moment was one of the hardest things she'd done in a long while. She missed him. He hadn't tried to talk her into any more adventures, and though she understood the gala benefit and Bo's move took priority, she couldn't help but feel disappointed. Something she shouldn't be feeling, considering how badly he'd hurt her. And how much she despised those adventures.

Okay, maybe not *despised*, but sorely disliked. Kind of.

Chapter Twenty-Four

Tyler didn't see Allegra after the gala began, at least not up close. He saw her for a moment when she came in to talk briefly to Peter, the board director who'd helped organize the benefit, but she'd quickly stepped back out to the mezzanine.

Distracted by the plate in front of him, Tyler set thoughts of Allegra aside and focused on his appetizer—a white truffle gnocchi dish. He took his first bite and groaned his pleasure. Peter's wife, Casey, sat beside him, giggling.

"So good." He lifted his fork for a second bite, but it didn't reach his mouth. Allegra walked into the Garden Room on the arm of a man. Heat sizzled through his body. As the pair walked closer, he recognized the man as the son of the governor. A player. Why was she with him?

Tyler didn't fault her for leaving the auction. She'd been working those tables for hours already, setting up before the event. She deserved a bite to eat. But he didn't think she knew anyone here, other than him.

Tyler crumpled his napkin as thickness built in his throat. How did he not even think to go get her and sit her at a table? Could a man be any more pea brained? It was like he'd missed an easy forty-yard pass. Something not even a rookie would do very often.

He scraped his chair back from the table. The others were in deep enough conversation and didn't notice his swift departure. He walked in the general direction of the couple, who'd just sat down at a table near the windows. When he reached Allegra and what's-his-name, he paused, unsure what to say. Until she looked up at him with those deep ocean-blue eyes. Tyler lost himself for a moment, all sounds fading as he stood mesmerized.

It took him a moment before he saw her lips moving. "Tyler. Are you okay?"

Jolted, he stepped back. "Uh, yeah. Sorry. Spaced out there for a second." He ignored the question in her eyes. "I just wanted to stop by and see how the auction is going out there." He thumbed over his shoulder in the direction of the doors to the mezzanine.

"Oh, fine." She slid her chair back a bit so Tyler could see the man sitting beside her. "This is Jeremy Fanton, the governor's son. Jeremy, Tyler Hawk."

"Yes, I know who you are." Jeremy stood, a lift to his brow and a wide grin on his face. A charmer. Tyler blinked to stop from rolling his eyes.

"It's good to meet you." He stretched out his arm to accept Jeremy's shake. "Are you enjoying yourself tonight?"

Jeremy looked down at Allegra, a glint in his eyes that

made Tyler want to tackle him right then and there. He was trained to block on running plays, and Jeremy was obviously making a running play on Allegra.

"I'm having an excellent night in the best company."

Tyler's stomach churned. If he weren't so stubborn, Allie would be on *his* arm. But it was better this way. At least, that was what he told himself. He couldn't exactly picture himself sitting on the couch binge-watching *Downton Abbey* every Saturday.

Parks and Rec maybe. He grinned. Chris Pratt was too funny. But he didn't think even the TV and movie star could keep him glued to the couch for more than an hour. And Allegra didn't seem the type to—

He watched as Allegra looked up at Jeremy, her soft kissable lips forming a smile. His heart beat in a staccato rhythm. He had to get away from them. "Well, have a good night."

Tyler turned and took one step before a gentle hand on his arm stopped him.

"Tyler, the auction is going really well." Allegra looked over her shoulder at Jeremy before she faced him again, lowering her voice. "The donations have been pouring in, on top of the auction. These people are seriously generous."

Gratitude released some of the tension in his neck. "That's great to hear, Allie. Thanks for your hard work. I doubt we'd have such generous donors if it weren't for you."

"Well, it wasn't all me, you know." She knuckled his arm before she returned to her table and Jeremy.

If only he could walk away from her as easily.

It was so hard walking away from Tyler, pretending to be lighthearted when all she really wanted to do was pull his mouth to hers. Tears burned the backs of her eyes.

Soft piano music played as she sat down beside Jeremy, who immediately picked up the conversation.

"So I was telling you about my cars."

She tried to listen, but she couldn't stop her eyes from lifting heavenward. *When will this man stop talking about himself?*

When they'd met at the auction table, he'd seemed nice. She'd watched as he inspected each item on the tables, read the descriptions of trips being offered, and made small talk while she typed his information into her tablet, including a generous amount for a donation on top of his bid. He'd then asked her to accompany him into the Garden Room for dinner and tried to make her promise to save him a dance. Not that she danced.

She glanced down at her two left feet. If he made her follow through with that, she was going to embarrass not only herself but Jeremy, and worse, Tyler. No way she was getting on that floor.

The waiter set down the main course. This would be her only chance for a long time to eat something other than packaged soup. Steam rose from the plate, carrying its delectable scents. Allegra's mouth watered over her Dungeness crab mac-'n'-cheese as she waited for the others to be served their plates. She bent her head to hide her finger wiping her mouth. She was pretty sure she'd just drooled on her fillet of Angus beef.

Beside her, Jeremy watched his plate being lowered. He scrunched his nose. "Are these baby tomatoes organic?"

Seriously?

The waiter shook his head. "I'm sorry, sir. I don't know. I'll go ask the chef for you, however."

"See that you do."

Oh, the arrogance of this man! Allegra ran a hand across her forehead.

"Is there something wrong with your plate too, Allegra?"

"What? No. Nothing's wrong at all. And your lamb looks delicious."

Jeremy sniffed. "Hm."

This was going to be a long night.

Chapter Twenty-Five

It was amazing how well Allegra commanded his attention. He was aware of her every smile, her every bite. Her every moment.

It was time to get himself under control.

Huh. Imagine that irony. Control. Maybe Allegra was on to something after all.

Tyler was finishing the last bite of his ice-wine poached strawberries when Bo leaned over. "Is there dancing first, or the announcement?"

"Dancing." He eyed Bo. "Hoping for a certain dance partner?"

Bo grinned. "Not as hopeful as I think you are for your certain dance partner." He pushed away from the table, leaving, Tyler presumed, to find Story.

Allegra was nowhere to be seen. She must be at the auction tables.

A waft of heavy perfume tickled his nose.

Oh no.

Tyler squeezed his eyes closed, praying with all his might that he was wrong about who was approaching him. Maybe she'd walk past him. One could hope.

"Hello, Tyler."

Or not.

Tyler opened his eyes and looked up at the tall blonde standing beside him. His stomach gurgled. Hopefully, he'd throw up all over her and have a good excuse to leave.

"Hi, Sondra."

Sondra bent over and wrapped her thin arms around his neck, giving him a long wet kiss on his cheek. "It's been forever. Where have you been hiding yourself?"

Uh…as a well-known football player in Seattle, where the city adored the Seahawks, he couldn't exactly hide. "Can't say I've been hiding." Though he wished he was holed away in some far-off country right about now.

Sondra's high-pitched laugh—one that garnered attention from those close to his table, even over the sound of the jazz band starting to tune their instruments—grated his nerves. How had he ever been attracted to her? He didn't know, but it was going to remain a mystery, because he didn't want to pick back up what she was throwing down. Once upon a time he wouldn't have given it a second thought—he would have taken whatever was freely offered to him—but no. Not now.

"Oh, Ty. You always have been a difficult one to track down." She sat in the seat Bo had abandoned. "Tell me. What have you been up to, other than this little foundation of yours?"

Could he speak through clenched teeth? He was about to

find out. "You surely know about my excursion outfit. This foundation also takes a lot of time." Huh. Who knew? He was pretty sure it didn't even sound like he was gritting his teeth. Much.

Her lips pursed before she rolled her eyes. When Sondra opened her mouth, she showed all her perfect veneers, as white as they could be. He'd once enjoyed kissing that mouth of hers. Now it made him gag. *Be nice, Tyler.*

"Psh. You're still running that little store? When are you going to go back to football? I'm sure you miss it." She ran a hand down his arm to his thigh, letting it rest there. "I know I miss watching you play." She lowered her eyelids halfway. Going for bedroom eyes, he assumed.

Tyler lifted her hand off his leg. "I'm done with football, Sondra. I retired, remember? It's why you dumped me." He ignored her pout. "Now, if you'll excuse me, I need to go check on something."

He stood, ignoring Sondra's protests, and turned to go find something to check on.

Searching for Tyler proved to be easy. The glamorous blonde bending down at his table caught her attention first. How was it possible for someone to be that gorgeous? Allegra's gaze drifted from her to the person she was talking to.

Of course. Tyler. She watched as the woman leaned close, giving him a hug and lingering kiss on the cheek.

Allegra looked down her own body. She was blessed with an hourglass figure that helped disguise some of the extra weight she carried, but she was no model like the woman hanging off Tyler. Maybe two models put together though... Three. She probably equaled three models. But who was counting?

Sighing, Allegra decided to give him a few minutes with the woman before she handed him the auction winners list. The jazz band began a lively tune, inviting the guests to take to the dance floor.

A finger tapped her shoulder. She turned to find...ugh. Jeremy.

"I'm so glad I found you. May I have this dance?"

Allegra glanced over her shoulder to see the woman's hand on Tyler's thigh. He was obviously still busy. She turned back to Jeremy. "Sure. Thank you."

His overly confident grin told her he didn't doubt what her answer would be. Jeremy took her hand in his and led her to the center of the parquet dance floor. She was thankful for the faster tune. He might not be, however, when he saw how poorly she danced.

She couldn't help the slow smile spreading across her face. Jeremy was sure to leave her alone after this.

Thank goodness.

It seemed Jeremy wouldn't give up though. When the first song finished, the tempo slowed a bit and Jeremy slowed with it. "Maybe with a slower song, your feet will be able to catch up."

Oh, he went for a charming look, waggling his brows, and his smile hitched up on one side, but it didn't work.

"Maybe a different partner would be more comfortable for

you."

How she tried.

"You're sweet. But I have no doubt in my ability to teach you." He leaned down, his words breathing hot air on her ear. "I can teach you about a lot of things."

The man was a dog.

Before she could respond to his advance, Allegra felt a tap on her shoulder. Saved by the tap!

She turned to find Tyler standing there, arms crossed against his chest and an annoyed look in his eyes.

"May I cut in?"

Well. His voice was certainly gruff. What had gotten under his skin? She figured he would be out on the dance floor with his blond beauty.

"No." Jeremy didn't give her a chance to respond, instead answering for her and gliding her away from Tyler.

He was beyond infuriating. "I can answer for myself, Jeremy."

"Oh, I don't doubt that you can. But I prefer to keep you for myself."

Her jaw dropped. "I don't think that's for you to decide."

Jeremy winked at her. "Somehow, I don't think you disagree."

Before that moment, she'd thought *So mad I saw red* was just a saying.

It was actually possible to see red.

Chapter Twenty-Six

Heat coursed throughout Tyler's body. His only condolence was the look on Allegra's face when Jeremy Fanton answered for her and whisked her away.

He watched Allegra dance for a minute. Oh, that woman needed help.

Badly.

Tyler shoved his hands in his pockets and followed the pair as Jeremy led her across the floor. He felt a headache forming as he watched Allegra shake her head at something the guy said.

He read her lips as she shook her head again, this time harder. *No.*

That did it for him.

Tyler stalked over to Jeremy and Allegra and once more tapped Allie on the shoulder, refusing to make eye contact with Jeremy. "May I cut in?" He wasn't sure, but what looked like relief flooded Allegra's eyes.

"No."

Tyler's body tensed. "I didn't ask you."

He was risking the anger of a donor, but at that point, Tyler didn't care. He'd replace the man's donation if Jeremy pulled it.

Allegra shot a hand up between them. "I do believe this is *my* decision." She met his gaze. "Thank you. I'd like that." She turned back to Jeremy. "But I do thank you for the dance." She smiled.

Tyler didn't know for sure, but he was confident that smile was a forced one.

Allegra's hand was warm in his as he led her to another part of the dance floor. He turned and took her other hand...just as the music finished.

Seriously? He couldn't catch a break.

Allegra laughed up at him. "Whoops."

"Yeah. Whoops." Her infectious grin made him laugh.

"Well, I guess now's the time I can pass along the auction winners to you."

She didn't let go of his hand as they walked out of the Garden Room and to the mezzanine. When they reached the tables, one of the foundation workers smiled and handed Allegra the tablet.

"We had a few last-minute bidders and some great donations on top of the bids."

"Fantastic. Thank you so much, Jeanine. Why don't you go on in and see if there's any food left?"

Jeanine nodded at Allegra, smiled at Tyler, and left them alone.

Allegra began tapping through the screens. "Oh, Tyler. This is amazing. I hope you'll be happy."

She turned her gaze to him, weakening his knees.

In that moment, all he wanted was to be kissing her. Heat crawled up his neck. He cleared his throat before responding. "I'm sure I will."

Allie tapped one last screen and then handed him the tablet. "That's the list of winners right there." She looked over her shoulder at the arrangement of prizes on the tables. "I can't believe some of these items. Seriously. A Caribbean cruise? And diamond earrings? This is highbrow, Boss."

He laughed at her playfulness. "Yeah, it is." He wet his lips. "Time to get back in and make the announcement."

Tyler held out his arm. She put her hand in the crook of his elbow and performed a small curtsy. "Let's do this."

The room buzzed with excitement as the guests watched Tyler take the stage. It was energizing seeing everyone in such high spirits, especially when high spirits usually meant higher donations. At least, that was what Allegra hoped.

Feeling a presence behind her, Allegra looked up to see Jeremy moving in beside her.

Oh brother.

She pasted on a smile. No sense in further offending the governor's son. "Hi."

"Hi." No return smile. Rats. Apparently she'd done a bang-up job on the dance floor.

"Jeremy, I'm really sorry for the way I handled Tyler's interruption. I should have finished the dance with you first."

Her skin crawled with the false platitude.

The incorrigible man sniffed. "Thank you. I appreciate that." He gave her a halfhearted smile. "Maybe after the auction winners are announced, we can go finish that dance?"

Ha! Not likely, bucko. "Of course." Sometimes she hated herself.

Tyler's low voice traveled across the room as he made his first remarks. His words dripped with passion for his organization, causing Allegra's chest to expand.

Wait...did Jeremy just say something? "I'm sorry, Jeremy. What was that?"

A flash of annoyance crossed his face before he schooled it. He leaned back down, his mouth close to her ear. Breath heated her neck as he spoke. "I said, you look pretty."

Did his lips just graze her neck? Allegra jerked back and stared. The insufferable man just stood straight and grinned.

Though she desperately wanted to tell him off, Tyler needed this man's money. She didn't want to do anything more to risk him pulling the donation he'd made at the auction table.

Allegra fluttered her eyelashes and offered a coy smile. "Thank you." *Not.*

She turned back to watch Tyler make his speech—just in time to see his eyes narrow in Jeremy's direction. Did Tyler see what happened? Well, too bad. He made his choice. What she did or did not do in regard to Jeremy—and it would be a *did not*—was none of his business.

Chapter Twenty-Seven

He couldn't stand it. Seeing Jeremy lean into Allie made him sick to his stomach. Tyler swung his gaze from the playboy back to the tablet in his hand.

"Finally, the winner of the seven-night, all-expenses-paid cruise to the Caribbean aboard Crystal Cruises' Crystal Serenity is..." The jazz members behind him started a drum roll. "...Robert Morrison."

Tyler waited as the audience clapped and congratulated Robert as he made his way to the stage. When he reached Tyler, the man stuck out his hand. "Thank you, Mr. Hawk. My wife is absolutely delighted."

This man had been a supporter of Tyler's foundation since day one, having a now-adult son who grew up with asthma. "Sir, it's my pleasure. I couldn't be happier that this trip went to such a beautiful couple."

After posing for some photographs for the foundation's website, Tyler reached for the mic again.

"I would like to thank each and every one of you for your

generous donations. It amazes me how much you care about those kids who don't just live with asthma but excel beyond it." He paused for the applause.

"Growing up, my parents loved me. Maybe a little too much." He smiled, and the audience laughed. "But they feared for my safety. They were scared that if I went out to play sports, I would have an attack that could land me in the ER...or worse, as a few fellow asthmatics have sadly experienced." His throat thickened as he remembered one of his childhood friends from asthma camp. Manuel had died from a severe attack two years after Tyler met him. It still hurt to think about it, but that was why Tyler set up this foundation. To help other kids avoid Manuel's fate.

"I'm thankful to God for putting my middle school coach in my life to encourage me to go out and play sports, eventually trying football...I think that paid off."

More laughter from the audience lifted his spirits. Tyler glanced back down at the tablet and frowned, his spirits taking an immediate plummet.

It really irked him to have to make the following announcement, but part of this gala was to honor those who made major contributions to the foundation.

"Finally, one very generous donor tonight deserves some recognition. Jeremy Fanton, as you all know, is the son of Governor Fanton. Mr. Fanton has made an extremely generous donation on top of his silent auction bid."

From his spot on the floor beside Allegra, Jeremy's face oozed with pride. Tyler's stomach churned.

"Thank you, Mr. Fanton, for your donation of"—he

paused—"twenty-five thousand dollars for the Tyler Hawk Breathe Deep Foundation."

All 160 guests erupted in applause, cheering for the man who had gone deathly pale when Tyler read the dollar amount. Jeremy looked to the beautiful woman standing next to him. Allegra stood, staring at Tyler, her mouth gaping. Why was she shocked? She was the one who'd written the amount down.

He reread the tablet screen in his hand: $25,000.

What was going on?

She was going to faint. No. No, no, no, no, no! This couldn't be happening. Allegra stared at Tyler, the pit of her stomach turning to ice.

The cheering in the room was loud, but beside her, Jeremy's voice, low and tight, sounded in her ear. The loudest accusation ever. "*Why* did he announce twenty-five thousand dollars in my name? Is he ripping me off? What's going on?"

"Jeremy, I swear...I'm sure I only entered $2,500. That's what you told me, right?"

"Yeah. So why did he"—he shoved a finger in Tyler's direction on stage—"announce an amount *ten times* that, Allegra?"

If tones could kill, she would be six feet under.

Her breath formed in short bursts. What was going on? Tyler must have read the number wrong. Surely they could quietly settle this after Tyler left the stage.

"Jeremy." Allegra laid a shaking hand on his arm. "Tyler

must have misread the amount. He's almost finished up there. We'll find him and speak with him."

"In private." His jaw twitched as he eyed those surrounding them. No doubt to see if they'd heard the conversation.

"Of course."

"If these people find out I only gave twenty-five hundred instead of twenty-five thousand…"

Tyler spoke for a few more minutes, thanking everyone again and encouraging them to stay and enjoy the rest of the evening. When he left the stage, Jeremy and Allegra were waiting for him.

"Tyler, can we—"

"Outside. Now." Jeremy turned on his heels and stalked out of the Garden Room.

Tyler eyed Allegra. "I knew something was wrong when I announced his donation. What's going on, Allie?"

Thankfully, Tyler's tone was kinder than Jeremy's.

She sighed. "His donation wasn't twenty-five thousand dollars. You must have read the number wrong. I think he's just embarrassed. He doesn't want to look bad in front of everyone if they all find out his donation was much less."

Tyler stopped walking and grabbed Allegra's arm. "I didn't read it wrong, Allie."

She put a hand to her stomach. "What are you saying?"

"Allegra." He lifted the tablet, showing her the screen. "It says twenty-five thousand dollars."

Was the room moving? The room was moving. "Stop moving."

"What?" The scowl on Tyler's face switched from side to side. His eyes widened, and he grabbed her upper arms. "Let's get out into the hall."

"It's hot in here. Too hot." Sweat broke out along Allegra's hairline.

"Come on, honey."

Tyler wrapped an arm around her shoulders and leaned Allegra against his side, holding her up as he walked her out. They walked to the mezzanine, where Jeremy paced alongside the auction tables.

"Let's go to that alcove over there so we have some privacy." Tyler pointed his chin in the direction of a dimly lit corner down the hall and away from where guests would start picking up their winnings.

When they reached it, Allegra leaned against the wall with her knees bent—well, as bent as they could be in the formfitting mermaid gown. She rubbed her face, not caring if her mascara and eyeliner colored her cheeks.

Jeremy turned on Tyler. "Tell me what's going on. Are you trying to make me pay for having Allegra's attention all night?"

"What? No!" Tyler raised the tablet in Jeremy's face. "You gave twenty-five thousand."

"No." Jeremy's clenched teeth muted his words. "I gave twenty-five hundred."

The two men looked at Allegra. Tyler shook his head. "The info I was given said twenty-five thousand."

Oh, how she wished she was home in her sweatshirt and yoga pants, burrowed under her blankets. "Tyler, Jeremy gave twenty-five hundred. I...I don't know what happened, but that's what he said and wrote down on the donor slip."

Allegra stared, mesmerized, by the color rising from Tyler's throat up his chin, cheeks, and ears. His nostrils flared. "Then *why* does this"—he shook the tablet—"give a different amount?"

She licked her lips, momentarily drawing Tyler's attention before his gaze met hers again. "I—"

"*You* entered the amount, Allegra." Jeremy's staccato voice drilled holes into her.

Her throat tightened. She had. She'd been the one to enter it into the processing software.

Chapter Twenty-Eight

Tyler rubbed the back of his neck. "We can fix this." He turned to face Jeremy. "Allegra can reverse the entry and put in a new one showing the right amount. We'll keep it quiet, so no one outside the foundation accountant will ever know."

Behind him, he heard a quiet voice. "Tyler..."

He looked over his shoulder. "Yeah?"

Allegra's face was white as a ghost. Her mouth moved, but no sound came out.

"What is it?" Impatience colored Jeremy's voice.

"Allie, what?"

"I...I ran hi...his credit card already."

Ice formed in the pit of his stomach. "Credit card?"

Allegra's eyes flicked between Jeremy and him. Tyler looked down at the tablet. Oh man. What a mess. He rubbed his neck again, where his headache was now fully formed.

"Jeremy, I'm so sorry. I—"

"I don't want to hear it." Jeremy jabbed Tyler in his back,

forcing him to turn and look. "You"—Jeremy's finger now poked Tyler's chest—"you better fix this. Now."

"Jeremy—"

He cursed, then waved his hand in front of him, effectively cutting her off. "No, Allegra. I don't want to deal with you. You're incompetent, and now I have to figure out a way to get my money back." He looked at Tyler. "*All* my money. Not one red cent will be given to such an inept foundation."

Behind him, Allegra gasped. "Jeremy, that's harsh! And it wasn't Tyler's fault, or even the organization's fault. It was *mine*."

"I don't care."

"But the kids!"

Tyler's heart sank.

"If I don't get all my money back within a day, I'm going public." Jeremy stared hard at Tyler, then left.

What was he going to do? He was thankful Breathe Deep had made as much tonight as it did, but this was still going to hurt.

"Tyler..."

He shoved his clenched fists into his pockets and turned to face Allegra. Tears left trails in her smudged makeup, and her hair was falling out of its bun. He steeled himself.

"I'm so sorry." Her voice cracked.

"Yeah, well..." What could he say? This was a major mistake. A $25,000 mistake. "Go home, Allegra. We'll talk about this on Monday. Give me the weekend to cool off."

She answered with a small nod and shuffled off, her eyes

downcast.

Tyler's chest felt hollow as he watched her leave. But he couldn't think about her right now.

He had bigger problems to worry about.

Saturday morning dawned with Allegra watching it from her bed, where she'd been—awake—since getting home from the gala hours earlier.

Well, not quite since she got home. First, she had to get to her bathroom so she could be sick. *Then* she'd crawled into bed. Well, after slipping her gown off and putting on some sweatpants, her dad's old holey sweatshirt from Duke University, and the thickest fuzzy socks she could find. She didn't bother taking her hair down or washing her face. Just crawled into bed, pulled her covers up to her chin, and sobbed.

What had she done? She couldn't believe she'd made such a huge mistake.

She was going to be sick again. She scrambled out of bed and ran for her bathroom.

An hour later, the phone rang. She picked it up off her bedside table. Tyler. Allegra's heart flipped. Was he going to fire her? He *should* fire her. Even if Breathe Deep's accountant could fix her error, it was costing the foundation more than money. It cost them a donor.

She slid her thumb along the bottom of her cell and lifted it to her ear. "He—" The thickness in her throat prevented her from continuing.

"I thought you'd be awake. Have you slept at all?"

Allegra shook her head before she remembered Tyler couldn't see her. "No."

He sighed. "I don't—"

"Tyler, I—"

"Go ahead, Allie."

She worried the edge of her blanket. "I'm so sorry. I don't know what happened. I've been thinking about it all night, and all I can think is that I accidentally tapped four zeros instead of three. I just...I don't know how to make this better."

The wall clock she'd received as a college graduation gift from her parents chimed the hour out in her living room. She had collected clocks throughout her teen years and into college. Her parents' last gift to her, however, was the only remaining clock. She'd sold the others to help pay for Caprice's high school senior trip. Capri had argued with her, but Allegra had been determined to give her sister the experiences she'd been able to have when she was in high school.

"You can't." Tyler's sharp voice brought her attention back. He sighed. "Allie, I think by now I know you, and I know what you're thinking. You're not fired."

Air whooshed out of her lungs.

"You were there as a volunteer for the foundation, not as an employee."

Oh. So did he *want* to fire her but didn't feel like he could legally? She pinned an arm against her stomach.

"Breathe Deep's accountant will fix what's going on and refund Jeremy's money."

"O-okay. I...thank you, Tyler."

"Mm-hm."

Allegra tilted her head back toward to her ceiling. He was angry. And disappointed. She didn't know what hurt worse.

Yes she did. The disappointment.

"Try to get some sleep. Let me know tomorrow night if you want to take Monday off to catch up on your rest."

The phone went silent. She pulled the cell away from her ear. Tyler had ended the call.

A latté. She needed a latté. And chocolate. And her computer.

Allegra spent the rest of the weekend under her bed blankets with her laptop in front of her, searching the job sites for openings. If Tyler really didn't want her there, she'd quit. But she needed a new job first. There was no way she could afford to quit before she landed another position. She needed to save every spare penny to cover upcoming tuition payments.

Sunday afternoon, Allegra hit Send on another résumé. What was she thinking sending it off to a company almost two hundred miles away?

Chapter Twenty-Nine

After spending Saturday morning with Breathe Deep's accountant, Tyler started his truck and drove to Bo's place for the last time. He couldn't believe his best friend and business partner was moving across the country.

He'd say his heart was breaking, but that wouldn't be so manly.

Right?

Right.

Flicking his signal to turn left, Tyler let his thoughts drift to this morning's meeting with the accountant to correct Allegra's mistake. His head had been throbbing all night until he and Barnes had figured out the problem and issued a refund to Jeremy Fanton. When he'd spoken with Allegra earlier that morning, he was still angry. Thankfully, the entry itself turned out to not be quite as big a deal as he'd feared. Losing that donation—and the donor himself—however, proved to be a hard pill to swallow. And he had no doubt

Fanton would tell his dad what happened, resulting in a potential loss there too.

Reaching Bo's place, Tyler parked and opened his door to a warm, sunny day. It didn't match his mood though, and he wished it were clouded over and raining so he would feel better about moping around.

He was losing his best friend and a major donation in one day.

Tyler knocked and was welcomed into an apartment full of boxes. "Hey, man." He grabbed Bo in a hug, pounding his friend on the back. "You ready for this?"

Bo couldn't hide the excitement in his eyes. He always was up for change. It was partly what made them best friends.

"Oh yeah. The question is, my friend, are *you* ready to do some heavy lifting?" Bo eyed Tyler's jeans and collared shirt. "Where are your moving clothes? C'mon, man. I'm not giving you a break here. You're gonna help me load up this moving truck no matter what."

Laughing, Tyler lifted his black duffel bag. "Let me go change, and I'll prove my worth."

The two loaded the big furniture, then boxes, into the rented moving truck. They'd just finished carrying out some sports equipment, when tires crunched some gravel in the parking lot. He and Bo looked up to see Story parking her beat-up car.

"You'd think I paid her enough to get a new car."

Bo didn't respond. His brows drew together as he watched the small woman open her door and remove her sunglasses.

Tyler busied himself as Bo and Story talked quietly. Bo

lifted his hands. Story shook her head and looked down at the ground. Whatever was going on, it was hurting them both.

Story turned and, without acknowledging Tyler, got back in her car and drove off.

"What was that about?"

"Just saying goodbye." His friend's flat voice said otherwise, but Tyler kept his thoughts to himself.

The rest of the afternoon was spent cleaning Bo's apartment. Then it was time to say his own goodbye.

"What time are you leaving tomorrow?" Tyler hefted the last bag of food into the back of his truck. He'd stop by the shelter on his way home.

"First thing."

"What? You're not going to let me take you for breakfast?"

"You mean your treat?" A flash of white teeth emphasized Bo's golden-brown skin.

Tyler laughed. Something he really needed today. "Yeah. My treat."

"You willing to wake up early on a Sunday?"

He punched his friend in the shoulder. "Bring it."

"Game on."

"Speaking of game..."

Bo rolled his eyes. "You better not be talking about Story again."

"You goof. I meant football. One last time. You don't have any big plans tonight, right?"

"Oh, you're on. I'll give you one last shot to try and beat

me."

Psh. "Nice try, old man."

⁂

That was it then.

Tyler met Bo for an early breakfast before he watched his best friend drive off, starting a new life without him in it. Okay, so he'd always be in Bo's life, but it was tough knowing he wouldn't be in his friend's day-to-day life.

At a stop light, Tyler looked at the clock on his dash: 9:30 a.m. When the light turned green, he eased onto the gas pedal and drove, no destination in mind.

Until he came across a one-story brick building and saw people walking in. He slowed to let someone cross the street and glanced out of the corner of his eyes. City of Light Church.

Huh. Well, he had nowhere else to be. He should park and go in.

The thought caught him off guard, but as he sat, letting more people cross, the better it sounded.

Tyler turned his steering wheel to the left and parked.

Walking into the building—it must have been an old factory of some sort, with its brick walls, exposed ducts overhead, and wood beams—he was greeted by a few people near the door, one of whom handed him a sheet of paper. He read it as he took a seat near the back of the church. A bunch of upcoming events. He flipped the paper over and saw only the name of a person and a title. *Where Is Your Safety?*

A chill went down his spine as an image of Allegra filtered into his vision. She was so beautiful. Not just physically—

though that was true—but her personality, kindness, charm, intelligence...everything he'd always looked for in a woman, she had. But with a major flaw: fear.

All through the singing part of the worship, Tyler thought about Allegra's fear. He'd never had patience for fear—his or anyone else's. To him, fear was something to be conquered, not a cop-out. But a lot of people didn't think like him. Including Allegra. And he'd always wanted a woman who would be adventurous with him, laugh in the face of fear. Allie had definitely made an effort, but she didn't enjoy it like he did. He relished risk and adrenaline.

The band up front stopped, and a woman walked on the stage and took a microphone. "Please stay standing for the reading of the Word, Psalm 18." She waited a moment, then began. "'I love you, O Lord, my strength. The Lord is my rock and my fortress and my deliverer, my God, my rock, in whom I take refuge, my shield, and the horn of my salvation, my stronghold. I call upon the Lord, who is worthy to be praised, and I am saved from my enemies.'"

The hair on the back of Tyler's neck stood. Saved from enemies...like fear?

The woman continued. "'In my distress I called upon the Lord; to my God I cried for help. From his temple he heard my voice, and my cry to him reached his ears.'"

Cried for help. So the Psalmist was afraid...and admitted it.

Tyler didn't hear the rest of the passage until the woman said, "The Word of the Lord."

The pastor stepped onto the stage at the front, his face

enlarged on two screens on either side of him. "When was the last time you looked at the Lord as your rock, your fortress, your deliverer, your shield, stronghold, and the horn of your salvation?"

When *was* the last time he'd done that? He'd been giving lip-service to God. He certainly believed in God, but when had he actually spent time with Him? Tyler thought back to his childhood. His parents had acted as his safety net, whether he wanted them to or not. From the time he'd met his middle school coach, Tyler had learned to push his boundaries, take risk, and...rely on himself. He'd considered himself his own stronghold, shield, and fortress.

A revelation tingled his skin. All these years, pushing himself to excellence and to experience the scary, and pushing others to get outside their comfort zones and experience adrenaline rushes, he'd been running from his own fears. The fear of mediocrity...of being his parents. Always afraid.

Chapter Thirty

She paced circles around her coffee table. Who needed a gym membership when she had a track in her own living room and heart palpitations all morning. When Allegra had arrived at work Monday, Tyler had been out, leading an excursion. Tuesday, he'd been in meetings all day with his foundation's board of directors, no doubt discussing the money the gala had raised. And her very costly mistake.

A latté. That was what she needed. After one last circle around the table, she moved to her espresso machine on the kitchen counter.

It was a siren's call.

She filled the water reservoir, ground some dark-roast beans, filled the frother with some half-and-half, and waited with bated breath while the machine worked its magic.

She thought back to Wednesday, when it happened. Tyler was out of the office again, leading another excursion. Allegra's phone had rung midmorning, but she'd paid no attention to it until lunchtime. She hadn't recognized the number in her missed calls, but when she listened to her voicemail, she'd dropped her fork in her leftover mac-'n'-cheese. An interview. The company she'd sent her résumé to in Portland wanted her to come in for an interview. Which she dreaded. But she'd arranged the time for just after lunch the next day, then emailed Tyler, asking him if she could take the day off. He'd replied later that night with one word: *Sure.* He was obviously still angry with her. His answer just confirmed what she knew. She needed to find other work.

The machine finished spurting its sweet nectar. She lifted her oversized mug to her lips and closed her eyes, relishing the taste. Allegra glanced at the clock on the microwave. Shoot. No time to relish. She needed to guzzle.

It was time to leave for her interview, and she felt sick to her stomach. Was she doing the right thing? She'd made a terrible mistake that cost Tyler's foundation thousands—and a donor or two—but she had to admit, the store was growing on her.

The excursions, not so much. But maybe she could get used to them. Maybe.

Regardless, her heart told her she needed to step away. She'd often heard that the heart was the greatest deceiver, but she didn't think that was the case this time.

She could admit it: she was running. Allegra smirked. Probably the only time she'd ever run.

She lifted her purse off the counter, set her mug in the sink to wash later, and grabbed her car keys. She locked her door behind her and hurried down to her car.

Allegra sat in her Pacifica, started it, and gave just enough time for her phone's Bluetooth to connect before she called Caprice.

Her sister's phone rang until voicemail kicked in. Allegra looked at the clock. New York was three hours ahead, which would make it lunchtime. Maybe Capri was out with some coworkers.

Allegra sighed. The drive would be long and lonely.

You have me to talk to.

Warmth spread through her body. *Yes, God. I do.*

During her drive to Portland, Allegra went between having her Bible app read to her and pausing it to pray. It was the longest—and sweetest—time she'd had with God since she could remember. As she drove I-5 into the city, she felt completely at peace. The nerves were gone. And she felt renewed.

Okay. Most of the nerves were gone. That interview still loomed in front of her, but at least that quiet peace eased her mind.

Mostly.

Allegra pulled into a gas station. She stepped out of the car when an attendant ran up.

"Ma'am..."

Oh how she hated being called that!

"I'm sorry, but there is no self-service allowed here. Oregon is full-serve only. Can I fill your tank for you?"

Hello! She could get used to this. "Sure." Allegra climbed back in her car and waited while the attendant pumped gas into her tank. She slipped him her credit card, signed the receipt, and found her way to the offices of Schmidt, Basham

& Monzon. Time to get it done.

Friday morning revealed another sunny day in Seattle. Tyler sat in a chair on his patio overlooking the waters of Elliott Bay from his Belltown neighborhood condo, his Bible open to the passage he'd just finished reading. He loved this city and was glad he'd stayed after retiring from the NFL. And his condo? He loved sitting on the patio, but the view from his living room left him speechless sometimes, especially at night. The Space Needle stood tall and proud—and large—framed by his windows. Belltown though...it was heavily populated with tons of restaurants, nightclubs, and boutiques, but it just made it that much more vibrant. More than all of that, the people who lived in Seattle were friendly and super supportive when he'd announced his retirement after a stellar season. He hadn't just played for the 12th Man—he'd become one.

Picking up his Bible, Tyler walked inside. He hadn't been in the office all week, so he was looking forward to sitting down with Allegra. And getting some work done. Mostly meeting with Allie. He grinned. This week had been a huge growth for him with Jesus. He still had a long way to go, but he was walking in the right direction, and it felt good.

Really good.

Arriving at Hawk's Flight, he greeted Story on his way to the back. He dropped his things on his low file cabinet and made his way to Allie's office. She was sitting behind her desk staring at her computer screen while chewing on a nail.

Wait. She was chewing on a nail? He'd never seen her

doing that. Was she nervous?

"Allie?"

She jumped in her chair. "Oh!"

"Sorry. I didn't mean to scare you." He sat down in a chair across from her. "You looked deep in thought."

She wasn't meeting his gaze.

"Yeah." She shuffled some papers on her desk.

She also wasn't saying much. Did she think he was still angry? "Allie." He held a hand out to her, but she ignored it. "I'm not angry."

Allegra bit her lip but still didn't look at him. He sighed. "Okay. I *was* angry. It was a big mistake, but it was fixed."

Finally, she looked up and searched his face. "But I cost you a donor."

His shoulders slumped. "Yeah." He bent forward, resting his elbows on the desk. "But I'm sure we'll find others to replace Fanton."

"Hm."

She didn't sound convinced.

Tyler opened his mouth to speak again. "Seriously, Allie. I'm honestly happy this happened. Governor's son or not, who needs a jerk like that on our team? I'm sure—"

Allegra held up a hand to stop him. "I need to talk to you."

That sounded ominous. And she interrupted. Not like her. Uh-oh. "What's up?"

The woman in front of him lifted her gaze to the ceiling before lowering it again. She bent to her side and pulled her purse up into her lap. Opening it, she drew out a thin, white envelope.

Uh-oh. Thin envelopes were never a good sign. And the frown on her face just confirmed that.

Allegra slid the envelope across the mahogany desk. He let it sit there.

"What's that?"

She swallowed. "My...my resignation."

If an earthquake happened right then, he couldn't have been more shaken. "Your *what*?"

She didn't say anything, just sat there, staring at her hands in her lap.

"Why? What's going on?" A thought occurred to him. "What about Caprice?" Maybe bringing her sister into this would shake her out of whatever was going on in her beautiful brain.

Allegra shifted in her chair. "I, uh...I had an interview yesterday."

His mind raced. An interview? Where? With whom?

Why?

"If I don't pay you enough, I can give you a raise. I've been meaning to do that anyway. You've been doing great work."

She was shaking her head before he even finished. "No, Tyler. It isn't that."

"What is it then?"

Her chin lifted, and she took a deep breath. "I would feel more comfortable moving back to an accounting firm. The where and with whom doesn't matter. I told them I could start in a month. That should give you enough time to find someone to replace me."

A month. First Bo, now Allie. He loved Bo like a brother, but Allie...she was irreplaceable. She was excellent at her job—not surprising. But it was more than that. She brought an element to the store that he hadn't known was missing. She'd brought laughter into the place. Well, a different kind of laughter than what Bo and Story had offered.

Allegra was different. She wasn't just physical beauty—no denying that though—she was joy and warmth...and companionship.

His muscles weakened like a newborn baby's. He was alone.

Chapter Thirty-One

Allegra stood at her kitchen table, taped off the closed box, and bent her neck from side to side. Packing was stressful, but not nearly as stressful as going to work. If she'd thought things had been tense before the gala, it was nothing compared to now. Tyler barely spoke to her. Story kept trying to find out what had happened to make her quit. And Allegra, well...she'd cried almost every night, the floodgates wide open since that day in the climbing gym. But moving was the right thing to do.

She opened a new box and carried it to the bookshelf in her living room, where she stared blindly at the spines of her dear friends.

Three weeks had passed. Three weeks full of advertising her job, her regular work, and interviewing replacements with Tyler. Three weeks of pure torture. With each day that passed, her heart grew duller. She was doing this. Actually leaving Seattle.

Leaving Tyler.

Allegra shook her head. No. She wasn't leaving Tyler. He'd walked away, for whatever reason, from what they could have had. But it was all for the best. Her relationship with the Lord, while not as strong as it should be, was heading in the right direction. And this move would be good for her.

The pink spine in front of her caught her attention. She removed the book from the shelf and carefully placed it in the box, repeating the action over and over with every book.

She hated packing, but doing it gave her somewhere to focus.

The cell on her coffee table behind her rang. She glanced at the screen before answering it. "Hey, sis."

"Hi! Are you finished packing yet?"

Allegra looked around her apartment, boxes lined along one wall. "Just about. I have one shelf and my bedroom left." Speaking of, she cleared off the last of the books and placed them in the box with the rest.

"I still can't believe you're doing this. I thought you really liked working for Tyler."

A sharp pain in the region of her heart caused her to draw a quick breath. She blew it back out slowly. "I did. But this job will be better. And Portland is a great area."

"I know."

Allegra entered her room and put her phone on speaker. She assembled a box and started filling it. "So how's work going?"

"Oh, Allegra!" The words burst from her sister's mouth as if she'd been holding them in for eons. "It's been *so* incredible! I can't believe how much I've learned. Thank you"—her voice came out in tears—"thank you for this, for paying for school. I'll never be able to repay you."

Her words were a balm to Allegra's soul. "You never need to repay me, Capri. I'm doing this because I love you."

"I know." Sniffles sounded over the speaker. "And I love you. And it's because I love you that I'm going to do something."

Um...what was her sister going on about? "What are you going to do?"

A beat of silence before, "I've contacted the financial office at school and asked them to change my account number and refuse your inquiries."

Allegra's stomach dropped. "What are you talking about, Caprice? If you changed your account number and won't let them talk to me, I can't—"

"Exactly. You can't pay my tuition."

"Caprice..."

"Allie, you've been taking care of me since the moment Mom and Dad died. And I so appreciate you paying my tuition, I really do. But I'm an adult now—"

Twenty hardly qualified as an adult in Allie's book.

"—and it's time I stepped up, paid my own tuition."

"How can you do that and maintain your grades? You can't, and I refuse to let you take out student loans. I don't want you burdened with that debt."

She heard Capri take a deep breath on the other side. "J. Wong offered me part-time permanent work. They want me to stay here, Allie."

"What?" Her neighbors might call the police over that screech, but it would be worth a disturbing-the-peace ticket. "A *permanent* job?"

Capri giggled. "Yep. Permanent. As in, part time for now and full time when I finish school."

Joy tingled her nerves. "Oh, sis, I'm so happy for you!" Too bad real life sank her stomach. "But you go to school in another state. How can you go to classes and work in New York?"

"Best. Part. Ever."

Allegra waited for her sister to continue, but apparently she was going to make Allie beg. "Oookay...what?"

"They've recommended me to a school right here. And I've been accepted. I can stay here in New York. And some of my roommates are staying too, so we'll get to keep this apartment."

Her sister's dream just came true. Allegra's arms pebbled with goose bumps.

They spoke for a few more minutes before saying goodbye. "I love you." Her sister's singsong voice was soothing.

"Love you too."

Drawing in a breath, Allegra surveyed her room. She was almost finished. She couldn't believe her time in Seattle was almost over. Her time with Hawk's Flight and Tyler.

Her chest ached. Only a few more days, and she would be out of Tyler's life.

~~~

Today was Allegra's last day. The thought drummed a steady beat throughout the morning.

"Hey, Allegra." Tyler knocked on her office door as she finished some last-minute training with the new employee, Ed.

"Hi, Tyler."

Ed rose from his seat. "I'm going to grab some water. Can I get you two anything?"

"No thank you." Allegra turned her gaze on Tyler. "What's up?"

"Do you have lunch plans?"

"Story is taking me for sushi."

"Oh." He rubbed the back of his neck. "When are you leaving for Portland?"

He still couldn't believe she was going. But no matter how he'd tried to talk her out of it over the last few weeks, she'd remained stubborn. She was going. But he didn't believe her for one moment that it was because the job farther south was what she really wanted. She never looked him in the eye when she spoke about it. So what was the real reason?

"After work."

His head jerked back. He couldn't have been more surprised if someone with a camera jumped out and shouted he'd been punk'd. As a matter of fact, he'd *prefer* that.

"It'll be late by the time you get there. Why not leave tomorrow morning? Then I can take you for dinner."

Allegra's shoulders rose high and then slumped down. "Tyler..."

"Come on. Let me take you for dinner." A thought occurred to him. "Hey...do you have anyone helping you move? I can follow you down there, grab a hotel, then help you move into your new place."

"No!" Pink crawled up her neck. "I mean, Schmidt, Basham and Monzon hired someone to unload my truck on their end. I hired someone to do it up here already, so the things are taken care of. I'm driving the truck down myself."

"Well...what about your car? I can drive it down for you, then fly back."

One of her cheeks popped out, and she inhaled a breath.

"No, Tyler. Thank you for your kind offer, but no." She picked up some papers and set them inside a folder. "Is there anything else? I still have a few more things to show Ed."

Yeah. Yeah, there were lots of *anything else*s. She was running. Fear once again had gotten hold of her. And here he thought she'd been making progress, at least until she gave him her notice. Now there was no talking to her.

Maybe it was just as well. If she couldn't break through her fear, she wasn't the person for him.

And if you can't have more compassion, maybe you're not the person for her. Wow. Being hit upside the head by God's truth sure didn't feel good.

Tyler shook his head as Allegra stared at him. "Um...no." *Lie.* "At least, not right now." *Little white lie.* What he really wanted to do was grab her by the shoulders, kiss her soundly, then pray together for God to guide them. But maybe...maybe she needed this time away.

He left her alone with Ed, entered his own office, and shut the door behind him. *Pray.* That was what he'd do. He'd pray for her. Maybe she'd come back. Maybe.

Chapter Thirty-Two

Late-August sunlight filtered through her kitchen window, casting natural light where she stood at her gas stove.

"You can't stay holed up in your apartment, Allegra."

"Says who?"

A sound like a woman gargling came over the speaker as Allegra stirred the pan of spinach wilting. Real food. She could actually afford real food on the salary she was earning now. She didn't think she'd ever get over that marvel.

Well, that and the fabulous feeling of not having to send money for Capri's school anymore. She hadn't realized what a burden she was shouldering until her sister set her free from it.

"Says me," Capri huffed.

Allegra looked around her corner apartment. The kitchen was near the entrance, but open, so she could be in that room and look out over the living room, where sliding doors led to a small balcony that overlooked the downtown area. It wasn't the most spacious or updated place, but it was affordable, close to work, and within walking distance from everything she could want.

"Have you found a church yet?"

The ultimate question. "Actually, yes."

"What? Why didn't you tell me?"

Allegra laughed. "I just did."

"So?"

She described her newfound church to her sister and spoke at length about the sermon the previous Sunday. "So see? I *am* getting out."

"Okay. To church. What about making friends? Going out for dinner? You know...having a social life."

Oh that. "Well..."

"I knew it! You can't live without friends, sis. Even the Bible says you need a tribe."

"A tribe?" Allegra removed the spinach and spooned it overtop the salmon she'd already cooked. Her mouth watered.

"Close enough. 'For if they fall, one will lift up his fellow. But woe to him who is alone when he falls and has not another to lift him up!' That's in Ecclesiastes."

"You're Googling on your computer while we talk, aren't you?"

Laughter filled the kitchen. "I've been found out."

"I love you."

"Love back."

After they hung up, Allegra curled up on her sofa with her plate full of wilted spinach and baked salmon and turned on the TV. Within fifteen minutes, her phone rang. Caprice again?

"What's up?"

"Don't hate me."

Umm... "Didn't I tell you I loved you when we hung up?"

"Yeees."

The drawn-out word filled Allegra's stomach with rocks.

"What did you do, Capri?"

"I, uh...I had a moment of what *I* thought was brilliance after we hung up."

"Uh-huh."

"Over the past few years while you paid for my schooling, I was able to save a little money."

"That's good. And it better still be in your bank."

"Well..."

The silence on the other end didn't bode well.

"Go on."

"So this moment of brilliance...I'm having second thoughts, but really, I think it'll be excellent."

More hesitation. Hm. This time she waited it out.

"I kind of signed you up for something."

"What *kind* of something?"

"Remember that you love me."

"Capri." Her clenched teeth made her sister's name come out like a curse word.

"Well, I figured you never got to do all the adventures Tyler made you sign the contract for when you started working for him, so..."

No. Her sister wouldn't do this to her. "What. Did. You.

Do?"

Nervous laughter rang in her ear. A pause. Then, "How do you feel about whitewater rafting?"

Her sister was going to die young.

Tyler slapped the last person's back to send her on her way.

Ziiiiipppppp.

The woman's initial screech turned into laughing as she sailed down the 2,400-foot zipline with a thirty-story descent. Tyler's heart started pounding. He loved this part, where he got to chase his final adventurer and experience the ride himself. Standing on the launch platform, he looked over Fitzsimmons Valley between Whistler and Blackcomb Mountains. He loved his adventures in Washington, but there was nothing like getting out of state into the province of British Columbia now and then to get him the change of scenery he sometimes needed.

And a change of scenery today was doing his heart some good.

He couldn't deny it. He missed Allegra. He'd kept up with news about her through Story's continuing friendship—could he admit he was even a little envious that Story had gone down to visit Allie in her new apartment? The past number of weeks without her around had been, well...

He really didn't believe she'd leave cold turkey, but she had. And he'd come to a surprising revelation. "She's more adventurous than I thought," he murmured.

"What was that?"

Tyler glanced up at the man behind him, who was monitoring each excursion group to ensure safety. Kind of a double-check in case Tyler or any other group guides missed something. "Sorry." He cleared his throat. "Just talking to myself."

The man nodded and turned as a new group approached. As the voices infiltrated Tyler's thoughts, one rose above the others as familiar. He turned to see who it was.

"Ty, man!"

He thought so. "Garret. How are ya? It's been a while."

Garret Browning led an outdoor excursion outfit much like Tyler's own, but in eastern Washington. He'd first met Garret when they both had a group paragliding off Tiger Mountain.

The thought of that mountain rushed in memories of Allegra. His chest pinched.

"I'm good, thanks. What about you? How's business?"

What? Oh. Garret. *Hold it together.* "Keeping busy." He gestured down the zipline across the valley. "I have a group on the other end waiting on me."

"Right on." Garret held up a hand. "I don't want to keep you, but I was going to call you tomorrow. I have a favor to ask."

"What's up?"

"I'm scheduled to assist a rafting trip down the White Salmon this weekend, but my wife has been having contractions off and on."

It'd apparently been too long since he'd last talked to Garret. He didn't even know he and his wife were pregnant.

"Congrats, man! That's awesome."

Garret chuckled. "Yeah, we're pretty excited."

Something within Tyler cracked. He'd never thought of having a family before, but suddenly, the urge overwhelmed him.

"Anyway, I really don't want to go off grid and leave Tricia. I know this is completely last minute, but do you think you could fill in for me?"

Tyler's pulse kicked up another notch. The White Salmon was a fun river to navigate. "Absolutely, man!"

Laughter preceded Garret's words. "Don't you need to check your schedule?"

Oh. Whoops. "Yeah. I guess I should," Tyler shrugged. "I can do that when we get back to the van, but I'm pretty sure I'm clear." It was unusual to have Labor Day weekend free. He and Bo usually planned a big excursion for that weekend since it was the last big hurrah before kids went back to school and the weather cooled down. But without Bo, he just hadn't had the heart to schedule it.

"Nice. I really appreciate it. And Tricia won't kill me, so I'll get to meet my little girl."

A girl. He pictured Allegra holding a newborn baby girl. His heart stopped.

"Ty?"

"Uh, yeah. Sorry. Text me with the details, will you?"

"You bet."

The radio on the safety guy's belt cracked. "Eagle's Nest, this is Fox Hole. You're clear for the next ride."

Hearing those words sent bolts of electricity from Tyler's

arms through to his stomach. He grinned at Garret. "My turn."

His friend laughed. "Enjoy!"

Tyler checked his helmet one last time, tugged on his harness to ensure it was still secured properly, sat back, and lifted his feet.

Ziiiiiipppppp.

His stomach dropped even as his heart jumped in his throat. Thunder rolled through his veins as strong as the 12th Man in the Clink was loud. His blood pounded adrenaline, shooting tingles throughout his body. He lived for this. At a top speed of around eighty miles per hour, this last zipline sped him over the tops of old-growth rainforest and plateaus, wind rushing his face. And the whole time, he could only wish that Allegra was with him to experience it. Not that she'd like it, but...yeah.

He wasn't doing so well without her.

Chapter Thirty-Three

"Hey, Allegra, do you want to go get some lunch?"

Allegra looked up from the spreadsheet she was working on. One of her coworkers, Renata Fernández, smiled down at her. Well, Capri *had* been on her about finding some friends, and Renata was one of the friendliest people at the firm. "I'd love to."

She stood, smoothing her knee-length navy pencil skirt, and shouldered her white bag over her bright-yellow silk blouse. They hit the sidewalk and aimed themselves toward a line of food trucks a block down from their office. The overcast day held in some of the warmth and humidity from the prior week, making for a frizzy mess of hair. Allegra tugged her mane back, wrapping elastic around the thick mop, creating a messy bun. It might not be the most professional, but it was better than going back to work with hair eight times its normal size.

"How about grilled cheese?" Allegra eyed the menu of the bright-yellow truck, her mouth watering.

"Mm. Sounds delicious."

They moved into the queue, the scent of melting cheese and butter wafting around the small crowd.

"So how are you settling in?" Renata's soft voice broke through Allegra's thoughts. The woman was probably a good ten years older than her, with sweet eyes and a bright smile. Her long dark hair was held off her face with clips, revealing skin devoid of any flaws. She was definitely a humble woman, but gorgeous. She and Allegra had hit it off from day one.

They moved up in line. "Life is good here." For the most part. She shoved thoughts of Seattle—and Tyler—from her mind. "My apartment is cute, and I love living close to downtown."

Renata eyed her. "Mm. And? What else are you doing to make a life here?"

Allegra's friend knew something had driven her from Seattle to Portland, but didn't know what. Though Allegra thought Renata might have some suspicions. She had met Story on her first visit to Portland a few weeks ago, though Allegra was sure Story never would have said anything.

"I tried that other church you told me about."

"Oh yeah? What did you think?"

"I loved it." And that was putting it mildly. The pastor had been funny but hadn't shied away from the hard stuff, and she appreciated that, especially after such a bleh faith for so long. The music was fab, and the way the church served the city was amazing.

"And what else are you doing?"

"Um…I visited Powell Books. Oh. My. Goodness. That

place is to die for. A *million* books? I almost cried."

Renata bent her head back and laughed. "Oh, Allie. You crack me up."

She spun toward the food trucks, and Allegra bit her lip. She was settling in, but making a life? Even with her church and having a new friend in Renata, a big part of her heart had a hole. A Tyler-sized hole.

"Hey." Renata turned back again. "I was thinking of going spelunking in Ape Cave this weekend, and—"

"Nope."

Allegra slapped her hand over her mouth. Whoops. That came out way too fast...and loud.

Renata's gaze landed on her, confusion and amusement at odds. "You don't even know what I was going to say."

"You were going to ask me to come, weren't you?"

"Okay, you got me. Why won't you come?"

"Bats."

Renata had the nerve to laugh. Hard.

"It isn't funny! What if they attack and eat me? I saw that movie *Bats*, you know."

Renata rolled her eyes. "First, the cave does not have genetically mutated bats. Second, they won't likely attack you."

Oh, Renata tried to slip that one word past her, but she was smarter than that. "You said 'likely.'"

Renata stepped up to place her lunch order, shaking her head. "You're coming with me," she called over her shoulder.

"No, I'm..." It was no use. If she'd learned one thing about her new friend, it was that her gentle spirit and soft voice were *great* disguises for a determined personality. She rolled her eyes. Renata reminded her of Caprice.

And of course, thinking of Caprice reminded her of that whitewater rafting trip coming up.

Huh. Everything was starting to turn red in color. Or was that just Allegra's temper coloring her vision? Her sister *was* trying to be helpful though. And it was very sweet and generous of Capri. But still...

She huffed. Would she ever escape adventure?

Allegra's black jogging pants were a mistake. She should have worn brown ones. To hide the dirt and mud. Ugh. At least her hiking boots were brown. But her poor hot-pink Columbia jacket. She'd be lucky if she ever got it clean again.

"Don't worry, Allie. Dirt washes out."

She hated how well Renata could read her already. And she loved it. Next time Story came to town, they were all having a major girls' night.

"Here." Renata handed her a knit cap with an LED light attached at the front.

Allegra shook her head. "No. The bats will be able to find me!"

Her so-called friend tucked her lips between her teeth, apparently holding back a laugh. "If the bats are flying toward your light, it's only because they see bugs they want for dinner."

"They want *me* for dinner, you mean," she wailed.

And her so-called friend lost it, laughing so hard tears formed. She was such a brat. Much like Caprice, who kept calling to count down the days until that whitewater trip.

She rolled her eyes. Her sister was going to pay.

Allegra followed Renata down the two sets of stairs and into the Upper Cave. The black-brown lava on either side and over them intimidated her. She'd done her research and discovered the Ape Cave was the longest continuous lava tube in the country, formed from Mount Saint Helen's. It was a pretty interesting formation—but not one she was thrilled to be hiking through. Still, she trudged on, avoiding touching the "slime" on the cave walls. Thank goodness for that rule she could happily obey.

"Uh, Ren?"

"Yeah?" Beside her, Renata tilted her head back so her light would strike the stalactites above.

"What if there's a volcanic eruption while we're in here?"

"Then we meet Jesus fast."

Allegra huffed. Renata obviously didn't take her concerns seriously. They would have to have a serious discussion.

Once they exited this death trap. Alive.

It didn't take long to reach the first rock pile. Navigating it took a few minutes—as did a number of others. Allegra knew what was coming though, and her stomach clenched. The eight-foot lava fall loomed ahead. Would it be uncouth to get sick in the cave? She sighed. It would probably interrupt the "delicate ecosystem." How in the *world* could slime be considered delicate? Goose bumps crawled down her spine. She was *not* cut out for this.

"Would you ladies like some help getting over that thing?"

Allegra jumped, a tiny screech shooting from her mouth.

She and Renata turned, eyeing two men. Both wore loose jeans and plaid flannel jackets, with what looked like hard hats and lights covering their gray hair. Twins.

Renata was able to catch her voice first. "Thank you, sirs."

"Our pleasure," the man on the right said. He stuck out his hand. "I'm Larry, and this"—he motioned to the man on his right—"is my brother, Gary."

Yep. Definitely twins.

"I'm Renata, and this is my friend Allegra. We would love some help. Thank you."

All Allegra could do was bare her teeth in what she hoped resembled a smile. The lava fall looked…difficult.

Gary climbed up, using the one foothold and the rope to get his momentum going. Once he reached the top, he bent over to call down to them. "Okay, one of you ladies come on up. Grab the rope and use your legs."

Who knew her rock climb with Tyler would be a little useful?

Renata went first. Allegra watched as her friend made easy work of it. Huh. Maybe this wouldn't be so difficult.

As soon as Renata reached the top, Gary grasped her arm, helping her up and over. He turned to look down at Allegra. "You're good to go."

She could do this. Sure.

Allegra thought of Tyler and how much he'd love this. No. She couldn't think of him. That would only distract her. She took a deep breath—cave air wasn't her favorite to breathe in—and grasped the rope.

It was a flimsy thing.

She pressed her right boot against the lava fall and pushed off, hand over hand on the rope. For at least two feet.

"Um...I don't know if I can do this," she mumbled.

"Nonsense!" Larry's voice rose from behind. "Of course you can. Hold on."

As she went to pull herself up, she felt movement behind her...then hands around her thighs.

She shrieked.

And swore she heard the wings of a thousand bats flapping.

She shrieked again.

Above her, Renata doubled over in laughter.

Beneath her, Larry grunted as he pushed her up from underneath.

Gary yelled over everyone. "Eat that rope!"

What!

"Feed that rope through your hands." Larry spewed the words between clenched teeth. If she wasn't in such a precarious position, she might take offense at his effort. Having a better budget to work with had given her healthier options for dinner, and she'd lost six pounds since moving to Portland.

But she pulled the rope through her hands, slowly climbing until Gary was able to grasp her arm and help pull her up the rest of the way.

At the top, she turned to Renata, whose eyes were suspiciously bright with merriment. "You'll pay for this, dear friend." She turned and walked on, knowing the exit had to be close.

Behind her, gales of laughter echoed. Allegra shook her head, but her lips twitched upward.

She had to admit it, this was probably the most fun she'd had in a long while.

Chapter Thirty-Four

The sound of water rushing by was faint, the trees blocking the sound—and sight—between the river and the parking lot.

Allegra's palms broke out in a sweat. She was *not* happy.

Or looking forward to this.

This is not *cool.*

She looked over her shoulder at the rest of the group. Eyes brimmed with excitement, laughter was loud, and hands flew through the air as a few people talked about their prior rafting trips. Allegra heard the word "capsize" more than once.

Nope.

She glanced over her shoulder again, looking to see if anyone watched her. No one paid any attention, so she grabbed her backpack and hefted it back in her car. She'd just opened the driver-side door when she heard the crunch of gravel under a set of tires.

A set of tires that belonged to a truck.

A truck that looked suspiciously like Tyler's.

No. No, no, no. There was no way it could be Tyler. This rafting trip was with a different company. Caprice had promised her.

Yet when the door opened and first one leg, then the other, appeared out of the truck, she knew in her gut those legs, with long shorts that exposed still-hard muscles developed during his football days, belonged to Tyler.

Allegra's heart skittered. *Stopitstopitstopit.*

As Tyler straightened, his gaze searched the group, halting when he spotted her. His eyes went as round as his mouth before a grin hitched the right side of his face, producing a shallow dimple.

Her heart didn't just skitter this time—it galloped. Hard. *I am in trouble.*

She watched as he turned back to his truck and grabbed a…backpack? Was he joining them? Oh man. If he was, then she was truly in trouble. Time spent with Tyler? After two months of living in Portland, away from the man, one would think she'd be over any residual feelings and attraction.

But no.

Tyler closed his door and walked her way. Her mouth dried when she saw his rather well-formed biceps rippling as he shouldered the bag.

Oh, heaven help her.

"Hey, Allegra." He grinned as he came to a stop in front of her.

"Um…hi. I wasn't expecting you."

He ducked his head sheepishly. "I promise I didn't know

you'd be here. My buddy, Garret, usually leads this trip, but his wife was pregnant, and he didn't want to leave her alone." He grinned. "Turns out she had the baby early this morning."

"Oh. That's fantastic for them. I bet they're excited. I hope mama and baby are healthy."

"Yeah, they are. Lorelei weighed in at eight pounds even. And she's quite the knockout."

If she didn't know he was talking about a baby, she might have been jealous. "What a pretty name."

"Yeah."

An awkward silence filled the air before they both started talking at once.

"Ladies first." Tyler bowed, as if she were a princess.

"No, I...I was just going to ask how you were doing. How's business?"

He opened his mouth as if to answer, then closed it and shook his head. His gaze met hers. The warmth and—tenderness?—blew her mind. He reached a hand and pushed a wisp of hair behind her ear. "I'm sorry you felt like you had to leave, Allie," he whispered. "I didn't want you to."

She nodded. "I know."

He raised a brow.

"Well, I know *now*."

"I never should have walked away from you." Tyler stepped closer, his face close enough she felt his breath when he spoke. "I'm sorry."

Could she take him up on his peace offering?

～⚭～

Allegra stared at him. She lifted a hand and swiped a loose

piece of dark hair out of her eyes as the wind fluttered around them. The chatter from the group faded as they moved down the path toward the river. It was just him and Allegra left in the parking lot.

"I..." Her chin trembled, indecision written all over her face.

"I mean it, Allie." He took another step closer. "I'm sorry." *Please believe me.*

She stepped back once, twice. A breeze caught that loose piece of hair and blew it across her lips. He stepped forward and with his thumb gently brushed it away, pushing it behind her ear. Her full lips formed a soft *o*.

Her full, kissable lips.

Allegra took one more step back and put up what may as well have been a brick wall between them. "Thank you. I appreciate your apology."

"Allie—"

She held up a hand to stop him, her face paling. "I can't," she whispered. She took a deep breath, her chest rising and falling, before she spoke again. "Capri paid for this trip for me out of her savings, hoping I'd get out of my house and have some fun." Allegra looked up at him, her gaze pleading with him. "I can't be anything more, but"—she hesitated, a battle clearly going on within her. "It'd be nice to have a *friend* to do this with."

A friend.

Tyler Richmond Hawk, former NFL star and successful businessman, had just been friend-zoned by the woman he lov—liked. Strongly.

This was shaping up to be a humbling day.

Chapter Thirty-Five

What was she doing? Allegra grabbed her bag out of her car and shut the door. She closed her eyes and took a deep breath. She could do this. Opening her eyes, she stepped forward. One. Two. Three steps.

Aaand, *stop.*

No. She couldn't do this. Rafting? On a category three and four river? Was she *nuts?*

But Tyler.

Remembering the affection and hope in his gaze sent goose bumps down her arms. She trusted him, trusted his ability to make sure she was safe. She trusted him more than she'd trusted a man in a very long time.

Her breath caught.

It was true. Even after he walked away from her. Even after she left her job and her home to move to Portland, she still trusted him. *I* trust *him.*

Picking up her pace, Allegra followed Tyler down the path to the river. She took care to watch her step as tree roots snaked beneath the ground, her feet crunching the rocks and dirt as she walked.

Oomph!

Dazed, she looked up. Tyler's broad back, T-shirt clinging to it, faced her.

She really had a knack for running into this man.

Tyler spun and grabbed hold of Allegra's shoulders. "Are you okay?"

"Me?" she squeaked.

"Yeah. You ran into me. You know. Hard."

The laughter in his eyes drowned her. She was a goner. *Snap out of it!* She'd told him she couldn't do this, that she needed him to just be a friend. Now to make herself believe it.

"Oh. I'm so sorry. I have a nasty habit of doing that, don't I?" She grinned up at him and took a step back.

He rubbed the back of his neck. "Are you sure we can only be friends?"

He was making this harder than he knew. "Tyler..."

"I'm only asking to be sure. I...I didn't mean to ruin what was starting to happen. I got..."

"Scared?"

His eyes widened.

"Tyler..."

His head tipped back and forth, like a bobblehead.

Allegra bit the inside of her cheek. "Okay. So what stopped you?"

Red flooded his ears. Was Tyler embarrassed? "I don't know," he mumbled.

She narrowed her eyes. Right. He didn't know.

Baloney.

Allegra watched as Tyler massaged his temples. Finally, "Fine. I do know why."

Waiting for him to continue, she raised an eyebrow.

He let out a breath. "You're not a risk taker."

Nausea threatened. She forced herself to swallow. What he said was true, but it still hurt.

"Oh, Allie. I didn't mean that the way it sounded." He sighed and grabbed her hands hanging at her side. "When you first started, you have to admit, you hated even the thought of risk."

She nodded.

"You did it though. You put yourself at risk a few times, but...*at the time*"—he emphasized the words—"it wasn't enough for me."

Everything within her broke to a million pieces, like shattered glass.

"Listen to me, Allie. I said *at the time*." He held her gaze. "Since my parents, I've had a hard time understanding why people let fear run their lives, especially when it comes to experiencing His creation in such incredible ways. It's why I have my business, so I can push people past their limits. But..." His Adam's apple bobbed as he swallowed. "I pushed you too far, didn't I?"

She let go of Tyler's hand and rubbed her cheeks. When did she start crying?

She opened her mouth to speak, but Tyler laid a gentle finger against her lips. "I have more to say," he whispered.

Tyler took her hand, and they started walking toward the river again.

"The Sunday before you quit, the day Bo left, I drove past a church and had the weird sense I needed to go. So I parked and went in."

She let him process his thoughts as they slowly walked, the voices of the group and the river getting louder. Just as they broke through the trees to the riverbank, Tyler tugged her hand to stop her.

"I realized I'd been living in my own version of fear."

Her heart thudded against her rib cage.

"I was afraid I would end up living life the way my parents tried to force me to. Safe." He paused for a deep breath, then continued. "I was also afraid of pushing you. I'm really not proud of my past, of how I treated girlfriends when I was playing football. I knew as soon as I met you that you were different, deserved to be treated like the gift you are. I guess I took it too far though." He blew out a breath, rubbing the back of his neck.

"I'm sorry, Allie. I'm sorry I hurt you when I didn't call, when I walked away from you. I'm sorry I let"—he scrunched his nose—"fear dictate my actions."

She dipped her chin. "Thank you."

"Will you forgive me?"

She smiled. Her heart still hurt, but Tyler was making an effort. The least she could do was the same. "Yes. Of course."

Tyler's gaze dropped to the ground. "That's more than I deserve. Thank you."

"Tyler, stop."

"What?"

She huffed. "Sometimes I get the feeling you don't think you're good enough."

He stared over her head at the trees.

Seriously? Did she just hit the nail on the head? She squeezed her eyes shut. The man could be so thick headed. "That's exactly what you believe, isn't it?"

He still wouldn't look at her.

"Tyler, that's a lie. You *are* good enough." She hesitated. But if she'd learned anything these past months, it was to take a risk. "You're more than good enough. Especially for me."

Allegra turned to face the river, avoiding his reaction to what she'd just admitted. A full minute went by before he spoke again.

"You don't have to do this, Allie."

She lowered her voice to a whisper. "I want—I *need*—to do this. What's that verse in Psalms? 'When I am afraid, I put my trust in you.'"

"Psalm 56:3."

Allegra's brows shot up.

"What?" He grinned. "It's the verse I clung to when I made the decision to quit college and enter the NFL draft. My parents weren't happy about it, and I was scared that I was doing the wrong thing. I knew I could always go back to school if it didn't work out, but it felt like a now-or-never moment."

Obviously he was successful, but... "And you were chosen?"

Tyler laughed. "Drafted. And yes. Second round, thirty-fourth overall."

Allegra sucked her lips in and let them out on a puff of air. "Greek to me. Sorry."

He winked. "So...are you ready to do this?"

"Ugh. Yes."

He laughed again, loudly.

And Allegra's spirits lifted.

Chapter Thirty-Six

Wow. Her admission that he was good enough—for her—lightened a burden he didn't know he'd been carrying. And she was coming. Pride and joy made him lightheaded.

After hearing about her parents and their adventurous lifestyle that ultimately led to their deaths, he could understand how these excursions were scary. But now—too late—all he saw was an honest, courageous, *beautiful* woman.

A woman he desperately wanted to hold on to. And maybe kiss. A lot.

Tyler followed as Allegra dragged herself to the rafts that would carry her downriver. They were launching from a quiet part of the river, but it was a long ride, full of category three and four rapids. This would be no joke.

Lord, keep her safe.

They dropped their bags into the supply raft and reached for the life vests and helmets. He watched as Allegra struggled to zip her vest up. Putting his equipment down, he said, "Here, let me help."

The cutest rose color flushed her cheeks. "I'm fine."

Tyler shrugged. "Suit yourself."

She arched a brow, and he grinned. "Pun intended."

Smirking, she focused her attention back on her vest. Her teeth grabbed her bottom lip and...was she muttering? He turned to hide his laugh. He reached for the helmet and pulled it on, tugging the strap firmly under his chin.

A huff sounded behind him.

"Please."

He turned. "Sorry?"

Her hands moved to her hips, and she rolled her eyes. "Can you please help me?"

"With what?"

"Tyler!"

Laughing, he reached out to tug the zipper up, only to realize it was in a...delicate...place. "Um."

Allegra looked down to where his hands hovered and gasped. "Oh!" Without thinking, she jumped back. And tripped over the edge of the supply raft.

And fell backward.

Onto the backpacks.

With a shriek.

Slapping her hand over her eyes, Allegra moaned. "If this doesn't beat all..."

Tyler's booming laugh drew the attention of the others and pulled them closer. He reached a hand out to Allegra as she peeked through her fingers.

"No thank you. I'm just going to stay here. In

mortification. Forever."

"You can't stay there forever, Allegra."

"It's comfortable."

His gut hurt from so much laughter. "It might be comfortable, but they need to load in the tents."

Muffled words sounded from behind her arm.

"What was that?"

"I said, 'They can pitch a tent over me!'"

"While that image is definitely amusing, I don't think it would be quite so practical. Come on. Get up." Tyler grabbed her hand and pulled, half expecting her to pull back, forcing him into the raft. He wouldn't mind the landing.

His knees almost buckled at the thought.

Hold me up, God. Please.

Allegra straightened before him, pink still tinging her soft cheeks, and avoided looking at him.

"You okay?"

"Fine," she muttered. "Let's just get going."

"Hold on. You still need to zip up."

One of the other women in the group stepped forward, grinning. "Let me help with that."

Allegra squinted up at her. "Thank you."

Once the life vest was secured, Tyler handed Allegra her helmet. "Put it on and tug the straps snug under your chin."

"I know how to put a helmet on, thank you. I *do* ride a bike, you know." She shoved it on and tightened the straps.

He laughed and smacked the top of her helmet. "Good job." He winked.

Allegra lifted her chin and stuck her tongue out. As she

did, Tyler spied a glint of gold on her neck. "Are you wearing a necklace?"

"Yeah, why?"

"You need to take it off. Anything loose—especially around your neck—could be a danger if the raft capsizes."

Allegra paled and hurried to remove it. "I'll run it back to my car."

"Good idea. I want you to be safe."

She fingered the necklace as she smiled at him. "Thanks."

Tyler watched as her gaze lowered to his mouth. His suddenly dry mouth. Very dry.

Oh, how he wanted to kiss her.

His head bent toward her, and her tongue darted out to touch her lips.

Almost there.

His heart pounded as he brushed his thumb across her cheek. Allegra sighed and leaned toward him, her eyes closing. Her lips parted, and he groaned. He lowered his mouth, anticipating the sweet taste of her kiss.

"Hawk!"

Both Allegra and Tyler jumped at the intrusion. His whole body tingled as heat flooded it. Allie stared at him with wide eyes.

"Yeah?" he called over his shoulder.

He turned to the leader of the trip. "What's up?" He ignored the knowing smirk.

"You two coming? Or should we leave you behind, O Great Co-Lead?"

Tyler turned to Allegra, lifting his brows. "You're sure?"

She took a deep breath and lifted her chin. Her courage endeared her to him even more. "I'm sure."

"Then let's go."

They turned and walked toward the group until Allegra halted. "My necklace! I almost forgot. I'll be right back." He watched her hips swaying as she stepped over tree roots until she disappeared down the path.

He had it bad, with a capital *B*.

She didn't think her heart would ever stop pounding. What had she been thinking? She'd almost *kissed* Tyler! After she told him she only wanted him to be a friend.

She was losing it.

Allegra exited the path into the parking lot. She sat down in her car, took off her necklace, then took a minute to catch her breath. That man had some sort of freakish hold on her.

Looking at her phone on the passenger seat, she wondered if she had time to make a quick call. Deciding she did, she picked it up and tapped Capri's name.

"Aren't you supposed to be on a raft right now?"

Allegra bit her lip. "We're just about to leave. But…"

"What?"

"Tyler's here."

"What?" Her sister's voice shrieked. "I promise you—I thought for sure I'd booked you with a different company."

She leaned her head back against the headrest. "You did. But the normal guy's wife had a baby, so he asked Tyler to fill in."

Caprice chuckled. "Of all the things… Sis, I hate to tell

you this, but it sounds like it was meant to be."

Her thoughts scrambled. "No. It can't be."

"I don't know. It seems too coincidental to me."

Allegra heard a flush in the background.

"Ew! Are you talking to me in the bathroom?" She scrunched her nose. Gross.

"Oh please. Don't tell me you've never done that."

She'd never tell.

"I've got to go."

"Have fun."

Fun. On a river. In a raft. With rapids. Right. "Uh, yeah. Thanks."

Caprice giggled. "And I'm praying for safety for you."

Because she needed it. For the rapids.

And Tyler.

Chapter Thirty-Seven

Allegra ended the call with her sister and put her necklace into the change tray, closed it, and climbed out.

"Allegra." She turned to see Tyler standing at the beginning of the path, hand still cupped to his mouth.

"They want to get going. C'mon!"

She slammed her door shut and jogged across the parking lot.

Thank goodness the life vest fit snug around her, or she'd be...bouncing. She looked up to see Tyler's wide mouth set in a grin, his eyebrows waggling. That man was Dennis the Menace himself.

She slowed to a fast walk, *much* more comfortable, and he winked at her. Actually *winked.*

The punk.

She couldn't help the return smile though. He was just too cute. Maybe Capri was right. Maybe there was a reason he was here.

The scent of dirt after a Washington rain—fresh and earth—greeted them as they walked silently side by side toward the river. The rushing water grew louder with each step, as did the murmurs and splashes of the group talking and getting into the rafts.

It was relaxing to walk beside Tyler. So weird. He was adventurous, a risk taker, yet she found comfort and peace in his presence. She liked it. A lot.

It was dangerous to her well-being. And her safety.

Lost in thought, she stumbled over a tree root.

"Whoa!" Tyler reached out a hand to stop her fall. "You okay?"

"Yeah." She gasped. "Fine. Apparently I'm *super* clumsy today. I don't know what's gotten into me." His hand was so warm on her arm. Distracting. She looked down at it. "Um..."

The heat of his hand was replaced by what felt like ice when he removed it. *Nuts.*

Warmth against her fingers, though, surprised her right before he grabbed her hand.

And then he started jogging back to the raft, pulling her along. *Double nuts.*

A few moments later, they exited the trees. Everyone but the leader of this trip was positioned in the rafts. Allegra's heart skittered to a stop. It was actually happening. Tyler kept pulling her along toward the raft. The chin strap on her helmet tightened as she swallowed past the lump in her throat. "I..."

Tyler looked over his shoulder. "What?"

She stared at him. *What would he think of me if I backed out?* She'd already said she'd go, but...*really?* She was an accountant. *Not* an adventurer. Not someone who went whitewater rafting.

Or rock climbing. Or paragliding. Yet she'd done those things because of Tyler. Surely she could do this. It was likely the last adventure she'd take with him. After this, she would live in peace. In safety. Without him.

Her throat thickened.

If she didn't do this, she'd regret it. So weird how far she'd come since that day she interviewed with him.

She stifled a giggle at the memory of knocking his water all over him. The look on his face! She snickered out loud, unable to hold it back.

Tyler turned. "What's so funny?"

Allegra stared at his chest, remembering how the water soaked his shirt that day, defining muscles earned when he'd played football. He must hit the gym every day to keep that physique up.

"Allegra?"

"What? Oh! I was just...remembering the day you interviewed me at the store."

A glint lit his green eyes. "Oh? You mean the day I performed in a wet T-shirt contest just for you?"

She burst out laughing. "I really *am* sorry about that."

"Yeah." He grinned. "I bet."

Allegra winked at him. *What did I just do?* The heat in her neck now burned her cheeks. She pushed past Tyler and headed for the last raft, determined to put this embarrassing conversation behind her. Tyler followed, and she could feel his cheeky stare. The brat.

She gingerly climbed in, taking a middle seat on one of the benches, while Tyler sat at the back. He shook his head. "Uh-uh, Allegra. You're paddling. Get on the side."

"*What*?" Did the shock show through in her voice? "I'll fall in!"

"Not if you listen to Ben's instructions."

"Who's Ben?" She squinted at the others around them.

"The leader." Tyler pointed to an older man with salt-and-pepper hair but a pure-black beard.

"Oh." She faced Tyler. "But what about capsizing?" Fear triggered a swarm of bees in her belly.

Tyler pulled her to the spot right in front of him and scooted her to the edge. He then placed a finger in front of his lips—oh, those lips!—and motioned toward the raft in front of them.

"Listen up, everyone." Ben waited for people to stop talking before he continued. "I'm Ben, your guide for this trip. In the other raft"—he pointed back to where Tyler and Allegra sat—"is Tyler Hawk."

A few *oohs* sounded. Yeah. The man was well recognized.

"He's going to be leading alongside me. We're going to be hitting some class two and three rapids before lunch. After lunch, we'll be getting into class four. I'll remind you again after our lunch break, but here's the lowdown. This is a physical workout. We'll be paddling for about six hours for two days, plus portage."

Tyler leaned forward from where he sat and stage-whispered, "That's *carrying*."

Allegra stuck her tongue out at him. A few people around her laughed.

Ben kept going. "Remember to tuck your feet under the tubes in your raft. The paddling will be tough, so you need to keep an ear open for my instructions. For you"—Ben pointed to Allegra's group—"your guide, Tyler, will repeat my instructions in case you can't hear me."

Allegra looked over her shoulder at Tyler and found him watching her. He lifted a brow in question, his eyes warm, his half smile surrounded by an overnight growth of beard. The sun glinted off his barely there beard, highlighting the red tint to his otherwise blond hair. He was really too handsome for his own good. His lips quirked up in a small grin, and she met his gaze. Humor—and a hint of something she couldn't define—lit his eyes.

"Ready?"

Before she could answer, Ben's voice caught her attention. "The most important thing today: *stay in your raft*. When Tyler and I catch sight of any rocks coming from downstream, we'll yell out 'Bump.' When you hear that, lean in and place your paddle in a T-grip on the floor of the raft." He demonstrated and requested everyone else do the same.

After they sat back up, Tyler moved beside her. "You'll be fine," he whispered.

Ben's voice boomed over the rush of the waters. "After the bump with the rocks, get back to your seat, ready to paddle."

Allegra's stomach knotted, forcing bile up her throat.

"If you fall out of the boat, *don't panic.*" Ben made eye contact with each person.

Allegra found Tyler's hand resting next to hers and grasped it. His immediate squeeze gave her some comfort.

"If you fall out, you'll likely pop back up right beside us. Grab the handles on the side of the raft so you don't get pushed downriver. If you end up a few feet from the raft, swim to it—on your back, nose and toes to the sky, head up so you can see where you're going, feet downstream and knees bent a bit, arms out to the side, keeping your butt up."

This was *not* reassuring her.

"If you're closer to shore than the raft, swim to shore. Get on your stomach, point to where you want to go, and swim hard until you're out of the river. Never stand up in a moving current!"

Sweat broke out on Allegra's hands and face, and it had nothing to do with the early morning sun bearing down on her.

"If the raft capsizes—"

Oh, here we go.

"—your swimming will have to be *very* aggressive. We'll likely be in a rapid at that moment. Remember: if you don't swim hard, you're at risk of drowning, hypothermia, foot entrapment, bruises, and scrapes."

Lovely.

"Again, if you end up in the river, *do not panic.* If you panic, you won't be thinking about getting back to the raft or to the shore, and that'll make rescuing you that much harder."

Ben's gaze pinned Allegra.

Thanks for that vote of confidence. She leaned over to Tyler and whispered, "Do you really think we'll capsize?"

She expected a joke, or at least a half smile of humor. What she didn't expect was his gaze intent on her. "Allie, while rafting is fun—I love it—it's not something to take lightly. The danger *is* there." He lifted a hand to her shoulder. "If you want to get out, now's the time. No one will judge. Least of all me."

Oh, the temptation. But... "No, I'm good." She tried to force some courage into her voice, but even she knew she failed miserably. "I can do this."

A tender smile formed on his sweet face. "I know you can. And I'll be right here with you."

And *that* made all *this* worth it.

Chapter Thirty-Eight

The rush of the breeze in her face and the water spitting up from the river invigorated her. Oh, the nerves were still on fire, but Allegra caught herself grinning more than once as the raft moved downriver.

Getting in the rhythm of paddling didn't take nearly as long as she had thought it would. Even Tyler didn't fluster her. Of course, she was too intent on not *dying* to pay him much attention. Especially going over the first few rapids. Tyler had told her they were category twos and one three.

Maybe she could handle this.

After three hours of rafting, the group paddled to shore for a lunch break. They climbed out, removing their life vests and helmets, and grinned at each other.

"Well?"

The flush of Tyler's cheeks and sparkle in his eyes caused flips in her stomach.

"What did you think? Are you more comfortable with it?"

Allegra laughed. "Um, I wouldn't say 'more comfortable,'

but I *would* say it's not as torturous as I thought."

Tyler took the helmet and vest from her hands, his fingertips brushing her skin. Warmth shot through her. A warmth that resulted in joy. While whitewater rafting.

Inconceivable, as Vizzini would say.

The group pulled out the lunch food and spread out over the open area along the shore.

"Eat with me?"

The earnestness in Tyler's eyes pulled at her heartstrings. *Keep your distance, Allegra.* But she didn't know anyone else in the group, but maybe she could get to know Ben. The guy seemed nice. She searched him out and found him sitting alone with another woman, leaning over to kiss her. Not going there. Only one choice.

"Sure."

They found a spot on a fallen tree and ate their sandwiches and fruit in silence, Allegra enjoying the sound of rushing water and birds occasionally chirping. It was peaceful here.

Her parents would have loved this.

An ache from deep within pushed from her stomach up through her throat until she let out a quiet gasp. Oh, how she missed them!

"Are you okay?" Tyler reached out and touched her arm, giving it a quick squeeze.

She glanced at him before looking back out at the river. "Yeah. I just...my parents. They would have loved this." She offered up a small smile. "Actually, they wouldn't have even wanted to stop for lunch. My dad especially. He would have been so excited to hit the big rapids farther down." A knot formed in her stomach. The big rapids. Oh man. How could she have forgotten? She'd been so focused during the first few hours of the trip, and so hungry for lunch, that she hadn't given the afternoon a thought. But they were due to start hitting the class four rapids. As quiet as it was at the moment, she could hear a distant roar that could only mean one thing: they were close.

Nausea curdled her gut. She turned to Tyler, only to find him watching her, his gaze intent. Looking for something.

"We'll be fine, Allie. Ben has taken lots of groups down this river. He knows it well. So do I. Just listen, and you'll be okay." He reached up and gently tugged on some hair. "Promise."

She swallowed the bile and slowly nodded. "Sure." Right.

Thirty feet away, Ben stood and cupped his mouth. "Break's over, everyone! Let's clean up and go!"

This was it. Time to face a demon.

Was she nervous or what? To anyone else, the smile that appeared on her face as soon as Ben called out was genuine. To him, however, it was pasted. As false as *one size fits all*.

Sitting in the raft before they shoved off, her leg bounced a mile a minute. He picked up a paddle and handed it to her. "It'll be fine, Allegra. 'Be strong and courageous.'"

She glared at him. "You do know that verse is in reference to Joshua taking over for Moses, right? Not *voluntarily* sailing through class four rapids."

He clapped his hands together and laughed. "Touché."

She didn't even crack a smile. She really *was* nervous.

"Hey, really. It'll be fine."

Allegra stared past him, not meeting his gaze. "Yeah. I know."

He reached for her hand at the same time Ben called for them to shove off. He scrambled to get to his seat but lost his balance and fell into Allegra, his face landing right in the space between her shoulder and her neck. She squealed and jumped, but not before he caught the smell of something faintly sweet. Like...flowers or something.

"Tyler!"

He jumped back, heat flushing his face. When did it get so hot out here? "Sorry." He avoided her eyes and pivoted to his seat at the stern.

Before she could respond, the raft caught in the current and was carried down the river. Slicing through the water with their paddles, the group's voices were hushed by the rushing river. Ben's was the only voice that carried.

As they neared the first rapid of the afternoon, Allegra yelled, "I hope you know I'm terrified!"

"It'll be fun. You'll see." He grasped her shoulder in a quick squeeze before taking full control of his oar again.

Ahead, the water started churning, white water shooting up in the air. It was hard to tell from this distance, but one area looked to be shooting up four or five feet.

"River center left," Ben yelled. Tyler repeated the command.

Allegra looked over her shoulder, her eyes wide.

"Just do what you're instructed, Allie. You've got this."

One blink, and she turned back around.

The water started bouncing the raft up and down. He felt like he was a kid on a trampoline. Tyler couldn't stop the grin from forming as his gaze met Ben's.

"Here we go!" Ben's voice once more carried over the water.

Chapter Thirty-Nine

It was coming. She'd had her chance to back out, and she'd refused, all for a pair of emerald eyes, permanent five o'clock shadow, and a solid chest.

Fine. He was also funny. And kind. And...well, working hard to learn how to be compassionate. But right now, she wanted to hit him.

Hard.

And then kick herself. She deserved torture.

A trip to the gym, even.

She shuddered. This rafting trip would be workout enough. Her thighs burned from keeping her in place on the raft, just as Tyler had warned, and her arms...who knew putting aluminum things—oars? paddles?—in water would be such hard work?

The raft lifted up on the other side, leaning Allegra closer to the water. She shrieked and would have thrown her oar in the air had Tyler not grabbed hold of her arm. "It's fine,

Allie. Just a bump."

She turned until she could see him in her peripheral and gave him a halfhearted smile. "Yeah. Right. A bump."

The water churned and started bumping the raft around more, turning it slightly from side to side. The rapid roared toward her, fast and furious.

Ready or not...

"No turning back!"

Ben's words rankled over her. Like she didn't already know there was no turning back.

The raft dipped forward, lurching everyone, causing a few yelps, and tilted to the left before it righted itself. Only to repeat the process. They started turning in the water, more and more facing the shore.

"Over right!"

From behind, Tyler yelled. "Stop paddling and throw yourself to the right, Allie!"

Shock held her still.

"Allie. Now!"

His voice finally penetrated her shock, and she threw herself to the other side of the raft. Adrenaline spiked through her veins.

It felt like forever before Ben called for everyone to get back to their positions.

"What was *that* all about?"

Tyler looked back to the rapid they'd just crossed, and she followed his gaze. A rock or log jutted up. She swallowed past the lump in her throat. "We almost hit that thing?"

He nodded, still looking at the obstruction. "With its

angle, if we'd hit it, it likely would have flipped the raft over and dumped us."

Her mouth formed a silent *O. Thank You, Lord.*

Thank you, God. Wow. That was a close call. If it hadn't been for Ben's sharp call, they might have capsized. The rapids were no joke, what with a steady amount of rain the last few days bulging the rivers.

The sun glared off the water as they continued downriver. He pushed on his paddle, acting as the raft's rudder. Allegra was as pale as white rice after that scare back there. Guilt churned his stomach. If he hadn't pushed her into these excursions, Caprice wouldn't have ever thought to get Allie on this trip. And she wouldn't have had that close call. Would she ever get over her fears? Unlikely now.

The waters smoothed out, and they had a gentle ride for the next little while. It was almost the end of day one. They'd be heading to shore soon to set up camp. It was probably a good thing. He knew Allegra could use a break, and to be honest, so could he. Adrenaline still thrummed his veins, though it wasn't at breakneck speed anymore. And oddly, he wasn't relishing the rush as he normally would.

In front of him, Allegra's back bunched and strained in a steady rhythm as she pushed and pulled on her paddle. Sweat trickled down her neck. She hadn't spoken to him since he pointed out the sharp rock that had almost ended their trip.

She slowed her paddle and bent her head toward her lap.

"You okay, Allie?"

Her body tensed before she took a deep breath and turned

to look over her shoulder at him. Her eyes glistened. Was she crying? There weren't any tears on her face though.

"Yep. Fine."

Uh-oh. He'd heard the rumors that when a woman said "fine," things weren't fine. But she didn't look mad. Maybe. Her eyes narrowed, but she could just be squinting from the sun.

A low growl sounded from her throat before she faced forward again. Huh. Weird. Maybe she *was* mad. But why would she be mad at him? He hadn't put the rock in their way. But...wait... He grinned. Maybe the woman wasn't as immune to him as she tried to make him think she was. He may have walked away after their kiss, but just maybe she couldn't shake that memory.

Just like he couldn't.

He opened his mouth to speak just as Ben called out the order to head for shore. To their left was a small area they could pull their rafts up to and hop out. From his experience on this river, Tyler knew that just beyond was a meadow large enough for all their tents, and a fire pit to cook over.

Tyler watched as everyone readied to exit the raft, including Allegra. She didn't look his direction once, not even when she turned toward him and bent over to grab her pack.

She wasn't immune.

Hmm. This could make for a very interesting trip.

He'd fought his feelings for Allegra since the moment she walked through his door for her interview. He saw what a workplace relationship—or lack thereof—did to Bo and

Story, and he hadn't wanted to risk losing Allegra as his employee. But it was even more than that, if he was going to admit it to himself. She wasn't a personality fit for him. They were oil and vinegar, chocolate and green beans…Seahawks and 49ers. He rolled his eyes. Not only did he still lose her, but worse, he lost any possibility of a deeper relationship with her. And it hurt. A lot. So much, the pain kept him awake at night and dogged him all day.

Huh…maybe personalities didn't have to fit like puzzle pieces.

But it would be too awkward to approach her this evening when they had to spend the night in a camp together, plus an entire day rafting tomorrow. No, he'd leave things as they were—well, not *exactly* as they were right now. He'd butter her up. But leave things the way she wanted—friends—just until tomorrow night.

One side of his mouth lifted. His skin tingled with anticipation.

His gaze sought her out only to find her peeking at him from behind a pack she was carrying. As soon as their eyes met, she looked away, readjusting the load.

Yep. Tomorrow night.

Chapter Forty

Camping was not for her.

Glamping, maybe, with its white canvas tents, cots with warm blankets, and cute white lights and rustic accessories everywhere. But camping? With actual sleeping on the ground? No. Not her.

Allegra moaned, rubbing her hip as she rolled onto her side and pushed up to a sitting position. She'd woken up a few times throughout the night but wasn't suffering from sleepiness. Just bruises from the lumpy ground. And burning muscles from the day before.

Allegra wandered to the campfire, where Tyler was helping Ben prepare breakfast for the group. "Morning," she croaked.

Coffee. She needed coffee. *Stat.*

Tyler grinned at her and held up a metal carafe. "Lifeblood?"

He got her. He really got her. "Yes."

He poured a tin cup full of the steaming black liquid and

handed it to her.

"Thanks."

"Are you ready to get back on the river?"

Allegra sat down on the ground beside him, crossing her legs. "Kind of." She viewed him out of the corner of her eye. "And before you ask, yes. I'm still terrified."

"And grumpy?"

"Ha." She rubbed her hip again. "I think I slept on a rock."

Tyler eyed her with empathy. Or pity. It was a toss-up.

"Have you ever been camping before?"

She stifled a laugh. "Um, do I look like I'm the type to have ever been camping?" She lifted a sore arm to accept the plate of eggs and bacon he handed her. "Thanks."

"No problem." He crouched down and planted himself beside her. Close enough that his arm brushed hers. His unique scent—that citrusy mix of grapefruit, oranges, and the sea—drifted around her. So refreshing. So him. She inhaled that part of him, determined to remember.

"Allie." He waited for her to look at him before he continued. "When we get back...do you mind if I come to Portland and take you out for dinner?"

She should have foreseen it, but shock still skittered a path down her spine. She scooped a forkful of eggs into her mouth, staring at him with eyes so wide, they dried immediately and she was forced to blink. She swallowed her eggs, licked her lips—a motion that drew Tyler's attention to that part of her face—and opened her mouth to answer.

"All right, people," Ben called out. "Time to clean up and

get back on board."

She tried to stop the groan, but it escaped.

Tyler laughed as he picked up the pail and started to douse the fire. "It won't be so bad, Allie."

Did he mean the river...or the potential date? She chose to focus on the river.

"Yeah, no. You're trying to tell me a class four rapid won't be so bad? After yesterday?"

He paused what he was doing to look her over. Sweat trickled down from his hairline, probably from the heat of the fire. The gray of his T-shirt somehow intensified his green eyes. And the growth of hair on his face...her heart skipped a beat. *Down, girl.*

"I'll be right behind you. Nothing will happen to you."

She shook her head. "Don't make promises you can't keep, Ty." She stalked back to her tent before he could reply.

Within the hour, the campsite looked as though no one had been there. The supply raft was loaded up with the tents and rest of the gear, and everyone had their life jackets and helmets on.

There was no turning back.

She was going to be sick.

After yesterday's scare on that last rapid, the thought of going over rapids that could potentially be worse than that one made her chest ache like she was having a heart attack. That couldn't be good. Maybe she should go see a doctor and get checked out. She wondered if there were any roads nearby where she could hitch a ride.

"I see that panic in your eyes, Allie."

She jumped. He'd appeared out of nowhere. "What? What panic? I'm not panicking."

"Uh-huh." He stepped closer to her, bent forward, and whispered into her ear. "I believe that as much as I believe you only want to be friends." He leaned back and winked before walking away.

Argh! That...that...*punk!* She marched after him. "For your information, I *do* only want to be friends. And I'm not panicking!"

His broad shoulders shook as he laughed. "Sure, Allie," he called back.

She turned on her heel and stomped off. There was just no reasoning with that man.

For the first hour, the water had been mostly smooth. A small rapid here and there, but otherwise calm. Tyler watched Allegra's back as she moved her oar in and out of the water. She had refused to acknowledge him since they got on the raft. He grinned. She was fighting hard. Too hard. Which could only mean one thing. Her walls were coming down.

The water started moving faster, and the raft bounced. Up ahead, the roaring rapid spewed white foam. He couldn't stop his grin. This was going to be good and fast.

The churning waters splashed up and over the rafts, soaking everyone in them. Allegra sputtered and called over her shoulder. "Tell me it won't be much worse than the class three!"

"Worse?" He laughed. "No. It'll be more *fun!*"

He didn't hear her response over the growing cacophony of the rapid, but he imagined she didn't take too kindly to his statement.

Ben's voice from the front raft didn't carry to theirs, but this was why Garret asked him to lead. He knew rapids well and knew how to get over them. He kept his eyes on Ben's raft to see how it was moving and what Ben was doing to steer through the fast-moving water.

A screech from his left alerted him to Allegra's fear. "Don't panic, Allie," he called. "Just listen for my voice, and you'll be fine."

White foam crested, and the raft bumped, jumped, and rocked. "This is it! Big water!" His pulse quickened as adrenaline rushed through him.

Up ahead, Ben's raft caught a bit of air. Anticipating that same motion for his raft, he threw out a command. "Hang on!" He watched to make sure they heard. Everyone stopped paddling and grabbed a handle.

Only moments later, the raft bounced up. It was on the landing that he saw the chute. If he didn't make the call, more than one person would end up in the water. "Get down!"

The group abandoned their seats and clambered down into the bottom of the raft, grabbing ropes, handles, and whatever else they could to keep from falling out.

Everyone except Allegra.

"Allie!"

She continued to sit there, her back completely straight. He crawled toward her and tried to tug her down. She wouldn't budge. He scrambled to get in front of her. Her face was drained of all color, eyes wide.

"Allie!"

Still no response.

Tyler got on his knees and grabbed her shoulders, shaking her. "Get down *now!*"

He didn't think she heard him until she screamed. Tyler glanced over his shoulder. No time left. He pushed her backward into the bottom of the raft.

In the next moment, he was swallowing water, aching for breath, and moving faster than he should be.

Using all the strength he possessed, he reached an arm out as he raced past Ben's raft, just missing his friend's rope. He kicked, moving first one arm, then the other, in an attempt to swim to shore, but the water was too strong, the river too wide, and he was fading fast.

Allie will never get back on a river again.

Chapter Forty-One

"Tyler!" Allegra's scream echoed over the river. Ben shouted from his own raft, then threw a rope. She saw Tyler's hand reach for it...

And miss.

Her hand cupped her mouth as tremors overtook her body. Water splashing—or was that tears?—made it hard to see. She heard someone yell "Got it!" and turned to see a person at the bow holding on to a rope that led to Ben's raft.

"Paddle to shore!"

Ben's firm command released everyone from their shock. Within minutes they were climbing off the rafts.

"Ben, where's Tyler? We need to find him!"

The guide looked as shook up as she felt. "We will. Just let me think for a minute."

"We don't have a minute!"

She stood, fisted hands at her sides, trying to blink her tears away. Crying wouldn't help Tyler.

"Stay here, everyone." Ben slipped the radio off his belt,

flicked a button, and walked away, speaking into the handheld radio.

Her stomach gurgled. She slapped a hand over her mouth and ran to the tree line, retching into some bushes. She dreaded turning around, but when she did, no one was looking her way.

Maybe…maybe she could go find Tyler.

Her heart thumped harder at the thought, but she didn't see anyone else doing anything. Ben talked on his radio, and the rest stood in small huddles, some wiping tears from their eyes. Like they even knew Tyler.

She glanced over her shoulder and into the woods. If she snuck through the trees, no one would be the wiser. Allegra swallowed. Hard. Who knew what animals were in there? What if she fell and hurt herself?

But what if Tyler needed help?

Beads of sweat formed over her lip. She had to do this. She *could* do this.

For Tyler.

Hearing chatter on the radio coming her way, Allegra stepped fully into the trees and ducked as Ben walked past.

"The river's more swollen than when we scouted yesterday. It must have been the rain last night." He paused. "Garret, I'm worried about Tyler."

Allegra gasped before she could stop it. She watched around the trunk as Ben stopped pacing, looking into the forest. When he started speaking again, she closed her eyes. *Thank you, Lord.*

She needed Ben to move so she could get away. Please,

please, please.

Several minutes later—several *precious* minutes—Ben walked toward the group.

Counting on the water to cover any noise she might make, Allegra picked her way over fallen branches and stones. The terrain was rocky, but she moved fast, fear for Tyler pushing her.

Limbs and branches slapped her, scratching her face, hands, and arms as she pushed through the forest. The river continued to rush by on her left as she kept an eye on it so she wouldn't get lost.

Hopefully.

Her stomach continued to churn. Would she find Tyler? And what would she do if she did?

Oh, this was a dumb idea. Dumb, dumb, dumb.

But she couldn't just stand there, waiting for Ben and whomever else to figure out a plan when Tyler could very well be stuck somewhere. Maybe underwater.

No! *Oh, God, please help!*

She paused a moment to catch her breath and think. A noise to her right alarmed her. A coyote? A cougar? *A bear?* She needed to move again. Now.

The rotting leaves under her feet kicked up a musty, earthy scent as Allegra continued down the banks of the river. In the distant, she thought she heard her name being called. Ben? Or Tyler?

The faint voice sounded again. From behind.

Definitely Ben.

Picking up speed, Allegra pushed forward, still keeping an

eye on the banks in case she spotted Tyler. Her legs and arms were sore from paddling for a day and a half, but images of Tyler lying somewhere, hurt...

Push on. Push on.

Everything hurt, especially his head. But why was he soaked? And cold. So cold.

Tyler tried raising his head, but sharp pain and flashes of light prevented him. Instead, he turned his head to the side and instantly choked on water rushing in. That was when he remembered where he was.

Shivers racked his body. He needed to get out of the water before hypothermia set in. How long had it been since he'd gone over the side of the raft? He looked at his waterproof watch but couldn't make sense of the numbers. He just knew he needed to move. *Strength, don't fail me now.*

No. That wasn't right. It was God he needed. God's strength. God...

Nausea jerked him awake. He mustered the energy to roll over onto his stomach and push himself to his hands and knees. He glanced upriver but didn't see the rafts. They must have pulled off to shore in order to look for him by land. Smart.

His heart raced, though he couldn't say whether from the onset of hypothermia or because of fear. *God, I'm definitely afraid.* He lowered his head toward the water, unable to hold it up. Tired. So tired. *Help.* His arms shook as they held him up. Tyler lifted his gaze and saw a small boulder he could grab. If he could reach it. He moved first one, then the other knee, shuffling his way through the water like a snail. But he was moving.

Finally, he reached out a hand and grasped the top of the rock. He slid his fingers over the top, then stopped to pray. "Please, God. Help."

He gritted his teeth...and pulled.

Chapter Forty-Two

Hunger rumbled her stomach, but Allegra wouldn't stop. She had to find Tyler.

She stepped over a log and continued to pick her way alongside the river. How long had she been walking? She hadn't worn her watch, so she had no sense of time. Except her stomach. Oh, what she wouldn't do for a croissant donut and Kit Kat latté right now.

Pressure built behind her eyes. Oh, Tyler. *Where are you?* The memory of the heat in his eyes when he looked at her yesterday morning sent her heart racing. It was time to admit it. She liked him.

A lot.

Okay, so it wasn't so much an admission as it was finally allowing herself to feel it. She had feelings—strong feelings—for someone who was like her parents. A risk taker. What was she thinking?

She was thinking with her heart for once.

A snap behind her yanked her out of her thoughts. She

whipped around and clutched her chest.

A rabbit. It was a rabbit. She giggled at her reaction, wiping her forehead with her arm. Turning back around, she continued walking, looking out over the river as she did.

If something was to ever happen with Tyler—she had to believe he was okay—could she accept his love of extreme sports? Would she be able to relax when he was out on excursions? She would never ask him to stop. He loved the rush too much, and she was loathe to take that away from him. So it would be up to her. Love Tyler the way he was, or let go and forget him.

Wait...*love*?

She stopped in her tracks. She loved him. "What am I going to do, Lord?" She sighed. First things first. She needed to find Tyler.

Cupping her hands around her mouth, she started calling Tyler's name.

No response. "Lord, I hope that's because he isn't in earshot yet, not because he's unconscious."

Exhaustion weighed on her. Tears trickled down her cheeks. She had to find him. And when she did? She'd give him that kiss they came so close to sharing before Ben interrupted.

Well, *after* she got help.

Okay, maybe before.

Her lips tingled at the thought. Oh yes. Definitely a kiss first.

"Tyler!"

He didn't remember hallucination being a symptom of hypothermia. But then again, he couldn't exactly think clearly right now. He thought he'd heard his name, but he was so tired.

Tyler finally reached the edge of the river and collapsed onto his back, too worn to give it more thought. Instead, he focused on Allegra.

Or tried to.

"Lord." His voice rasped. "Keep me awake."

His head throbbed. *Make it stop. Please.*

He forced his eyes open and stared at the blue sky. Clouds floated by, in no hurry to go anywhere. He was thankful the trees provided some shade from the bright sun.

Allegra. He needed Allegra.

A groan escaped as a stab shot through his head again. He raised his hand and rubbed the spot that hurt the most. When he brought his hand back down, it had a smear of blood.

Well, that wasn't good.

His eyes drifted closed, but a prodding from within forced them back open. God was working overtime to keep him awake. *Thank you.*

Tyler let his mind wander back to Allegra. Guilt traced a sharp nail down his chest. She'd been afraid something would happen on one of the excursions he'd forced her into. He had promised her she'd be safe, but he didn't know what happened after he fell out of the raft. Did she go over too? His breathing choked. He couldn't catch it.

Hyperventilating. He needed his breath.

He took a deep breath through his nose and tried to let it out slowly through his nose. It didn't work out so well, but he kept trying. After a few moments, he was finally able to breathe again.

Calm.

Allegra. She was fine. She had to be.

Tyler!

Huh. He was so sure she was okay, he was hearing her voice. Good. He needed that confidence.

Time to try to get out of here. He pushed up on his elbows and leaned his head back, eyes closed.

Rest a moment.

Pushing up with his hands now, he made to sit up, but a wave of dizziness and nausea stopped him.

He had to do this. He closed his eyes and pushed up again, this time sitting all the way up before opening his eyes. The world was tilting, but the nausea passed as he sat still, waiting for the dizzy spell to stop. But he was still so cold.

He forced his focus back to Allegra. He'd missed her over the past weeks. He hadn't realized until she was gone just how much she'd brightened each day. He'd known back then that he liked her, but there was nothing like falling into a river and suffering from the onset of hypothermia, stuck on an embankment, to really show a man he was falling in love with a woman.

Falling in love? He grinned. Yeah. He was falling in love.

Actually, nix that. He was *already* in love.

"Okay, God," he whispered. "It's up to You. I can't get out of here without You, and I can't see a way to convince Allie to make a life with me."

Would you be willing to change?

His stomach dropped. Would he? Would he be willing to give up doing what he loved for a woman he loved? "Oh, Lord. Will I have to choose?"

Silence met his question.

"Tyler!"

He opened his mouth to talk to God again. That was the first time he'd ever audibly heard God's voice. But then his muddled brain finally connected that it was a woman's voice calling for him.

A woman?

"Allegra?"

Chapter Forty-Three

What was that? Allegra paused in her search. She thought she'd heard something...or someone. She waited to see if it happened again.

Then a faint call. "Allegra."

Was that Ben? It was so hard to hear over the water. She leaned against a tree, scrunching her eyes closed to concentrate. And waited.

Nothing.

The heart could only take so much battering. Likely, it was only a figment of her desperate imagination. She rubbed her hands over her face. The shade from the trees, welcomed only a few hours ago, was now her enemy, hiding the sun she so desperately needed to stay in the sky for her search.

Hair fell across her face. She pulled the elastic out of her falling ponytail and redid it. It was taking a lot longer than she thought it would. Setting her mind to prayer, she started walking again.

"Tyler!"

She called for him every few minutes, always stopping to listen for an answer, but no call came. Where could he be? Or had she passed him already?

Her heart skittered to a stop. There was no way she'd walked all this way already, searching, and missed him. No. Please, no.

The sounds of the river mixed with those of the forest. If she wasn't so worried about Tyler, she might actually find it peaceful. Allegra laughed out loud. Her? Find a forest peaceful? But the more she thought about it, the more it wormed into her heart.

She'd run away, but still Tyler had done some hard work in her heart and changed her. She shook her head. No, that wasn't right. It wasn't Tyler who'd changed her…it was God. She'd been able to swallow some fear and go with Tyler on his harebrained adventures. She'd even gone spelunking with Renata.

She swallowed hard. Though Capri had set up this whitewater trip, it was Allegra who'd made the choice to go. By herself. She smiled. She had to admit she was thankful Tyler showed up though.

She'd become a little less fearful and more open to friendships outside of her books. God had made His presence known in His gentle, quiet way. She just hadn't wanted to listen until now. She hadn't wanted to trust until now, with so much at stake.

But how did one trust? Her parents gave her no reason to trust them. They'd loved her and Caprice, but they'd valued their love of adventure more than their daughters. They put their desires before the welfare of their children. And though it was an accident, they died, leaving their daughters to fend for themselves. Thinking back, however, she saw now how God had provided for them. No, her parents hadn't left a life insurance policy, but God had given her a job that paid enough for her to live on and send her sister to college. And when that job failed, He provided Tyler. Not just the job, but the man.

So focused on her worry for Tyler, Allegra tripped over a rock and fell to the ground, landing on her hands and knees. Exhausted, she let her head hang between her shoulders and prayed. "God, please keep him safe. Help me. I'm sorry, Lord. I'm sorry I haven't trusted You. I'm sorry I've been so focused on me and my abilities that I've completely ignored how You have been caring for me." Moving from her knees to sit, she bent her legs and propped her arms against them. She needed to rest, or she wouldn't be any good to Tyler when she did find him. "Lead me, Lord."

"Allegra."

Her head snapped up. It was hushed, but she'd definitely heard her name, and it didn't sound like Ben.

She scrambled to her feet and called out. "Tyler!"

There was a moment of quiet before she heard her name again. "Allie." Weaker this time.

"Tyler! Where are you?" She moved closer to the edge of the river, hoping to see him in the waning light.

"…here." Faint. "I'm here."

Allegra picked up her pace and began to jog, calling Tyler's name as she went. She scanned everywhere between the river and the tree line as she went. She didn't have to go far before she spotted a gray T-shirt, wet, dirty, and torn.

"Tyler!"

Tyler lay curled on his side, trying to stay warm. And awake. But it was getting harder.

"Tyler!"

He stirred and tried to call out, but his voice stuck. He felt himself fading. He tried to focus on praying but couldn't get his thoughts straight enough to make sense. Thank God Jesus interceded for him. He closed his eyes, just to rest them for a second.

"Tyler!"

He forced his eyes open. Was he hearing things, hallucinating, or was she actually nearby? Tyler opened his mouth to try again. "Allegra." It was weak, but he heard his voice.

"Tyler!"

It was her. How... Never mind how. He licked his lips. He was cold. And his voice wouldn't work again. He forced a cough and was able to push his word out. "Allie."

He heard her call again, asking where he was. It took everything in him to answer. He knew she'd find him even if he didn't, but he needed to keep talking to stay awake. "I'm over..." His voice croaked. "...here. I'm here."

The last bit of energy drained. He hoped she heard him, because he didn't think he'd be able to speak again. He closed his eyes. *Please show her, Lord.*

What felt like hours later but was likely only a minute or

two, he felt soft, warm hands on his face.

"Tyler! Oh Ty." Hot tears dropped on his cheek.

Oh, God, thank You.

Chapter Forty-Four

As Allegra bent over Tyler, she ran her hands down his arms, legs, and chest—not that that was so much a hardship. But he was freezing, lips discolored. Her frantic gaze slid across her body and the forest, searching for something to cover Tyler's body. The only thing she could think of was her shirt. And, um… That just wasn't possible.

A scene from a TV show came to mind. A couple were stuck out in a snowstorm, and to stay warm, they, well, they stripped and cuddled. She felt heat flush her cheeks. No. That wasn't possible either. She started rubbing her hands up and down his arms, trying to create some friction. Tyler didn't respond though. He needed help. Now.

"Help!" Maybe Ben was close by and would hear. She moved to Tyler's other side and lay down, facing him. He opened his eyes. "Hi. You sure know how to make a girl work hard."

His eyes closed again, but she gave a small smile. A harsh

tremble shook his body, and he groaned. Allegra scooted closer to him and wrapped an arm over him.

Through chattering teeth, he said, "Don't mind if I do."

"Punk," she whispered.

He didn't respond.

"Ty, stay awake."

He mumbled something, so she moved her head and put her ear near his mouth. "What was that?"

"I lo…"

She leaned back and looked at him. He was out. She turned her head away from his face, drew a breath, and yelled again. "Help!"

The sun continued to lower in the sky as Tyler slept, shivering now and then, but she noticed color starting to return to his face.

She tried again. "Help! Ben!"

Allegra pressed her face against Tyler's cheek. "Hang on, Ty. I'm sure Ben isn't far behind."

Noises from the forest—birds singing, crickets chirping, small animals scattering—soothed her as she called for help a few times a minute. Her throat was starting to get a bit sore from the yelling, but there was no way she'd stop. Tyler's life might depend on it.

"Help!"

Tyler became restless against her. He opened his eyes. "You're…loud."

She grinned. "I prefer relentless."

Exhaustion lined his eyes, but his twinkle was still there. "I prefer you."

Laugher escaped. "You goober."

He leaned away from her and rolled onto his back.

"Tyler, you need warmth."

No response. Allegra sighed, sat up, and leaned over him. He was out again. She cupped her hands around her mouth and called out. "Help!"

Next to her, Tyler shivered again. Maybe she should try to build a fire or something.

Oh, who was she kidding? Unless she had a lighter, she didn't have a clue how to light a fire, let alone keep one going. *This* was why she didn't venture outside. She didn't belong out here. What had she been thinking? And now *she* was the one responsible for Tyler? *Oh, God. I don't think I can—*

"I can hear you panicking."

"What?" She gasped. "I'm not panicking."

"Yeah, you...are." He turned his head toward her and opened his eyes. "Allie...this isn't in our...hands."

"I don't know what—" Oh. He meant... "It's in God's."

"Yeah." He closed his eyes again. "But you can still...call for help."

She couldn't stop the laugh. But he was right.

"Help!"

It was comfortable having Allie beside him. More than comfortable. It was home.

Even out here in the woods, suffering from mild hypothermia.

He was so in love.

Unfortunately, that had to wait a little while longer. He was bone tired, and all he wanted to do was sleep, which was why they had to get moving.

"Allie." He so badly wanted a drink of water but couldn't stomach the thought of drinking something cold.

Hot breath fanned his cheek when she spoke. "I didn't know you were awake."

He cracked a smile. "Hard not to...be with all the ruckus...you make."

She sputtered a laugh. "You're such a brat."

"So I've been told." He licked his lips. "We need...to move, honey. Back the...way you came."

He felt her sit up next to him. "Tyler, you can't even keep your eyes open. How do you think we're going to be able to move?" She leaned over him, the warmth from her body now hovering over his chest. "I'm not leaving you."

Hmm. Maybe they didn't have to move after all.

He sighed. "I'll need...your help, but I can...walk, I'm sure. Just help me...up." He cracked his eyes open to watch her stand and move in front of him, reaching her hands out. "No, sweetheart. You're...not going to want to stand right in...front of me. I, uh...might get sick."

Allegra's eyes widened, and she scrambled to his side. He grasped her hands and pulled himself to sit up.

His stomach rebelled, but he sat long enough that it passed.

"Ready?" she asked.

Dusk was settling in, dimming the light with which he could see Allegra's face, but her shining eyes gave him comfort and strength.

"Yeah. I think so."

With a ready hand, she helped him to his feet, steadying him when his world tilted on its axis.

"Thanks."

"Always."

The shiver that racked his body had nothing to do with her lush lips forming around that husky voice. Or did it? Hmm.

Chapter Forty-Five

They'd been trudging alongside the river for only a few minutes when Allegra called for help again. It was slowgoing because of Tyler's condition, but she was sure Ben couldn't have been far behind her.

She had no problem, however, admitting she was scared. She eyed Tyler. He was so pale that his blond two-day growth looked dark against his skin.

"How are you doing?"

He grunted in response.

Allegra kept her right arm around his waist while grasping his left hand with hers to keep him steady on his feet. He'd already stumbled a few times, but thankfully caught himself. The more they moved, however, the weaker he seemed. He shouldn't be spending all his energy this way.

"Help!" If she kept calling at regular intervals, hopefully that would lead Ben to them.

"Thanks, Allie." His words came out on huffs of breath.

"Always."

They paused for Tyler to rest against a tree. "When we get...out of here, we...need to talk."

She caught her breath, as if it were bottled up in her chest. "Yeah?"

Tyler nodded. "Yeah. I want...you back at Hawk's Flight."

Oh. Her entire being deflated.

"And we need to talk about us." The glint in his eyes told her he knew exactly what he was doing to her.

She bit her lip. "Us?"

"After we...get out of here, Allie. I...need us both...off this ledge."

Ledge? What ledge? Apparently his thinking wasn't quite on point. But his request to talk about them...was this going to turn out the way his promise to call her did? Because that didn't go quite as planned.

"Allie."

She met his gaze.

"I promise. I...won't back out like...I did before." He held out a shaking hand. "No more fear."

Her heart tripped as she grasped his offered hand and their skin made contact. She shook her head. "No more fear."

Allegra pulled him off the tree and moved to support him again. They only made it another fifty or so feet when he had to stop for another rest. Her mouth dried. She needed to get him help faster than he could move. *What should I do, Lord?* She searched up and down the river's edge, hoping to catch a glimpse of something she could use to help Tyler.

"Ty?"

"Mm?"

"Were you ever in Boy Scouts?"

He cracked open an eye to look at her.

"Ah. Football ruled your life. No time for Scouts, huh?"

"Sorry," he mumbled.

So he was no help there. Shoot. If anyone could get them out of this situation, it'd be a Boy Scout. She sighed.

"Allie! Tyler!"

Her pulse skipped a beat, then raced. "Tyler! Did you hear that?"

"Hear...what?"

Never mind him. He was almost completely out of it again. It was up to her.

"Help!"

A moment passed before she heard it again. Distant, but if she kept calling, they'd find her.

"Allie?" That was Ben—she was sure of it.

"Ben! Over here!"

She leaned over Tyler. "Ty, they're coming. Just hang on, okay?"

An incoherent mumble was all the noise that came out of his mouth.

"Beside the river!"

Allegra kept calling Ben's name, guiding him and whoever else was searching with him to their position. Finally, beams from flashlights lit the trees.

"Here! Ben, we're over here!"

"You have Tyler?"

"Yes!"

"Oh, thank God!" The relief in Ben's voice was palpable.

Within minutes a group of three pushed through the shrubbery and onto the embankment. Tears welled behind her eyelids as Ben radioed to someone that he'd found them.

She watched as Ben leaned over Tyler and began to assess him. "Hey, man, can you hear me?"

"Dude...you stink. Let...Allie check me out."

Tyler met her gaze with a wink.

There'd be no problem at all checking him out.

A deep rumble of laughter sounded from Ben's chest. "Yeah, I think you're going to be okay. Let's get you out of here."

The two men who accompanied Ben stepped forward and put their arms under Tyler's, lifting him off the tree. Ben spoke up. "Do you think you can walk, or will you need me to grab your legs?"

"Walk" was all Tyler managed.

They started out walking. Each time Tyler stumbled, however, Allie cringed. "Maybe you should carry him. He might trip and fall and break—"

"Allie...I'm okay."

Right.

That lasted only a few more minutes before Tyler stumbled again. She opened her mouth to speak, but Ben beat her to it.

"No way, buddy. We'll move faster if we carry you. And the faster we can get you warmed up, the faster you get to go home with your girlfriend."

Allie's jaw dropped. "I'm not his girl—"

"Sounds good to me." A low chuckle sounded from Tyler's

throat.

The bum!

Ben moved in front of Tyler and counted to three, then lifted Tyler's feet off the ground. The speed definitely picked up, though it was by no means fast. They stuck to the edge of the river for a short while before veering off west into the forest.

"Where are we going?"

Ben grunted. "We had one of the supply trucks paralleling us on a logging road." The men paused to give Ben time to climb over a fallen trunk, lifting Tyler over it. "We're not that far."

By the time they reached the truck, the sun had dipped completely and darkness surrounded them. The driver climbed out of his seat and helped load Tyler into the passenger seat, buckling him in. The rest of them climbed into the bed of the truck, holding on to the sides as they made their way down into town and the hospital.

Chapter Forty-Six

The bumps and jostles of being half carried, half dragged out of the forest to the trucks waiting on an old logging road likely did more damage to him than the actual hypothermia. Thank God it was a mild case though. It could have been so much worse.

Tyler stretched his arms above his head, pulling on his IV tube. Oh yeah. He was in the hospital. He opened his mouth wide and yawned, rolling his head to the left.

And there sat Allegra, chin on her chest, sleeping.

Her dark hair was pulled back in a low bun, wisps framing her face, one piece stuck to her cheek. His heart tugged. He wanted so badly to reach out and tuck it behind her ear, but he couldn't reach. Instead, he lay there, watching her sleep as her chest rose and fell with soft regularity.

She was so beautiful. And it wasn't just her physical beauty.

He wondered if she realized just how strong she'd been today. He hoped so. And if not, he would make sure to tell her. But first, he needed more sleep...

When he next opened his eyes, Tyler was alone in his room. Where had Allegra gone? And would she be back? He'd meant it when he said they needed to talk. Yes, he wanted her back at Hawk's Flight, but it was more than that. He would understand if she felt she needed to stay in Portland—she'd only been there two months and no doubt wanted to give her new employer fair time, plus she likely had a signed lease on an apartment there. But even if she didn't return to the shop, he would prove to her that they should be together. He would hire someone to lead weekend excursions so he could drive down to Portland every weekend if he had to. He just knew he wanted her in his life. For good. As his wife.

But first he needed to convince her that a relationship with him was a good idea.

He tucked the blanket under his chin. He was warming up, but there was still a cold edge. He let his mind wander to what the future might hold. *Would* hold. He was convinced she was the right woman for him.

Images of dark-haired little girls with green eyes and blond-haired boys with blue eyes filled his mind to the point his chest ached. Or was that hypothermia? No matter. But better to push those thoughts aside and focus on just getting a date with the love of his life.

Sipping on the coffee she bought from the vending machine out in the hallway, Allegra leaned against the wall outside Tyler's room. The steady beeps coming from the machine hooked up to him were a huge comfort. She knew, once he'd been put in the truck, he'd be okay, but still...to have the beeping confirmation relaxed her muscles and helped her breathe easy.

With her phone back in her car parked at the river, she had no way of contacting Bo or Story to let them know what happened. Maybe the nurse would let her call Story, and she would call Bo.

But considering whatever it was that was between them, Story may not be so inclined to call him. Ah well. Worth a shot.

After speaking with a nurse, Allegra picked up the phone the woman placed on the nurses' station counter, and she punched in Story's number.

It was three rings before Story answered. "Hello?" She sounded out of breath.

"Hey, it's Allegra. Did I get you at a bad time?"

"No, I was just coming in the door from the laundry room down the hall. What's up?"

Allegra shared what happened, then asked, "Would you mind calling Bo?"

At Story's hesitation, she spoke again. "I'd call, but I don't think the hospital would appreciate long distance. Please?"

"Okay." She may have agreed, but Story didn't sound thrilled.

"Thanks, Story. I appreciate it. Tell him Tyler is fine. I just wanted him to know what happened."

Story asked a few more questions before they hung up. Allegra wandered back into Tyler's room, fully expecting him to still be sleeping.

"Hey, what are you doing awake? You should be resting." She pushed the chair closer to his bedside and sat down.

"Lying in a bed *is* resting." He grinned. "But still, don't expect too much from me."

"Never do."

"Hey!"

Laughter bubbled up. "Kidding! I'm kidding."

"Uh-huh."

"Hey," she said. "Story is calling Bo to tell him what happened."

Tyler's eyebrows scrunched together. "That's not necessary. I'm fine."

"I know, but still." She placed her elbows on his bed and rested her chin in her hands. "He'd want to know, just like you'd want to know if something happened to him."

He rolled his eyes, but conceded. "Fine."

The room remained silent for a few minutes, with Tyler's eyes closed and the machine's steady beat. Allegra watched the slow rise and fall of his chest. She was exhausted herself, but she didn't want to leave until the nurses kicked her out, and so far, they seemed too busy with other patients to care.

"Allie."

She moved her gaze to meet Tyler's. "Yeah?"

"About us..."

The lump in her throat was too big to swallow past—or speak through—so she nodded.

He lifted a hand to her face and ran a finger down her cheek. Her breath quickened as all her focus went to his touch. But...

"Tyler, I can't. My job."

"I'll do whatever it takes," he whispered, "to make this work. I've already thought about it and—"

The piercing shrill of the phone on his bedside table interrupted what Tyler was about to say. Disappointment warred with relief as Allegra picked up the phone.

"Hello?"

She listened before handing the receiver over to Tyler. "It's Bo."

"This conversation isn't finished, Allie."

She smiled before leaning forward to place a kiss on his cheek. She waited until he acknowledged Bo, then walked out of his room, relieved to know he'd be fine.

It was time for her to go home.

Chapter Forty-Seven

Walking out of the hospital the next day felt incredible.

Maybe a little dramatic, but considering what could have happened, Tyler was thankful he only needed to be warmed up with some blankets and an IV, and have a good sleep. However, Allegra's disappearance when he took the phone to talk with Bo was disconcerting.

Walking beside him to drive him back to his truck, Story was quiet. "Have you spoken to Allegra?"

She looked up at him with surprise. "Well, yeah."

"Where did she go last night?"

They reached her beat-up car, dents and scratches everywhere. It didn't bode well for Story's driving abilities, but she'd never mentioned being in an accident. Huh.

After she unlocked the doors, they climbed in. Story turned her key in the ignition and looked at him. "She went home, of course." Cranking the car into gear, she reversed and left the parking lot. "Where else would she go? You know she only lives, like, an hour from here, right?"

The distance between here and Portland never crossed his mind. "Uh, no. I didn't give it much thought."

Music filled the silence for the rest of the drive back to Tyler's truck. When they arrived, Story left her car running but turned to face Tyler. She stared at him, hesitation written all over her face. Then she spoke.

"You know...I think she loves you."

He took a deep breath and slowly exhaled. "I know I love her."

The smile that played on Story's lips said it all. "Then get out of my car. And I don't want to see you at work until tomorrow, Boss."

A low chuckle rumbled his chest. Tyler leaned in to Story and wrapped her neck in a hug. "Thanks."

"Go on." She shooed her hands toward him.

He complied, pulling the door handle and climbing out. "Drive safely."

"Back at you. And, Tyler"—she leaned toward the passenger door—"even love is a risk. Make sure your heart is a safe place for her." She waved a hand in front of her face. "Now be gone." Story leaned further, pulled the door closed, and left him in the parking lot with his thoughts.

Instead of heading to his truck, he decided to move down toward the river.

The warm breeze was soft against his face as he sat down at the river's edge. The sun reflected off the water, creating what looked like thousands of diamonds glittering. Birds sang all around him. It was peaceful.

And lonely.

He wished Allegra were with him to just sit, relax...and kiss. A grin stretched his mouth. This would be a perfect spot to get married.

His heart picked up its pace. He couldn't imagine a better woman for him than Allie. She was everything he didn't want but everything he was beginning to realize he needed. She was gentle, funny, compassionate, and generous. She cared. And while she may not have that adventurous spirit when it came to pushing herself through extreme sports, she was adventurous in giving her heart. Even to the point of caring enough to face her fears and come looking for him in the woods. And getting him to safety. At night.

Amazing.

Tyler stayed where he sat for another ten minutes, just taking in God's creation. It was calming, being in that place. But the memory of Allegra last night when she walked out of his hospital room pushed him to his feet and into his truck.

It was time he faced his own fears and started what could be the biggest adventure—or mishap—of his life.

Allegra hit the snooze button on her alarm more times than she could count. After leaving the hospital so late the night before, then driving an hour back home, she was exhausted. She stretched her arms over her head, arched her back, and yawned.

She needed a latté. *Stat.*

After turning on her espresso machine, she made her way back to her bathroom to jump into the shower. She was in no mood to go to work, but that wouldn't look good when she'd only been working there for a couple of months. That meant no calling into work sick.

Rats.

The shower didn't wake her up, so with bleary eyes, Allegra made her way back to her kitchen and the vessel full of lifeblood—her coffee.

"Thank you, Jesus, for whomever discovered the coffee bean could be ground into such sustaining energy."

She hoped He took that prayer seriously. She knew she did.

She filled the portafilter, tamped down the ground coffee, and stuck her favorite huge mug under the machine, then set about foaming the milk.

Finally, it was ready. Such a sweet fragrance. Such joy. Such…deliciousness. Just as she took her first sip—*bliss!*—her phone rang.

Double rats. She'd hoped for a few quiet moments to spend with God before leaving for work. A quick glance at her caller ID squashed that idea though.

"Caprice, shouldn't you be in class?"

"I'm in between right now. I want to know how your rafting trip went."

Allegra sighed. "It was eventful." She went on to tell her sister everything that happened.

"So is Tyler okay?"

"He was when I left the hospital last night." She glanced at the clock on her microwave. "Hey, I need to run to work. Can I call you back later tonight?"

"Sure." The disappointment in Capri's tone caught her off guard.

"Is everything okay?"

"What? Yeah. Everything's good. More than, actually."

"Hold on." Obviously her sister had news she wanted to talk about. Allegra set the phone down on the counter, tapped the Speaker button, and opened her cupboard door to grab a travel mug. "Okay, you obviously have something you want to talk about. You're on speaker, but I warn you—I'll be walking out the door in a minute and getting on the elevator, so if I lose you, I'll call back when I get in the car."

A sigh sounded over the line. "Thank you."

Within minutes, Allie sat her in car, connected the phone to Bluetooth, and headed to her office. The drive wasn't far, but in the morning rush, it would take a few minutes longer than normal.

"Okay, I'm ready. What's going on?"

"I met someone."

"What?"

Caprice giggled. "He works at J. Wong too and even goes to my new school. He's so cute."

"I'm happy for you, but when do you even have time?" She couldn't help the question. Tyler definitely helped her loosen up and take some risks, but she couldn't ignore her personality entirely.

"Oh, sis. Just be careful. And don't let your schoolwork slide. And don't be late or do anything to upset your job, especially now that you're paying your own tuition."

Allegra practically heard her sister's eye-roll. "Yes,

Mother."

"Brat."

"But you love me."

Yes she did. Allegra ended the call just as she pulled into a parking spot. She turned off her car and sat, looking at the building where she worked. She missed walking into a place like Tyler's, where everything was so relaxed. But that was neither here nor there. She had a job to do, and do well.

Chapter Forty-Eight

A few hours sitting at her desk working, and she still felt discombobulated. Even after two more cups of coffee.

Her coffee—her Christian crack—was failing her.

As she sat back down in her cubicle with yet another mug of caffeine, the phone on her desk rang.

"Good morning. This is Allegra."

"Allie, it's Story."

"Story? Is Tyler okay?"

"Yeah, he's fine. I just dropped him off at his truck."

So the hospital released him. Good. "Great. So how are you?"

"Fine. On my way back to Seattle."

"Too bad it's Monday. I would've loved to have you stay for the weekend." She could use the girl time. "So is Tyler right behind you?"

Her friend was quiet for a moment. "Uh, no. I think he may have stayed at the river for a bit."

Allegra furrowed her brows. Why would he stay there? She would have thought he'd be anxious to get home and rest. He no doubt had another excursion going on sometime this week. And why would Story have left him? The man had just gotten out of the hospital. "Do you think that's safe?"

Story laughed. "Oh believe me. He's just fine. Better than fine, even."

Better than fine? Good. "Okay. If you're sure."

"Are you busy there today?"

Allegra looked at the reports spread across the desk in front of her. It was more busywork than actual necessity. "Not terribly."

"Good."

"Good?"

"Oh." Her friend paused. "Um, yeah. I'm sure you can use a quiet day today."

"A comfortable bed is more like it."

Laughter filtered through the phone held to her ear. "Well, don't let me keep you. And I'll make sure to come down for a visit one weekend soon."

They hung up, and the clacking of keyboards and murmurs of her coworkers' voices as they talked on the phone or with one another set a backdrop of...boredom.

A job she once loved, once thrived in, now bored her to tears. What in the world?

It was like working for Tyler had opened her eyes—and heart—to something more thrilling, to more variety in her days. Spending so many hours yesterday searching for Tyler, finding and caring for him, helping him get up and move, then seeing him to the hospital, she'd learned something about herself. She had courage.

Empowerment surged through her. She felt rejuvenated. Alive.

Allegra spun her chair, doing a little dance, and accidentally let out a squeal. She popped up to peek over her cubicle walls to see if anyone heard her, thankful when no one paid any attention. *Phew.*

She plopped back down and stared at the reports in front of her. She did love numbers and working to solve problems that had absolute answers, but this environment was no longer enough. She craved a casual atmosphere, camaraderie, laughter.

Tyler.

She leaned her elbows on her desk and pushed her hands through her hair. Tyler. There was no sense in denying that she missed working with him.

Scratch that. She missed *him.*

She loved him.

Now the question was, what was she going to do? She'd only been at Schmidt, Basham & Monzon for a couple of months. Tyler was on his way back to Seattle because she'd friend-zoned him, but that didn't mean there wasn't a place here in Portland that had a similar atmosphere to Hawk's Flight. At this point, she'd even take the extreme excursions.

Her pulse picked up at the thought. Was she actually *excited* at that prospect?

Tyler arrived in Portland faster than he probably should

have. That was the danger of a lead foot.

After speaking with Story and getting the name of Allegra's office, he looked up the address, entered it into his GPS, and made his way there. He stopped once for flowers—gardenias, if he remembered her favorite right. She'd mentioned it one day when she saw wild gardenias in photos of his diving trip in Australia.

Heart palpitations as he drew closer to her building threatened to send him back to the hospital. Could he do this? Could he talk her into leaving Portland and coming home? To him?

He threw his truck into park and sat with the engine running, arms crossed over the steering wheel. Never in his life had he been so doubtful of his ability to do something. It wasn't his parents holding him back now—it was himself.

When Allegra left the night before, he'd told her their conversation wasn't over. She'd just smiled, kissed his cheek, and walked out. She didn't look back at him or hesitate or anything. Maybe she truly meant what she'd said about just wanting a friendship from him. But even that didn't ring entirely true. He'd felt the warmth radiating from her whenever she neared him, saw the longing in her eyes.

Unless he just had an ego the size of Texas.

But he couldn't shake the feeling that she'd been holding back again.

All his life he'd fought for what he wanted. He fought his parents when they kept saying no. When he finally had some backup in his coach, he'd won that fight. He'd fought his asthma whenever it tried to get the better of him as he played football, but he'd always won. Yeah, it might have sometimes taken a trip to the hospital to beat it, but he'd still won. He'd fought the competitive field to make it into the NFL, and he'd won, if his success was any indication. But this woman...

She was worth fighting for, but only if she truly wanted to be won. If she didn't, it was a battle he'd lose. Maybe he should give her a little time.

Man, where were these doubts coming from? His clenched fists tightened. Maybe he needed his own time to pray things through some more.

He pulled the gearshift into reverse. He wasn't chickening out—he didn't do that—but he needed a more solid plan than just showing up with flowers.

Hopefully, some time with God would make that plan clear.

Chapter Forty-Nine

One Month Later

She was going to throw up. What she was about to do was so unlike her, so contrary to her personality, yet it was the only way she could think of to show Tyler just how much she loved him.

She only prayed he loved her too.

After a month of scrimping every last penny she could—and thankful for Capri's wisdom and sense of responsibility in refusing Allie's school payments—here she was, back in the Seattle area on a cool and cloudy fall Saturday.

What was she thinking?

Allegra shook her head. She must have marbles for brains. Or a really deep love for Tyler. But she hadn't even talked to him in a month, and here she was, about to—

The turnoff for the Virginia Mason Athletic Center, where the Seattle Seahawks practiced, was just ahead. The butterflies in her stomach performed somersaults as she made the turn and approached the building. But these butterflies were no match for the ones she would have the next day if all went according to plan in the next few minutes.

Once parked, she walked into the building and up to reception.

The lovely redheaded woman smiled up at her. "May I help you?"

"Yes. I'm here to meet—"

"Allegra."

She clutched her chest and whipped around. "You scared me!"

"Sorry." Bo laughed. "A bit jumpy, are you?"

She was going to knock that twinkle out of his eyes if it was the last thing she did. "Not at all."

He lifted a brow and smirked. "Uh-huh." Turning his back to her, he called over his shoulder. "Follow me."

Together, they walked down some corridors and through a set of doors where they landed on the indoor training field. Across the field, large white flags proclaiming the Seahawks NFC champions for several years hung above a yellow goal post. Dozens of large fluorescent lights hung overhead, and white yard lines crossed the field at regular intervals. So this was where Tyler had spent most days practicing.

Allegra looked around at the men in practice uniforms. They were huge. "Who's the pennyback for the Hawks now?"

Bo whipped his head around and stared at her, incredulous. "Pennyback? What are you..." His eyes widened before he threw out a bark of laughter. He was barely able to catch his breath, he was laughing so hard.

She crossed her arms over her chest and glared. "What's so funny?"

"Pen...penny..." He couldn't finish. Tears formed at the corners of his eyes. He was so loud with his laughter that he drew the attention of the players on the field.

"Bo." Those men jogged over to where she and Bo stood.

Um...coming closer, they were bigger than she even imagined.

And Bo still wouldn't stop laughing. What in the world was so funny?

The men all eyed Allegra while smacking Bo on the back and asking him about his coaching job. Though Bo was a hockey player, being best friends with Tyler had given him the opportunity to become good friends with quite a few guys on the Seahawks team.

Bo finally stopped long enough to make some introductions. "And this, Allegra, is Drew Perkins, the, uh...pennyback."

"Nice to meet you." She shook his hand.

"Pennyback?" His quizzical gaze settled on Bo. "What on earth—"

"So Allegra here needs to ask you guys a favor."

As a whole, the group of men shifted their gazes from Bo to her. Yikes. That wasn't intimidating at all.

Drew spoke first. "What's up?"

Taking a deep breath, she began to tell them her idea.

―∞―

Church had been great, but Tyler was ready to go home, grab his bike, and do some cycling. Sunday turned out to be a beautiful day, especially after the clouds and drizzle of the day before. It would probably be one of the last warm days of fall, so he planned to take advantage of it. With his new coleader out with a group doing some downhill biking up in Vancouver, he had a quiet day to himself.

Man, he missed Allie.

The past month had been long and hard. Driving away from her office building in Portland without seeing her was probably the right decision, but it didn't make it any more palatable. He had needed the time, though, to really pray through his feelings and his fears. Finally owning up to things he was scared of broke a bond he hadn't known he was tied to. Freedom had never been so sweet. And now…now that freedom included the permission he'd been seeking from God to propose to Allegra.

Yep. His face stretched in a grin. Theirs wasn't a conventional relationship, and they would need time before actually getting married to just date and be together, but he knew without a doubt she was the woman for him.

It was risky, but wasn't that adrenaline what he'd been living off for his whole life?

His phone ringing next to him on the seat jolted him from his thoughts.

"Hello?"

"Hey, man, what's up?"

"Bo, how are ya? I'm heading home to grab my bike and go do some riding."

"Nice. Where're you going for that?"

"Where else? I-5 Colonnade."

"Oh man, I miss that place."

They spoke for a few more minutes before Tyler parked his truck in his building's parking garage. They said their goodbyes, and then he ran into the storage to grab his bike. Placing it in the truck bed, he threw his helmet and other protective gear on the passenger seat and made his way to I-5 Colonnade. The mountain biking park was full of skills, with trails, berms, jumps, tracks, drops, and wall rides. His blood pumped just thinking about it.

When he arrived, Tyler drove around the lot until someone left and he was able to park. Despite the full lot, he was thankful the park itself didn't look terribly busy. His adrenaline was pumping, and he wanted to spend it all in this park.

He went straight to the advanced area. The traffic from the interstate overhead was loud, with horns honking and tires rumbling, but that noise and the exhaust from all those vehicles didn't deter him.

After working his body hard for a while, he biked down a rocky path into some quieter green space…where he saw one of his football buddies.

"Drew, what are you doing here, man?"

They pounded each other on the back. "Hanging with some of the other guys. Are you doing some biking?"

"Yeah." Sweat trickled down into Tyler's eyes. He wiped his forearm across his face. "You wanna go for a ride?"

His former quarterback chuckled. "Nah, man. I'm good."

Somewhere behind Tyler, pop music began to play. Loudly. He glanced over his shoulder to the direction the music was coming from.

Was that...wait...what were his old teammates doing here?

He turned back to Drew, but his friend was jogging toward the others and joining them. Before Tyler knew what was happening, his buddies started dancing and lip syncing to...was that Christina Aguilera? He blinked.

Okay, he was being punk'd. Christina's voice belted out "Ain't No Other Man" while Drew and the guys mouthed the words and actually danced. Oh man, they were dancing to it. What was going on?

He couldn't help but stare. Others in the park were drawn to the music and started to pull out their cell phones to record. No one would believe that a group of Seahawks were flash mobbing. He felt a rumble of laughter in his chest and let it out.

Oh man. This was too funny.

Chapter Fifty

This was it. The song was about to end. Allegra stood behind the team, cracking up as they danced. For such big guys, they surprisingly had a lot of good moves. As the song neared its ending, nausea threatened to overwhelm her, but no. She couldn't—wouldn't—let it.

Before she left Story's place, where she'd spent the night, Allegra had dressed carefully. When Bo told her where Tyler was going to be, she'd known Tyler would be wearing biking shorts and gear. She didn't want to overdress, but she still wanted to look good for him. She'd slipped on a coral hi-low strapless dress, matching sandals, and some simple gold jewelry. She'd brought a gold shrug with her to keep her warm, but the adrenaline was pumping so hard and fast, she didn't need it.

The guys in front began to part. She pushed her hand behind her back and squeezed her gift for Tyler. There was no way she would have been able to get this without the Seahawks coach's help, but it'd still cost her more than she could truly afford. She tried to swallow past the bile in her throat. If this didn't work out, she could likely sell it on an auction site and get her money back.

She hoped.

The last of the guys parted, and there was Tyler, straight down the tunnel the men had created. His mouth dropped open when he saw her. She couldn't hear him over the fading notes of the music, but she was pretty sure he'd said her name.

Allegra walked down the man-made tunnel. She was going to lose her latté all over him. She never should have had one at Story's place, but she'd needed some sort of fortification and didn't think she could handle food. The closer she got to Tyler, the more she thought she would hyperventilate. Some of the guys whispered encouragement as she passed.

"Go get him, Allie."

"You've got this."

"You sure you want him and not me?"

That last one expelled the breath she'd been holding, and she laughed.

Allegra finally reached the man of her dreams. She squeezed her eyes shut.

"Allie?" A curious smile played on his lips. "What is this? What are you doing here?"

This was it. Now or never.

Could she do this?

He watched Allegra coming down between the guys but

couldn't believe his eyes.

She was here? And what was the music about? Was she here to bike with him? But how did she know he was here? And why was she dressed so, so...beautifully?

Tyler took a step forward but froze in place when her gaze met his. Her skin was pale, and she kept clenching and unclenching her left fist. Was she getting ready to deck him for not seeing or speaking to her in a month? He was sure the guys would get a kick out of that one. But then why the flash mob? With that song?

His pulse froze in place, then began to pound as she stopped in front of him, gaze lowered.

"Hi."

Everything and everyone disappeared at her whisper. "Hi."

She lifted her gaze to his when he spoke. At that moment, he felt lighter than a kite.

"Tyler." She bit her lip, then laughed. "I had this whole thing planned for what to say, and go figure, I can't remember one word."

He moved a step closer to this amazing woman and opened his mouth to say something. But a soft, slender finger touched his lips and erased his mind of everything but that feeling. Allegra's lips parted, and desire shot down through his core.

"You've taught me so much since I met you. And..." Her voice drifted into silence.

His heart hammered against his chest. Tyler lowered his face so he was a breath away from her. He leaned in just a little farther, and their lips brushed. The faint mew from her encouraged him to deepen their kiss. Ignoring the cheers and hollers of his former teammates—possibly former friends—he pushed his hands through her loose hair, so soft, then drew them down to cup her shoulders and pull her closer. Finally, his hands drifted down her arms and slid around her waist.

He pulled back, breathless, and touched his forehead to hers. "What's behind your back?"

A slow smile hitched her cheeks. She brought her hand in front of her and handed up a football. "A..." He looked closer. It wasn't just any football—it was signed by Steve Largent and... "Is that..."

Pride shone in her eyes. "It's signed by Steve Largent. And lots of other Seahawks players from back in the day."

He cupped her face. "Allie, that's worth a lot of money. Why?"

"I love you, Tyler."

In a thousand years, he would have never expected those words to bring him the strongest adrenaline rush he'd ever felt. "I love you too, Allie."

With their heads still pressed against each other, she lifted her gaze to his. "Marry me," she whispered.

Those two words did him in. He grinned, then bent and slid one arm behind her knees and hauled her up to his chest. "Yes. Yes!"

Around them, the guys from his team yelled as they charged them, clapping Tyler on his back. Someone turned the music back on, and a bunch of cornerbacks, linemen, and a quarterback began to dance. Tyler turned his back to them

and placed his lips against Allegra's again.
"You're the adventure of my lifetime."

Epilogue

One Year Later

The summer evening sun cast a golden pink glow on the few clouds overhead. Birds chirped all around, and the distant sound of the great White Salmon River provided a backdrop to the soft murmur of guests as they were seated.

Allegra couldn't stop the tears that escaped and trickled down her cheeks.

"Oh, stop it! You're going to ruin your makeup." Caprice grabbed a tissue from Story and reached up to blot the tears. She grinned. "No tears when you're about to marry *the* Tyler Hawk."

Behind her sister, Story rolled her eyes. "*The*? Please."

Allegra laughed. Her emotions were all over the place today. "Is everything ready over there?"

"The only thing they're missing is you." Caprice winked. "And I must say, I totally approve of Tyler's choice of groomsmen." She fanned her face with her jeweled bouquet.

Allie cast a glance in Story's direction. The smile had

slipped from her friend's face. Bo being near must be playing with her heart. She reached over and pulled Story into a hug. "You two will make your way," she whispered in her friend's ear.

Story leaned back. "Today's about you." She sniffed. "Let's go do this."

Allegra watched from behind a tree as first Story, then Caprice, walked down the white rose petal–covered aisle. Then Bo's cute nephew, Hudson, followed in gray dress pants, brown suspenders and shoes, and a white shirt open at the collar, carrying a football with a wide white ribbon tied around it and wedding rings attached.

She glanced down at her own engagement ring. Though she'd been the one to propose, he'd surprised her later that evening with the ring, saying he'd had it for a month. A month! She grinned at the thought. The pear-shaped diamond, set in rose gold on a thin band, glowed with such beautiful clarity. Tyler had surprised her only a month ago with another ring that framed the point of the pear perfectly with a gold crown. The rose-gold band that would be added in only minutes was also thin, with micropavé diamonds. It was a stunning set, one she never could have imagined. But as beautiful as these rings were, her husband-to-be was more so.

The music did a soft change—her cue to start her walk down the aisle to become Mrs. Allegra Hawk. Warmth radiated throughout her body. She couldn't wait to say "I do."

Her blush dress rustled as she stepped around the tree. The light jagged layers of tulle floated in the soft breeze that skimmed across the open back of her dress, kissing her skin. Quiet gasps sounded as she walked down the aisle, "Storybook Love" from *The Princess Bride* playing. Holding her bouquet of pale-pink and white peonies—imported from Alaska where they were currently blooming in the August sun—and some sprigs of pearls, Allegra took the first step toward her future.

Chandeliers and white lights with clear beads strung through the trees glittered in the setting sun as she walked toward Tyler. Beyond the guests to her left, a wood swing hanging from a tree by rope gently swung under more white lights. Off to the right, the dance floor awaited the celebration of their guests.

And in front of her... Tyler stood, hands clasped in front of his chin as he watched her with a wide grin, never letting his gaze falter. How she loved him.

As she stepped up to him, Tyler took her hand in his, and together they faced the pastor.

Tyler watched as Allegra visited with each guest, smiling, laughing, and constantly seeking him with her gaze. He still couldn't believe this incredible woman was his wife.

The dance floor was lit under the white lights strung above it, and on it, people were ready to dance. A lighthearted Justin Timberlake song came on, and he couldn't help it. A king on the dance floor he wasn't, but he was going to do his best to spend every second with his bride that he could. As he swept her into his arms, he waggled his brows. "Are you ready for our honeymoon?"

The cutest blush colored her cheeks. "Tyler." She looked around, no doubt hoping no one had heard.

"Well?" He grinned. "Are you?"

She slid her gaze up to his, a coy smile in her eyes. "More than." His beautiful bride winked at him.

He threw his head back and laughed before gathering her up in a hug in the middle of the dance floor.

"So..." She pushed back from him. "Where *are* we going for our honeymoon?"

"Guess." They'd been playing this game for the last six months when he told her he wanted to plan the entire honeymoon himself. She'd fought it at first, insisting she didn't want to do anything that would end her life too soon. He'd only winked at her and walked away.

She wasn't the one whose life would end too soon. It'd be his when she found out.

"Paris," she said.

"No. Guess again."

She pursed her lips in thought. "Barbados?"

He laughed. "Nope."

"Hmm." She tapped a finger against her lips. "Honolulu?"

"Not even close."

Allegra threw her hands up in the air. "I give up. I don't have any clue at all. At least give me a hint."

Tyler considered her. "Okay, a hint: Beastquake."

Her brows furrowed. "Beastquake? Huh?"

Bo peeked his head over Allegra's shoulder. "Think

Seahawks, Allie."

Allegra jumped, knocking her shoulder into Bo's chin. Served him right.

"Bo, you scared me."

"Sorry."

Allegra watched him walk off, then turned back to Tyler. "Do you think he and Story will ever get together?"

Ah, she was momentarily distracted. Good. He shrugged. "I don't know, but right now I don't care. I only want my wife in my arms."

"Mm. And your wife only wants to be in your arms." She stood on her toes and planted a long kiss on his mouth. "Now, about that hint."

"We have a game to go to tomorrow. You need to learn about football." He laughed. "Drew's a *quarter*back, not a pennyback."

Tyler ducked to avoid the hand coming to smack him on the arm. He stood up, laughing.

"Tyler Richmond Hawk, you tell me where we're going for our honeymoon right now."

"Allegra Isabel Hawk." He nuzzled her throat, the taste of her skin sending bolts of electricity through his body. "On the adventure of a lifetime, my love."

The End

Acknowledgments

It takes a village, you guys. And what a *huge* village it took to get this book baby of mine off the ground.

First and foremost, Jesus gets all the praise. It's Him who gave me the gift of stringing the 26 letters in the English alphabet together to form somewhat coherent sentences. And I love Him all the more for it.

It took my mother getting after me for years...and years...and years... (well, you get the drift) to write. In her words, "If you don't use the gift God gave you, you'll lose it." I tried ignoring her for a while, but the fear of Mother is too strong in this one. Ha! Seriously, though, if it weren't for her constant encouragement, I don't know that I would have stepped up to this calling the Lord gave me.

My husband, Mark, probably deserves the most thanks after God. He's the one who put up with burned meals—and eventual takeover of cooking dinner—and lots of hours of me pouring over my manuscript and wrestling with every word...oh, who am I kidding? He sat beside me and shook his head at all the hours I spent on Pinterest when I should have been writing. And he nagged me to write. (He said I could call it that, and I told him he could nag me.) I love you so, so very much, baby! You're my real-life, daily hero.

Ethan, Van, and Elliette...I love you guys. You've all given me greater compassion, deeper feelings, more sensitivity...and lots and LOTS of white hairs. I *love* that you're my kids. <3

My sissy, Dale. I'M FUNNIER. Also, I love you. You need to move here. (Obey the younger sister.)

Jo-Ann, I can't, and won't, forget. Thank you.

Then I met Jennifer Slattery, an incredible author who lives near me. She's very pushy for someone so tiny. LOL! She's a woman who sees potential and giftings and won't let it go. I'm so thankful she pushed me, and sat in the coffee shops (#hardship) with me to brainstorm. Speaking of brainstorming, Stephanie Ludwig, thank *you*, too! You gave me so many great ideas that are seen in this book. And the Wholly Loved Ministries team (including Jennifer): Chaka Heinze, Dawn Ford, Lyndsey, and Ashley. You all are amazing women.

Carol Moncado...THANK YOU. Without your help, this baby would have looked like a wreck. I so appreciate you!

Of course, I would never leave out my beautiful, sweet, and über-talented critique partners. Shawna Robinson Young, Teresa Tysinger, Holly Michael—my original three—Amy Wozniak, and Angela Jeffcott, you all are so extremely beautiful and talented. God knew exactly what He was doing when He put our little group together. I would still be telling *waaaaaaaay* more than showing if it weren't for you. Not to mention my habitual passive voice.

Sarah Monzon...oh, my Sarah. From your encouragement to your simile help, from your nagging (I gave her permission, people!) to your sweet, precious friendship, I am so thankful to have you in my life. And I'm super happy you introduced me to Jennifer Rodewald! As of this writing, you're the only two who've read this whole shebang...and have made me feel somewhat confident enough to put this out for the world to read.

Great. Now my nerves are kicking in again. Excuse me for a minute while I go throw up.

Sarah also introduced me to Dori De Vries Harrell, editor extraordinaire. You guys. She's magnificent. Thank you, Dori, for taking my clunky, weird words and making me look good. I so appreciate you!

Cheryl St.John, thank you for meeting me for coffee at our now-gone Stories Coffeehouse. Your encouragement and wisdom and gentle sweetness that day has stayed with me. You're a beautiful woman.

Pepper Basham, Meghan Gorecki, Melony Teague, Rachel, Rachael, Beth, Marisa, and my Wonder Twin (my DubT, Carrie), y'all are crazy. And I love you all the more for it. Thank you for being so...violently exuberant about having me for a roomie at CFRR. LOL! And for being so incredibly supportive about helping the word get out about this book baby. Speaking of being incredibly supportive—and excited—thank you, Amber Lynn Perry!!! I adore you, beautiful friend.

Tamara Leigh, I'm soooo not forgetting you. I can't. Your books introduced me to inspirational romantic comedy (chick-lit!). *Stealing Adda* is still one of my favorites. And of course, your medieval, well...you know how much I love your books! Even more, I love you as a woman and friend.

And never, ever, ever would I forget Denise. Since toddlerhood, man. Ups and downs, heartbreaks and joy. Spiritual deserts and lots of growth. We've seen it all. Your friendship means the absolute world to me. I miss you! Please move to the United States. (Hey, I figured if I put it in black and white and in a book for the whole world to read, it might add some pressure on you and Jay to move here. I'm not wrong. Just give in already.)

And dear reader...thank you. Thank you, thank you, thank you. This is a dream come true, and I couldn't be more thankful.

I missed people. I'm human. Please forgive me. So many more than just this group helped me, prayed for me, encouraged me, and messaged me hearts and balloons on Facebook. I love you, too. Thank you.

PS – Everyone I named in this acknowledgement whose last name I mentioned is an author! An author you should totally go check out. Very, very worth it. And because I'm so helpful (ha!), here's the list, in order of appearance:

Jennifer Slattery
Stephanie Ludwig
Chaka Heinze
Dawn Ford
Carol Moncado
Shawna Robinson Young
Teresa Tysinger

Holly Michael
Amy Wozniak
Angela Jeffcott
Sarah Monzon
Jennifer Rodewald
Cheryl St.John
Pepper Basham
Meghan Gorecki
Melony Teague
Amber Lynn Perry
Tamara Leigh

Also, these *incredible* book bloggers who are mentioned, in order of appearance...because that's how I roll:
Rachel (Bookworm Mama)
Rachael (Rachael's Reads)
Beth (Faithfully Bookish)
Carrie (Reading Is My Superpower)

If you enjoyed Tyler and Allegra's story, I would so appreciate if it you head over to Amazon and Goodreads to leave a review! Even if it's just one very short sentence like "I loved it!" You'd make this debut author cry. A good cry. Promise.

To connect with me, I'd love for you to come "like" my Facebook page, follow me on Twitter, pin me (not literally!) on Pinterest, and visit my website.

Facebook: facebook.com/mikaldawnauthor
Twitter: twitter.com/MikalDawn

Pinterest: pinterest.com/mikal_dawn
Website: mikaldawn.com

To stay up-to-date on releases, you can sign up for my newsletter (you'll get notices of sales, including special preorder pricing! And I won't spam!) on my website.

Thank you so much!!

Mikal Dawn is an inspirational romance author, wedding enthusiast, and proud military wife. By day, she works as an administrative assistant for an international ministry organization, serves in her church's library, runs her kids to football, Tae Kwon Do, and figure skating, and drinks *lots* of coffee. By night, she pulls her hair out, wrestling with characters and muttering under her breath as she attempts to write. And drinks lots of coffee. When she isn't writing about faith, fun, and forever, she is obsessively scouring Pinterest (with coffee in hand, of course!) for wedding ideas for her characters.

Originally from Vancouver, Canada, Mikal now lives in Nebraska with her husband, Mark, their three children, and one ferocious feline who can often be found taking over her Instagram account.

www.ingramcontent.com/pod-product-compliance
Ingram Content Group UK Ltd.
Pitfield, Milton Keynes, MK11 3LW, UK
UKHW040038031025
8188UKWH00037B/148